HARD CHEESE

Paul Halter books from Locked Room International:
The Lord of Misrule (2010)
The Fourth Door (2011)
The Seven Wonders of Crime (2011)
The Demon of Dartmoor (2012)
The Seventh Hypothesis (2012)
The Tiger's Head (2013)
The Crimson Fog (2013)
(Publisher's Weekly Top Mystery 2013 List)
The Night of the Wolf (2013)*
The Invisible Circle (2014)
The Picture from the Past (2014)
The Phantom Passage (2015)

*Original short story collection published by Wildside Press (2006)

Other impossible crime novels from Locked Room International:
The Riddle of Monte Verita (Jean-Paul Torok) 2012
The Killing Needle (Henry Cauvin) 2014
The Derek Smith Omnibus (Derek Smith) 2014
(Washington Post Top 50 Fiction Books 2014)
The House That Kills (Noel Vindry) 2015
The Decagon House Murders (Ayatsuji Yukito) 2015
(Publisher's Weekly Top Mystery 2015 List)

Visit our website at www.mylri.com or
www.lockedroominternational.com

HARD CHEESE

Ulf Durling

Translated by Bertil Falk

Hard Cheese

This book is a work of fiction. The characters, incidents, and dialogue are drawn from the author's imagination and are not to be construed as real. Any resemblance to actual events or persons, living or dead, is entirely coincidental.

First published in Swedish in 1971 by Forum as *Gammal Ost*
HARD CHEESE
Copyright © Ulf Durling & Forum 1971
English translation copyright © by John Pugmire 2015.

For information, contact: pugmire1@yahoo.com

FIRST AMERICAN EDITION
Library of Congress Cataloging-in-Publication Data
Durling, Ulf
[*Gammal Ost* English]
Hard Cheese / Ulf Durling
Translated from the Swedish by Bertil Falk

As we all know, cheese goes into everything. And there are so many varieties for experimentation.

In Swedish, the phrase "gammal ost" is shorthand for the expression "att ge igen för gammal ost," which means to take revenge because of a longstanding grievance. While there is no equivalent phrase in English, we do have an expression "hard cheese," which means "bad luck," but intended in an unsympathetic or ironic way. It seems quite appropriate for the story

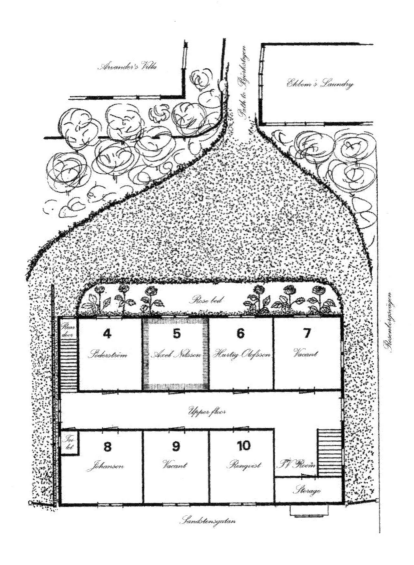

Plan of The Little Boarding-House

PART ONE
Åbrogatan, Monday, October 27th

1

Normally the reports of our meetings take quite a different form. The doctor makes a summary on an A4 page, he reports the summary the following Sunday and lets us approve it with our signatures. Since we have been functioning for more than five years and have met almost 200 times, the documents have become so plentiful that a new binder, a blue one instead of the old black one, had to be purchased this year. During the week, the binders, card index and complete collection of reports are kept locked up in a desk drawer at the doctor's house, and he brings them to every meeting. Since our journals are confidential, no outsider has seen them up to now. However, before we parted this morning, Carl noted that our common deductions had been of such an interesting and noteworthy nature this time that they deserved to be made public. At that, I undertook the task of reporting everything extremely carefully, even the most trifling details, and I promised a thorough report, even of those aspects where we had disagreed.

With all due respect for Carl's consideration for the public, I rather think he meant the police.

Our desire for secrecy is perhaps conditioned by the suspicion that, if they knew about our activities, people might have a good laugh at our expense. Tolerance of anything that might be considered unusual or different is low nowadays, not least in our town. Young people, on the other hand, are permitted to behave as they like. Nobody seems to react against how they are dressing, or against their long hair. In any event, nothing is done by the responsible authorities. If a bunch of hoodlums disturbs the peace at night by kicking up a racket on the main street a long time after midnight, they are rewarded with a brand new youth club costing hundreds of thousands of crowns. But if my cousin happens to break a leg, then the social authorities don't even have a domestic helper for him. Had not his daughter-in-law taken care of cleaning and shopping for food, he would have died of neglect and starvation.

Well, I don't want to carp and normally I am a peaceful and

reserved person—not exactly a cheerful senior citizen, but fairly satisfied with my life. Yet sometimes one has the right to get worked up, and it so happens, though not often, that I fire off a short reader's letter to the newspaper. Who, for example, has forgotten how last year I spoke out in connection with the delayed gritting of Åbrogatan, where I happen to live, and where, after the first snowfall had been followed by frost in the night, the street had become glassy? Had I not preferred to keep a low profile as "One of Many," I would almost certainly have received many a personal thank you. Of that I am quite sure.

My profession has taught me to do everything with care and attention. Nature has furnished me with doggedness and, thanks to my inquiring mind, I have been able to acquire considerable knowledge in all sorts of subjects.

Since my educational background is modest, I've devoted myself to individual studies, read a great deal at the adult educational association and learned a lot from radio lectures. I was a frequent visitor to the town library, and my private book collection consists of two thousand volumes, paperbacks as well as hardbacks. For many years I've been an active committee member of the town's ornithological society and have joined in many worthwhile field trips. For ten years I occupied the position of president of the local branch (The Watermark) of the Philatelic Society. In short, a life filled with intellectual activities, while constantly increasing my book-learning. As a result, despite my age, I feel full of life myself, vital and not at all played out.

In all modesty, I pride myself on possessing a fair amount of acumen, for which I've been complimented many times. Few would guess I was the most senior member of our little group. My dealings with my two closest friends have reinforced my feeling of preserved youth, as has the absence of all those inconveniences that arise over the years; I'm thinking, for example, of shortness of breath and the frequent need to urinate.

Over many years of careful monitoring of my health, I have not so far detected any foreboding signs. Carl, on the other hand, is afflicted with a mild form of diabetes, and the doctor himself recently underwent an operation for bowel obstruction. I still have my own teeth.

Strictly speaking, I hate talking about diseases, but I must nevertheless add that when I was hospitalized at the end of the

1950's, the chief physician as well as Sister Astrid were surprised to see how rapidly I recovered my strength. I'd been afflicted by the influenza rampant at the time and had been admitted to hospital with a high temperature (38,4 degrees Celsius), painful vomiting and much faintness. Already by the next day I could resume reading my book, *The Moonstone* by Wilkie Collins, in a Swedish translation.

It had been my intention to make a short introduction to each of the three of us, but somehow I seem to have gone on a lot about myself. Anyhow, twelve years ago I retired with a pension from my position as foreman at Lindquist's Printing, Ltd. At the time, I received a gratuity and a gold watch with the inscription: "For good and loyal service, from the friends of the company." Mister Lindquist made a short speech and everyone applauded and drank *skål* to my health in sherry.

In those days I was living at Västra Långgatan 29, but when my wife died two years later I moved to the present comfortable two-roomed flat, modern and with a moderate monthly rent. The bigger room, 28 square metres, is arranged as a library and it is there we gather on those Sunday evenings when I have the pleasure of being the host.

As a rule we have a cup of coffee and continue with a half bottle of Swedish arrack punch or port wine. The proceedings rarely drag on: two or three hours at the most. We begin at 19.30 and when we meet at my place I make a point of cleaning the flat beforehand. I often buy a sponge-cake and brush my smoking-jacket, which I always wear on these occasions. One last important detail is an overhaul of my six double rows of crime fiction on the southern wall. It would be extremely embarrassing to find some disorder had occurred, which would be noticed. We are used to browsing among each other's bookshelves, e.g. when the host is out picking up the evening's refreshments, or when some member finds himself compelled to go to the bathroom.

It can happen that I have not managed to clean the flat or even to check the bookcase, but on those occasions I will have been polishing my draft late into the Saturday night and then rehearsing the next day in order to be able to use the half an hour I have at my disposal in a fluent and easy manner and in an entertaining way, after the confirmation of the minutes of the previous week. In order to avoid criticism on factual grounds during the concluding speech, one must not overlook any important detail or place inadequate material at the group's disposal as a basis for forming a judgment. Thank heavens, such occurrences have happened only rarely during the entire time we have been active.

It may be of interest to learn how I met Carl Bergman for the first time, and how that meeting gradually led to the establishment of our club.

We bumped into each other outside the town library, where we were both headed. Since the presence of a bookseller at the municipal lending-place of books seemed to me to be somewhat paradoxical, I made so bold as to ask him about how his interest in books came to be so strong that he could not stay away from their dust even in his leisure time.

We had, of course, seen each other many times in his bookshop and I had earlier, before I retired, had the pleasure of placing some orders through him for the company. Our conversations then had been agreeable but fairly impersonal.

Now he confided to me that he, too, had ceased working within his chosen occupation and had now begun to read what he had not managed to read earlier. In the hallway he took out a bag of apples and offered me one to taste. Then, when we walked between the shelves, it turned out that we were both aiming for the same book. We were standing there, each with an apple, and he was holding Agatha Christie's just- published *The Clocks*. It was of course, just a coincidence, but I couldn't help asking him whether he understood how funny the circumstances were.

'What do you mean, Mr. Lundgren?' he enquired.

'Maybe Mr. Bookseller is unaware of the weakness the authoress is said to have had for apples? It's said that she consumed enormous numbers, perhaps from her own garden, when she was writing.'

'I didn't know that, and neither did I know that Mr. Lundgren was so familiar with what I thought was my own little special field.'

We continued talking about the detective novel on our way home and agreed to meet the next week at the same place, so that I could borrow the book after him.

It was also during that first stroll that I took the opportunity to entertain him with an amusing story, the one about the mystery-addicted borrower. In case the anecdote is unfamiliar, I shall retell it here: when our borrower had read all the detective novels at the library, he one day (by mistake) went home with the telephone directory. The following week, when he returned the book, he told the astounded librarian: "The plot was indeed a little thin, but what a gallery of characters!" I still remember that Carl laughed heartily and at length.

Thus began our close relationship. Apart from the doctor, nobody has mattered more to me than the bookseller Carl Bergman. I think highly of him and I admire his wide reading when it comes to our common field, the mystery novel.

Carl is short of stature, always well-dressed, has a pleasant and amiable manner and expresses himself in a refined way. His courteousness can doubtless be traced to constant contact with customers in Bergman's Book and Stationery Shop, a most valued establishment in the city.

It has a wide range of items and the service is first-class. Carl bought the business in the beginning of the 1930's and he ran it until 1963, when he retired due to old age and health reasons. Obviously his trade had been a paying concern. He is pretty well-off and has built a two-storey house in the eastern part of the town.

I have often been his guest in connection with our Sunday meetings and also on other occasions. His wife, a charming person who, of course, does not take part in our meetings, is in the habit of welcoming us at the door; she always calls attention to something pertinent regarding the weather and asks me about my health. I mention it because my health mostly is excellent.

The Bergmans have three adult children, two of them daughters, married and living in the capital. Their son Gunnar is with the police department in town. He has, according to Carl, a talent out of the ordinary and, after completing training at the Swedish National Police Academy with high testimonials, advanced to become a detective sergeant. I met him myself *ex officio* last year at the police station when I reported the vandalizing of my bike, a Crescent; both cycle tyres had been cut to pieces in a most revolting way. The hoodlum had not been captured, however, in spite of the efforts of the police force. A few months ago I met Bergman junior at his father's home and I reminded him of the cycle vandal. He assured me, in a very friendly and confidence-inspiring way, that my case had not been classified and was still open. I am glad to have contributed to drawing the police force's attention to this sort thing, which of course is not unique of its kind.

Carl and I thus began to meet in the library and made it a habit to walk back together, discussing books we both had read. Almost always these were detective novels. We discussed plots, murder motives and the deductions of the detectives; compared different modes of procedure and different styles; and analysed problems and compared notes as to similar cases.

At this stage, it's important to explain our fundamental attitude to detective novels. We are supporters of the classic problem-story tradition, with sharp-wittedness as a condition for the detective (or the reader) to be able to solve the riddle. We demand literary standards and a serious attitude from the author. The plot may be complicated but not illogical. The reader must have a fair chance to put his or her intelligence and cunning to the test. All the suspects must be introduced in a fair and honest way, and all solutions and explanations must be well justified. We demand that the detective solve his task using his gray cells, not with his clenched fists.

Already in those days we were more or less in agreement in all essentials. We had, and still have, different favourites among the writers. Among mine I count above all Freeman Wills Crofts and Cyril Hare, while Carl prefers Margery Allingham, Josephine Tey and, among the Swedes, Vic Suneson. We have a common *faiblesse* for Ellery Queen and John Dickson Carr.

Later on, the doctor introduced more modern voices that we learned to admire, such as Patricia Highsmith and John Bingham. We even included novels by Raymond Chandler and Ross Macdonald—whom I personally find to be too brutal and outspoken—through some minor technical changes in the procedure of presenting the report.

At the time of writing, the card index comprises no less than 58 writers' names, from Edgar Allan Poe to Harry Kemelman. In the collection of reports, there are, all in all, 193 cards from as many meetings entered into the minutes. The first one was held on March 14, 1965. At that time I had already met the doctor a couple of times.

Carl said to me during one of our walks that he wanted to introduce me to one of his friends. He asked me to visit him the next day and then it turned out that he had invited the doctor.

I knew, of course, of Dr. Efraim Nylander, but thanks to my health I had never had a reason to consult him. The previous year, he had handed over his position as district medical officer to Dr. Rydin and had opened a private practice on his previous premises. I suppose he couldn't give up contact with his profession and his patients.

Given that medical science has made considerable strides during the last few decades, and that the doctor's workload made it difficult for him to keep up to date with its evolution, his prescriptions could occasionally appear to be somewhat out-of-date. If he sometimes, for conservative reasons, prefers liniments and old-fashioned cures to some of the modern medical preparations, he makes up for it with a very personal attention to the patient's situation. Many people prefer the informality of Dr. Nylander's approach over sitting for an hour in the waiting room of the Out Patient's Department at our new and well-equipped hospital and then, after five minutes of consultation, receiving a prescription from a graduate in medicine. He still has many patients, whom I would gladly join if, contrary to expectation, ailments should knock at my door. For obvious reasons, I prefer to belong to his circle of friends.

Imagine my surprise when I found Dr. Nylander at Carl's place that evening in the beginning of 1965 and it turned out that, for many years, they had exchanged viewpoints and opinions about detective novels and that they now and then met in private.

The doctor is a bachelor and for many years his flat has been cared for by a charwoman, Mrs. Storm. He is a somewhat stout man, weighing more than 100 kilo, and he is almost bald-headed, with only a tonsure of white hair. Since for at least half of his life he has been wearing a doctor's white coat, he seems to be awkward in a jacket. He almost always takes it off it in the evenings. Perhaps he wants to hide the fact that the jacket is creased. He wears a pair of broad, red suspenders and claims they don't keep up the trousers but they do press down his shoulders. His head has a tendency to become a part of his chest, since his neck either doesn't exist or is hidden by his double chins. When he is laughing, his body vibrates in a strange way and his eyes seem to disappear into a pucker between the forehead and the cheeks. Everything to do with the doctor is very big and noisy.

He is in the habit of saying: "I generously offer myself."

In my mind's eye, I see him as Dr. Fell, but Efraim doesn't drink as much beer and is not yet using a cane. He is the youngest of the three of us, and when he turned sixty-nine this summer, I gave him *The Collected Works of Sir Arthur Conan Doyle*. My expensive gift was very much appreciated.

Anyway, our first evening passed most pleasantly. The doctor illustrated his reading in criminology convincingly and entertained us with strange cases from his experiences as a doctor. After Mrs. Bergman had looked in and said good night, a bottle of whisky was put on the table as well as soda to mix with it. We engaged in lively and rewarding conversation until midnight, and when we walked home I noticed the doctor staggered slightly. I had consumed as much as he, but I was nevertheless steady on my legs.

The next time we met was at Efraim's home on Gjutarevägen, and, following that, at my place. It was not until May, however, that we decided to meet more regularly, using the form we have observed ever since.

On that memorable occasion the doctor brought the black binder for the first time. Carl summarized the content of Christianna Brand's *Green for Danger*, which he had read in English during the previous week. After that, there followed a discussion conforming to the conditions Carl had set out. It was up to Efraim and me to point out the murderer and explain the relations between the gas cylinders, which were an important part of the solution.

I think that one may safely say that it is not that important for a reader of detective stories to deduce the correct solution well before the end of the story. He would rather prefer to be led astray and surprised—and, in addition, experience some healthy mental gymnastics.

The doctor actually maintains that we need small moments of stupefaction as a counterbalance to the trivialities of every day life, and that the helplessness we sense in the presence of the inexplicable gives us a salutary indication of our own limitations. We experience a pleasant lack of responsibility in the face of the unfolding events, which gives us a feeling of security amidst the dangers, the fears and the hatred. He furthermore states that reading horror stories is excellent, in that it satisfies unconscious and unspoken needs, giving us an outlet for our aggressive urges and criminal instincts.

I have problems believing that beneath my timid surface there lurks an unabated thirst for blood, but I am nonetheless flattered by the thought that someone could envisage in me a Mr. Hyde in disguise.

The above considerations, which are the fruits of our discussions, might seem exaggerated in the eyes of others. That's why I thought long and hard before deciding to write about our private activities.

If I've been able to convey some small idea about our small club and about ourselves, then the intention of my opening remarks will have been achieved, and I can proceed to recount the events which took place during our last meeting, yesterday, October 26.

The preceding evening I had gone to bed with E. C. Bentley's

Trent's Last Case and I must have fallen asleep just before midnight. My night's sleep was calm and undisturbed, to which a glass of warm milk with a few drops of cognac, downed after the late evening news, may have contributed.

2

Carl called yesterday afternoon, around four o'clock. My first thought was that he had been prevented from attending that evening's meeting, but, on the contrary, he wanted to make sure that I would be there. And when I met the doctor at the corner of Allégatan and Parkvägen at a quarter past seven, I was told that he had also had a call from our host during the afternoon and thought that he had prepared something really dainty for us and hadn't wanted us to miss it. In response to a point-blank demand about the book title for that evening, Carl had replied evasively, saying that at first he had thought of A. A. Milne's *The Red House Mystery*, but that now he wasn't so sure.

It surprised me somewhat that the doctor had been indiscreet enough to try to find out what mystery novel our friend had thought of, but Carl's phone call had probably provoked his curiosity. It is not our custom to reveal the topic beforehand and Carl's eagerness to ensure our presence during the evening made me even more curious. Nor did I understand why *The Red House Mystery* would be worth all the fuss, especially since that novel is said to include a secret passage, something I have always had reservations about within this particular genre, and which has most probably contributed to the fact that I have never read the book.

Carl himself opened the door. He was home alone since Margit was baby-sitting for their son's family. Their daughter-in-law was in bed with the flu and their son was working overtime. We would thus be undisturbed during the evening, which I appreciated, especially since the expectations at this point were great, and disturbances during meetings have a tendency to confuse reasoning and destroy the mood. Carl's wife, who was an excellent woman, is always very unobtrusive and considerate. She is in the habit of putting the coffee tray in the entrance hall and discreetly rattling the spoons in order to attract Carl's attention. At those times when he doesn't hear her low-key signal, the doctor usually clears his throat and announces that he is thirsty. In the event that even he has been distracted, I myself have, in my crafty way, prompted Carl by cautiously enquiring whether someone has recently been eavesdropping in the hall.

In the living room, there were teacups, a cake and biscuits already on the table. While Carl fetched milk for me from the pantry—I prefer milk to cream because of the lower fat content—the doctor said something witty about the number of teacups and I retorted amusingly by pointing out that the windows, luckily, were indeed closed. We were, of course, alluding to *The Ten Teacups* by John Dickson Carr, and given that this esteemed writer was one of our favourites, I felt the evening had got off to an auspicious start.

After we had all sat down, the doctor on the couch with the binders and other documents by his side, I in the easy chair and Carl in the armchair, the meeting was declared open.

"Herewith the minutes of the 35th meeting of the group in 1969, held October 19th at 19.30 hours at the home of factor Lundgren, Åbrogatan 2. Present: Johan Lundgren, Carl Bergman and Efraim Nylander...."

The doctor read in a booming bass voice of great penetrating power. One may think that it is too legalistic to repeat these recurring facts at every meeting, especially since we were always plenary, but we like doing the agenda this way and we don't intend to change.

"After Dr. Nylander had read out the minutes of the previous week's meeting, Mr. Lundgren presented an interesting summary of *The Listening Walls* by Margaret Millar (see Meeting Minutes 193, Binder 2) followed by a lively discussion."

I shall skip over the rest of the minutes, since neither Carl nor I had any objections. In my capacity as last week's host, I thanked the doctor for his observant summary and proposed that he should continue to serve as secretary, which was agreed unopposed. He has, moreover, filled that position with honour ever since we began. The minutes were then filed and my written summary of the book was added to the collection of reports. A new card was added to the card index under M.

During the proceedings I had detected signs of impatience on the part of Carl, who had changed his position in the armchair several times and was now nervously fiddling with his watch chain.

In order to convey the right mood, I should perhaps add that a thin rain was drizzling against the window. It had, incidentally, rained a lot during the previous week, especially at night. In the darkness, one could barely discern the greenery of the foliage, with streaks of red and yellow here and there. On nights like this, a particularly fresh fragrance rises pleasantly from the soil.

Carl then took the floor and, after a dramatic pause rather like the doctor's—when he lights his cigar, pretending that there is no draft and looks concernedly at the glow—he began:

'Well,' said Carl, 'I had actually intended to put your ingenuity to the test with a totally different problem, but I propose instead that we examine a case that is still unsolved and which happened in real life, right in our immediate vicinity.'

Not understanding what Carl was talking about, the doctor and I remained silent. I was perplexed and Efraim appeared nonplussed.

'This afternoon,' continued Carl, 'I received a visit from my son Gunnar and his children. As his wife was confined to bed, it was up to him to take them out. He seemed preoccupied and irritable.'

'It's hardly surprising that his wife has a raging fever and stomach pains,' the doctor observed. 'Half the town is in bed with the flu.'

'That's what I thought. When I asked him how Kerstin felt, he dismissed the question curtly. "She's fine," was all he would say. But a little while later he had a change of heart. Gentlemen, do you know *The Little Boarding-House*?'

'Of course,' we replied.

The Little Boarding-House is a two-storey wooden house about a five-minute walk from the railway station, at the intersection of Sandstensgatan and Rosenborgsvägen. It has about ten rooms and is run by a certain Mr. Blom. Needless to say I have never stayed there, since the establishment does not enjoy a good reputation due to the drunkenness the guests often display.

Parenthetically, I must state that the owner is an awful person. Once, as I strolled along Sandstensgatan, I found him sweeping the pavement outside his shabby residence and took the opportunity to suggest that he should perhaps also have his windows cleaned, and asked him if he was familiar with Arnold Bennett's *Grand Hotel Babylon*. It's not a mystery novel, as far as I know, but may be readable all the same. In spite of my friendly attitude, he looked offended and swore at me! He actually said "Go to hell!" Later, when we happened to meet at *Stora Torget,* I ventured to entertain him with a little anecdote of mine. Scarcely had I opened my mouth when he told me to shut up and turned his back on me. He is thoroughly mean, rude and shameless, believe me.

'At eleven o'clock today,' Carl continued, 'Gunnar got a call ordering him to go there immediately. He understood that something unusual must have happened, since he was disturbed during the weekend and everyone at the police station knew that his wife was sick. It turned out that the boarding-house owner had been alerted that morning by the cleaning-lady. She had wanted to finish her work promptly, but couldn't get into one of the rooms. Now, the rules say that any guest wishing to have his room cleaned must hang the key on a hook outside the door no later than ten o'clock in the morning. The cleaning-lady arrives around seven o'clock and is normally finished before twelve. This morning she found that the key to one particular room was missing and, when she eventually knocked on the door, she got no response.'

'Excuse me for interrupting,' I said, 'but aren't guests normally allowed to stay in their rooms until twelve o'clock?'

'True enough, but the cleaning-lady only works part-time and guests who stay on at the hotel have a choice between getting up before ten o'clock, or making their beds themselves. This particular guest had been staying there in an upstairs room for a couple of weeks, and the cleaning-lady became concerned when it seemed that he didn't want his room cleaned as usual. She suspected something was wrong and, since the guest was an older man and not in the best of health, she suspected that he had fallen ill during the night. Some of the other guests had gone down with the flu. Even when Blom knocked on the door there was no response, and they were unable to get into the room. The key was still in the lock and the bolt could be seen through the chink in the door-frame. At last they decided to call the police. Detective Ivehed arrived just before eleven o'clock, determined there was good reason to get inside as fast as possible, tried his keys without success, and then forced the door open. They saw at once that the man, a certain Axel Nilsson, must have been murdered. He was lying fully dressed beside the bed and it appeared he had hit the back of his head on the footboard. There was blood on his face and on his shirt-front. A bottle of wine on the table had been knocked over and the contents had spilled onto the table-cloth and down onto the floorboards—.'

'—and onto Nilsson's face and shirt,' the doctor suggested.

'That's right.'

Carl looked at us triumphantly.

'Wait a minute,' I said. 'An older man in a lonely hotel room feels sick and perhaps vomits during the night, gets up with the intention of going to the bathroom, stumbles on his way there, hits the back of his head on the footboard and passes away as a consequence of a heavy concussion of the brain. Surely that's the first thing to spring to mind after hearing your account?'

'I agree with Johan,' the doctor announced. 'How old was Nilsson?'

'They think he was about fifty.'

'They think? Didn't he have any identity papers? What year of birth did he give in the hotel register?'

'1917, I remember now. It fit with the driving license and the passport, which was issued in the USA. According to the entry stamp, he arrived in Göteborg harbour on the twelfth.'

'Fifty-two years old, then. That is hardly an older man. If it were, that would make the three of us decidedly ancient. The vascular systems in older and middle aged people often have a reduced elasticity, which creates the risk of a fall in blood pressure at sudden changes of position. That would bring about a sense of dizziness and, every so often, regular fainting fits with people who are so predisposed. These tendencies are strengthened if one is hungry or physically exhausted. As Johan says, he could have been awakened by a strong urge to visit the bathroom, perhaps because of diarrhoea as a result of the flu we talked about, and had not realised how weak he actually was. So when he got up quickly in the darkness, he banged against the table and upset the bottle so the wine ran out, then fell backwards against the headboard. Isn't that possible?'

Carl had been listening with an encouraging smile.

'Yes, entirely possible. The light was off and the room was indeed dark. But there's something else which needs to be taken into consideration, gentlemen. Allow me to continue. When Ivehed forced the door open and saw the devastation and the body that seemed to be covered with blood, he prevented anyone else from entering the room. At that point several upset guests had gathered outside the door. There was reason to suspect foul play, so after he had made sure that Nilsson had no pulse, he mounted guard over the broken door until my son arrived. He came just after eleven, made a preliminary search of the room, covered up the dead man and called for reinforcements. I shall return to the room itself and what was found there later, but first I want to share with you what I heard about the preliminary questioning of Blom.'

'Was there any reason to suspect that death was not accidental?'

The doctor sounded impatient and one got the feeling that he was not at all happy with Carl's apparent lack of interest in Nilsson's blood pressure.

'No, not exactly. Blom had said, during a conversation that had taken place downstairs in the owner's private quarters, that Nilsson checked in at the boarding house on the thirteenth of this month. He hadn't brought much luggage, just a suitcase and a briefcase, and he claimed to be returning home after a visit abroad. He was a rather thin man with a moustache and appeared to be worn out. His clothes, which hung loosely on his body, were baggy and outmoded. He limped and Blom was convinced that he had alcohol problems, for his speech was thick and he sometimes reeked of hard liquor. He seemed to be sleek and unpleasant, oily and ingratiating, with a habit of blinking cunningly and maliciously behind thick spectacles. He conveyed an untrustworthy impression overall, being quite reticent about himself, but asking the host all kinds of questions about the other guests or about circumstances in the city, so that Blom came to the conclusion that Nilsson must have known the place before, but had been away for quite some time. The evening before, he had, for example, asked how long a couple of female guests would be staying, and had seemed to be happy to learn that they would be leaving soon. However, one of them caught the flu on Saturday and they both decided to stay on.'

'What had he against those ladies? Did they drink?'

There was obviously no reason for any illusions about the guests of the hotel.

'No. They were very decent schoolmistresses. They had the rooms on either side of Nilsson's and entertained each other reading out loud in one or the other's room until the small hours. Nilsson had to listen to that night after night. He thought they were reading from a book about animals, for once he caught a reference to a pack of wolves hunting a woman. That's what he said to Blom, at least.'

'Blom seemed to think that Nilsson was sick. What was he suffering from?'

'Gunnar asked the same thing. Yes, Nilsson looked to be older than his age: pale, with hollow cheeks and a perpetual air of tiredness. Most of the time he stayed at his room. He had bad eyesight and he seemed to refrain from long walks because of his legs, at least if there was no need for a visit to the state-controlled liquor store. He seemed to avoid meeting people as well and would slip quickly into his room when anyone appeared.'

'Did Blom get to know anything about his personal circumstances?'

The doctor was visibly interested, which surprised me, since I myself at the time could not conceive of the death being anything but the result of a pure accident.

'Very little. He was probably single and independent. What was surprising was the contrast between his strikingly simple clothes and few belongings, and his relative prosperity. For almost two weeks he had occupied a double room which he had paid for in advance. He was probably in need of space because of his walking problems. We should note in passing the boarding house was not cheap for what it was: 24 crowns a night for a single room and 38 for a double.'

'Have they determined where his money came from?'

'No. They found some cash in the room, but just a few ten-crown bills. Besides, he had told Blom that money was not a big problem for him but that he wouldn't be staying long at *The Little Boarding-House.*'

'What could he have meant by that?'

'That he had a source of income we didn't know about, any more than we knew of his plans.'

'Did he receive any visitors? Did Blom know anything about any relatives or acquaintances?'

'I can answer the second question with a no. Regarding the first, it seems he had a visitor during the night of the murder.'

'A woman?'

Yet another interjection from the doctor. He had up until now been responsible for all the questions. I had been silent, for there was something about the name of the dead man that had drawn my attention. Some memory associated with the name lingered on, just as when one strikes a chord on the piano and the overtones gradually die away, but the keynote lingers and can be discerned a long time after the initial impression has gone.

'No woman, no. Blom didn't know who it had been, but he gave the following account: from about eight o'clock, he had been sitting in reception doing his accounts. There were several vacant rooms, but no new guests had arrived. Everything was calm. Around nine o'clock a few of the guests had gone out, either to the cinema or to a café to watch television. The hotel television was out of order, so the lounge on the first floor was empty. You may be aware that on Saturday nights there is a German criminal TV series called *Babeck*. Shortly after eight o'clock, loud voices could be heard coming from Nilsson's room. There was Nilsson's own, indistinct but indignant, and another, coarser, male voice, trying to be calmer. They were both angry and wrangled and cursed vehemently.'

'Why didn't the host interfere? Didn't any of the other guests complain?'

'It went on practically without interruption and even Gunnar was surprised that Blom had not at least knocked on the door in question. You mustn't forget that *The Little Boarding House* doesn't enjoy a very high reputation, and Blom seems to have turned a blind eye to much that went on. He decided he would interfere if the noise went on after ten o'clock when, according to notices in all rooms, silence is expected. The guests are asked to observe other rules like not consuming intoxicants, not accepting visitors after ten o'clock and not keeping pets in the rooms.'

'He was not very particular when it came to that first rule, was he?'

'No. Knowing of his guest's fondness for alcohol, Blom must have suspected that they were drinking upstairs, but he chose to do nothing.'

'What happened then?'

There was no mistaking that the doctor's curiosity was thoroughly aroused. He was leaning forward in the sofa and had forgotten to stir the sugar in his second cup of tea.

'At about ten minutes to ten Blom went to his own room—which, by the way, is situated exactly under room number 5, Nilsson's room. For fifteen minutes he listened to the news on the radio, which is situated in the window-recess, after which he went upstairs in order to subdue the hullaballoo. He listened outside Nilsson's door, but now it was totally silent, from which he drew the conclusion that the visitor had gone. The door was locked. He confessed that he looked through the keyhole without seeing anything. He remained there for a few minutes, but—no, I'm forgetting, it was not totally silent. Nilsson's radio was on. There was some kind of lecture being broadcast.'

'So Nilsson had a radio?'

'Yes. He'd placed it over by the window. He'd come across an old Philips somewhere.'

'But how and when had Nilsson's guest been able to leave the premises?'

'That's what Blom found incomprehensible! Nilsson could still be heard swearing at ten minutes to ten, when Blom had completed his monthly accounts. That was why he'd been in the reception area, which also functions as an office. That's where he keeps his ledgers and binders. The disturber of the peace must have left during the fifteen minutes Blom was listening to the news, but he could not have gone out through the front door because the doorbell had not rung, and Blom himself had been guarding the back door from his room. He is quite adamant about that. After listening outside Nilsson's door, he locked the front door and put on his radio again. Programme 3 had dance music, which he listened to. At one o'clock he locked the back door and went to bed. He had hung up the back door key on a hook on the inside of the door and it was still there in the morning. The cleaning-lady enters that way with her own key. Blom seems to be very careful when it comes to making sure that no undesirable elements get into the hotel. From his window he can see anyone trying to get in through the back door. Thus, at ten o'clock every evening he locks the front door and hangs out a sign above the doorbell referring guests to the back door. At one o'clock he locks the back door and anyone who comes back after that has to ring the front doorbell. No keys are permitted to leave the building, since they have a tendency to disappear with the guests. Room keys must be hung up outside the respective rooms or handed in at the reception, where they are kept on a wooden board.'

The doctor had been looking troubled throughout this explanation.

'There's something odd about this. It doesn't quite fit.'

'What is it that doesn't fit?'

'Well, why is it necessary to guard the hotel like this? What's Blom protecting it from? We know about the rowdyism which takes place at *The Little Boarding-House* and that it's possible to take women up to the rooms. At the same time, we hear of the owner lying in wait at a window until late at night, seemingly for the purpose of going against what he's actually making a living from.'

'What is he making a living from? Isn't it his hotel business?'

'Of course, but how? He's living on occasional guests, for example travelling salesmen, but also on people on shady errands, men who need a room for their love affairs and on more-or-less alcohol addicts, whose drunkenness is accepted by the host. In order to make a living from these kinds of people, he has to count on them bringing in extra guests.'

Carl and I were silent. He was right, of course. But the doctor had still more to say.

'All that talk about surveillance of front doors and back doors seems to me to be for the benefit of the police. Blom wants to appear in as favourable a light as possible. The police most probably keep an eye on him and he doesn't want any trouble. He wants to project the image of a clean-living man, a protector of morality and a true enemy of alcohol. As far as I'm concerned, the reputation of *The Little Boarding-House* doesn't square with the picture he's trying to paint of himself. And how can he expect anyone to believe he could possibly keep the back door under surveillance between ten in the evening and one in the morning so that nobody could get in unobserved? Does he spend three hours glued to his bedroom window? It doesn't fit.'

'I know it sounds strange, but that's the way it is. Blom swears that nobody got in or out during that period without his knowledge. He says that his window stands ajar and through the small slit he could even have heard if the gravel outside had crunched.'

The doctor still looked sceptical but preferred for the time being to let the matter rest there. Carl continued his report, which now had been interrupted a couple of times, and his tone intimated that the objections had probably taken some of the pleasure from the climax he had so carefully prepared.

'In any case, since Blom hadn't seen anyone else coming in and out, he concluded that Nilsson's visitor must have been one of the guests.'

'Bravo,' cried the doctor gleefully. 'Exactly what I've been thinking all this time. Continue.'

'The person Blom suspected was a certain Ivar Johanson, a travelling salesman in furnishing fabrics. His room is upstairs, on the opposite side of the corridor from Nilsson's. He had been in the hotel the entire evening and had, by the way, been on the telephone, which is on a table in the corridor upstairs, when Blom began knocking on the door of room number 5 the next morning. Johanson had then asked what was up and, when he realised that nobody was answering in the room, he recommended calling the police.'

'What did Johanson say when the police asked him if he'd been in Nilsson's room?'

'He firmly denied it, as did all the other guests, by the way. However, he added that he had knocked at the door around nine o'clock, because "people seemed to be having a good time in there," but he was not admitted. He had heard Nilsson saying "yea, yea" but nothing else. He felt rebuffed and returned to his room. Another guest, Warrant Officer Renqvist, happened to be passing at the time and confirms he saw Johanson at that particular time.'

During Carl's latest pronouncement the doctor's face had gone from red to crimson and from crimson to lilac. That is an unerring sign that a laugh is on its way and, sure enough, it began as a chuckle in his chest and developed into that loud, noisy snorting that inevitably leaves him utterly exhausted and his forehead covered in perspiration.

'Imagine,' he chortled, half choking, 'that touching sight! Johanson, thirsty and longing for company, roaming the corridor, tooth-brush glass in hand. He knocks on the door of number 5, but Nilsson thinks that it's the host who wants them to calm things down, so he just calls out "yea, yea," meaning: "We'll be more quiet." At that very moment, when Johanson is about to say "It's only me, Ivar," the military person arrives and Ivar has to turn around, hiding his glass under his coat and, in a hypocritical way, muttering something to the effect that he had just got matters under control.'

'That's how it must have happened, but in the morning Blom still thought that Johanson had left the room around ten o'clock that night, that the party was over by then and that Nilsson had begun listening to the radio when he was alone. Johanson, moreover, declared that he had heard the radio on in room 5 until well after midnight.'

'Did Johanson and Nilsson know each other?'

'Only in passing. Johanson asserts, in any case, that he never set foot in Nilsson's room, since he wanted to avoid being disturbed by the schoolmistresses reading aloud from *The Saga of Gösta Berling* by Selma Lagerlöf.'

I suddenly recalled the episode in the book when Anna Stjärnhök's sleigh was pursued by wolves. (In passing, I would like to call attention to the fact that Miss Lagerlöf received a well-merited Nobel Prize in 1909. She also wrote a number of other masterpieces, such as *Jerusalem* and *The Emperor of Portugal*.)

Carl continued:

'Just after ten, then, there was finally quiet in room 5, the door had been locked from the inside and Nilsson was listening to his transistor radio. That's what the hotel owner claims, anyway. But in the morning Nilsson was found dead and the door was still locked from the inside. Who could believe he was not already dead when the unknown visitor, somehow or other, managed to leave the room and perhaps the hotel? Blom claims that nobody could have left the house unnoticed, and all the other guests deny that they had ever been in room 5. It's difficult to determine who's lying, but even more difficult to explain how someone could have managed to get out of a room locked on the inside, leaving behind a corpse listening to the radio. Just before ten o'clock, Blom could still hear the quarrel from room 5, and one hour before ten Nilsson had answered Johanson's knocking at the door and his voice had been unmistakable. Furthermore, he had been downstairs with Blom at the reception only fifteen minutes before that, because he wanted a strip of sticking-plaster.'

'Plaster?'

Now both the doctor and I were on the alert. This we had not heard before and plaster means, as we know, blood and trauma.

'Was Nilsson injured?'

'The hotel owner doesn't know. He offered to go upstairs with cotton and disinfection fluid, but Nilsson declared, blinking his eyes in that strange way of his, that he only wanted plaster. Blom says he smelled strongly of alcohol.'

'Did he have any wounds when he was found in the morning? Was there any plaster on him?'

'No. Gunnar says flatly that he examined the body thoroughly without finding anything that would have needed a plaster. And the plaster itself was nowhere to be found.'

'So, it could mean that it was the murderer who had been wounded!'

I used the word murderer though the murder, as such, had not been proven as yet.

'That was what the police thought, but they couldn't find any plaster in the house or the slightest wound on any of the guests.'

We sat silent for a while. It was pitch dark outside and the wind was rising. One could sense the trees slowly swaying from side to side, but only because of the stars they blocked out as they moved. It was somewhat cooler now and Carl put more logs on the fire, which had already been lit when we arrived and which he had maintained at regular intervals since.

It was almost ten o'clock and I believe we all thought about how Blom would soon be locking the front door of *The Little Boarding-House* and then be on the lookout for self-invited guests from his room at the back, or perhaps pricking up his ears for crunching noises on the gravel path.

The doctor had long ago hung up his jacket and rolled up his shirt-sleeves. The lighting was deliberately subdued, in order to create the right atmosphere. I lit one of the doctor's small cigars, though normally I am very abstemious when it comes to tobacco. I savoured the moment before I spoke:

'Gentlemen, this means, unless I'm very much mistaken, that we have here a case of—.'

'— the locked room,' Carl chimed in.

He could not deny himself the pleasure of pronouncing what were, to us, three almost magical words.

We looked at each other, amazed and dumbfounded. It reminded me of one Christmas Eve when, as a child, I looked in disbelief at a set of tin soldiers I had dreamed about but never dared hope for.

'Yes,' repeated Carl. 'It does indeed appear to be a case of the locked room.'

The doctor stared thoughtfully out of the window, then at the fire, then down to his stomach where he had neglected to fasten a shirt button. Now he rectified that slowly and methodically, and, trying unsuccessfully to appear detached, said:

'If you could prove that Nilsson did not die a natural death, it means, damn it, that he was killed in a locked room around ten o'clock last night. The man was alive until just before ten, as witnessed by Blom. At five minutes after ten, the room was silent except for the radio. The door was locked from the inside and remained so twelve hours later. Nobody could have left the room. After the quarrel, the visitor disappeared as imperceptibly as he had arrived, leaving behind a corpse whose head had hit the edge of the bed. Yes, it might be, but I repeat that several things have to be checked before we know if it really could be a murder in a locked room in our specific sense.'

'Suicide?' I asked anxiously.

Unfortunately, it has happened more than once that a well-structured locked room with a corpse inside has turned out not to be the scene of a crime. The author has let the dead person commit suicide under circumstances that point to murder. When you have been struggling with an insoluble murder mystery for 220 pages, such a solution is a downright disappointment. Such a trick of the trade, however diverting, is nothing short of despicable.

'Poppycock!' scoffed the doctor. 'One might knock back a bottle of pills, hang oneself, or shoot oneself to death, but one doesn't throw oneself at a footboard. Let's keep a sense of proportion! No, if it wasn't an accident, it can only be murder and nothing else.'

'Not only that,' added Carl, 'the murdered man must have got up and switched off the radio during the night, since it was not on this morning.'

A stunned silence followed that remark, during which Carl brought out a bottle of chilled Swedish arrack punch he had been keeping in readiness for the occasion.

3

Space does not permit a detailed analysis here of "the locked room" in detective fiction. I must refer the reader to the very thorough account in *The Hollow Man*. The room where the murder has taken place must, however, be sealed, the entrances at all events under continuous surveillance and the method of the murderer a mystery. At the end, the solution is revealed and the author forced to explain how the wool has been pulled over the reader's eyes.

I opened the discussion by declaring:

'To begin with, we know that the door was locked and that the key was in the lock inside the room.'

'That's right,' Carl agreed. 'The hotel owner swore in the morning that it was there. He had looked through the keyhole without getting clear sight into the room.'

'Wait a minute, interjected the doctor. 'A dark keyhole is not a proof that the key is on the other side. A towel hanging over the door handle would produce the same effect.'

'Blom is adamant that he saw the key in the hole. Furthermore, they tried the door and found it locked and the bolt was visible. Besides, after smashing the door, they found the key on the doormat.'

'So it fell down on the mat when Officer Ivehed threw himself at the door?'

'Yes, it must have slipped out of the keyhole when the door buckled under the impact. Moreover they had knocked and pounded on the door in a heavy-handed way for a long time. As you know, a key could be seated quite loosely if the door had been locked by turning the key only one revolution.'

'Is it out of the question that the door could have been locked from the outside and the key put into the keyhole on the inside later, using some ingenious mechanism?'

My remark did, of course, not mean that I believed in that possibility, but I wanted to have it eliminated. Carl brushed it aside immediately.

'By attaching a thread to the bow of the key—or of a spare one—

and pulling the key back into the room through the lower chink of the door after having locked it from the corridor? Slipping a strong thread though the keyhole is no great matter and neither is locking the door without cutting the thread inside the hole, but just try to get the key in place by pulling the string so that it leaves the floor of the corridor, glides into the room and up to the inner opening of the lock and finally into the hole in a proper way! It would take a lot of practice and dexterity and the laws of leverage and balance would almost have to be suspended, all in all a miraculous achievement. Moreover, they did not find any thread loop around the key-bit and the space under the door does not even permit the passage of a nail-file so ... no, gentlemen, it is definitely not possible.'

'An extra key was mentioned. What happened to the spare one?'

'Thanks for reminding me. It disappeared with a guest about a month before Nilsson arrived. Blom has forgotten the name of the person and, when asked about it, he hadn't got his ledger to hand. Anyway, the door needn't have been destroyed if he'd been able to push the key on the inside away by inserting a duplicate key from the outside. Before Ivehed broke the door open he was asked to try his picklock, but it failed. It could have been then that the key fell down inside the room.'

'Why didn't the picklock work? The police use it everywhere. And why, for that matter, didn't they call a locksmith?'

'They were pressed for time. Gunnar thought that Ivehed's picklock hadn't worked because the key on the inside was in the way.'

Nobody could think of anything more to say about the door. It would have been convenient if it could have been locked from the outside but, given the appearance of having been locked from the inside, that seemed to be out of the question. We were all rather surprised that Blom hadn't had an extra key, but Carl assured us that the hotel owner had been credible on that point. A previous guest had simply forgotten to return it when leaving.

We now proceeded to discuss the windows overlooking the garden, from where one could see, beyond the gravel which surrounded *The Little Boarding House*, a passage leading to Björkstigen, a parallel street to Sandstensgatan. From Nilsson's windows one could see a fence to the left of the path, partly obscured by shrubbery, behind which stood the home of Director Arvander. To the right of the path stood Ekbom's Laundry; Miss Ekbom's kitchen window peeped out from behind a hawthorn bush. A wide flower bed ran the length of the wall beneath Nilsson's window. Anyone who passed in or out through the rear door on the left side of the house had to go round a wooden espalier, which protruded from the corner. Obviously the purpose of the espalier was not so much to prop up the miserably maintained and almost dead Virginia creeper, as to facilitate the hotel owner's secret surveillance of the rear door.

Blom had further improved the view from his lookout by mounting a window mirror in the window recess and a lantern above the rear door, providing efficient illumination for a distance of several metres from the rubber mat on the doorstep.

Gunnar had asked Ivehed to tiptoe on the gravel path while he himself lurked near Blom's open window. The footsteps could be distinctly heard five metres away.

Carl took his time as he described these circumstances. A strangely agreeable mood prevailed. The fire and the arrack punch had warmed us pleasantly, but not in such a way as to make us drowsy. Quite the contrary: our thoughts became clearer and new questions and speculations occurred to us in the same way that the temperature of a hothouse accelerates the growth of plants and vegetables.

The doctor made notes with his fountain-pen in his usual illegible handwriting. As for myself, I was able to readily absorb every new detail and analyse it thoughtfully without effort.

'Do you happen to know the size of the windows?'

'When both halves of the window were open, there was an aperture of about one and a half metres square. They could be locked from the inside with window latches.'

'Were the windows actually locked?'

'No, but they were pulled-to. The curtain wasn't drawn.'

We pondered for a while. Then came the inevitable question:

'So the room was not truly locked?'

'If you want to be pedantic about it, no. But since nobody could have got in or out, it was effectively hermetically sealed.'

'How high above the ground is the window?'

This time I was the one asking the question.

'Gunnar measured the height to be three and a half metres.'

'Then it must have been possible to jump out!'

'Not really. Anyone trying it would inevitably have ended up in the flower bed, which is two metres wide. Theoretically, a physically fit younger man could have leapt from that height without landing in the earth. However, in our case he could either have jumped from the window-ledge, which did not show any signs that a person of normal weight had stood on it, or from the window-sill, but the cloth there was not creased or dirty, as it would have been after a take-off. It was further cluttered with a tight row of hideous pot-plants and bric-a-brac. There was no space for feet with all that congestion. We have no choice but to assume the murderer didn't get out that way.'

'That sounds convincing enough. No rain gutters, niches or bay windows of any kind?'

'None. The outer wall is completely smooth.'

'I suppose it's pointless to ask if there are any other ways out of the room?'

'Absolutely none. No extra doors, no stove with a flue you could climb up, no hole in the floor, and no secret passage.'

That was, of course, what I had suspected, but according to our rules we have to ask for such information. I glanced furtively at the doctor, who obediently began to speak.

'If the room was impossible to get out of, then we have to assume that Nilsson was alive when he was left alone. He listened, as we know, to the radio and switched it off later that night.'

'Do you mean he died a natural death?'

'No, it means the murder was committed later.'

Neither I nor Carl followed. Carl managed to object first.

'Are you saying that the murderer got into a still-locked room later that night, a room inside a hotel nobody could enter without the knowledge of the host--?'

'No.'

'—and then left the room, like a ghost?'

'No. We can only regret that we don't know exactly when Nilsson died, but the trick's the same, in principle, whenever it was perpetrated.'

'You're sure you're saying that the murder took place after the visitor had left the room?'

'No, it was *accomplished* later. Suppose that Nilsson gets a blow to the head during a fight, but that he rapidly recovers. The quarrel continues and there's seemingly no reason to worry about Nilsson when the other person leaves at a quarter to ten—while the back door is still unwatched. Blom thinks the visitor is still in the room since Nilsson moves about for a while, swearing under his breath, before he switches on the radio and takes a rest. Then, probably after several hours, the after-effects of the concussion of the brain set in. At first he doesn'' notice his faintness and the increasing headache. The wine has limited his ability to register, and the feeling of sickness and dizziness get the upper hand when he gets to his feet. He manages to switch off the radio but faints by the table, falling flat on his face on the table, causing the bottle to overturn and the red wine to flow out. Whereupon he slides backwards and hits his head on the footboard. Previously, he had locked the door himself behind his heavy-handed guest.'

'Are you saying that even a slight concussion could have such severe consequences?'

'Yes. Usually a concussion doesn't cause major problems but, if you're unlucky, an unpleasant complication may set in.'

'Can you please be a little more specific?'

'I am talking of an *epidural haematoma*, a haemorrhage between the membranes of the brain, which can be caused by even a mild blow on the head. The patient gets better while he recovers from the concussion itself, but a vessel further inside the brain has been injured and blood is pumped out. When that inner bleeding gets big enough, he will become unconscious; it can happen within a few hours or after a couple of days. If the condition is discovered at an early stage it's possible to operate and staunch the bleeding, but Nilsson was lying there the whole night.'

'Could the perpetrator have anticipated such a development might happen?'

'Certainly not.'

I have to admit that the doctor's solution to the locked room puzzle was certainly an elegant variation on our beloved theme, but hardly what we were accustomed to from the literature. In books, the murderer outwits the police or the detective until the very end. He is not taken by surprise, as he was here, by circumstances without malice aforethought.

I thought of the poor devil who, twenty-four hours after his apparently innocent blow, was still completely unaware that an autopsy within the next few days would reveal that he had committed manslaughter.

The doctor seemed very pleased with himself. He was sitting comfortably on the sofa, puffing smugly at the Corona he had lit previously during my exposition.

'Can you think of anything wrong with my theory?'

He was addressing Carl, who had extracted the factual information from Gunnar earlier in the day and was clearly in the best position to form an opinion.

'Not offhand. Just to recap, you believe that Nilsson had a visitor in the evening and that the unknown guest managed to reach the room unnoticed. There he is served red wine and cheese—.'

'Cheese?'

This was the first time cheese had been mentioned. The doctor immediately became concerned.

'Yes, in the wastebasket they found a piece of cheese, which was probably eaten with the red wine. It was a Chianti, you know, in a straw-covered flask.'

'Hold on!' I exclaimed. 'What if the visitor left poisoned wine behind?'

'Nonsense!' snorted the doctor, rather brusquely. 'That would be the most clumsy murder by poison of the twentieth century, preceded by two hours of rowdy argument just to attract attention! No, it can't be that simple. Let's go back to the cheese. How do the police think it was cut up? With a cheese slicer or a knife?'

'I've no idea. Why do you ask?'

'Because if one of them had a knife, it could have been the weapon that caused the wound we suspect the murderer needed a piece of plaster for! Was there blood anywhere?'

'That I don't know either. Ivehed's first impression was that Nilsson was covered in blood, but that was before he smelt the wine. It had dried up in a couple of places, but there were small pools on the linoleum and on the table. The towel in the wastebasket was also—.'

'What towel?'

The doctor jumped to his feet as though his pants were on fire, dropping the glowing cigar on the carpet in his excitement. He contented himself with kicking it out of the way onto the parquet floor.

'There was a wet towel in the wastebasket, together with the cheese.'

'Wet from what? Red wine?'

'That's what Gunner thought.'

The doctor looked very satisfied.

'My friends,' he said, 'they sacrificed one of the hotel's few towels for the purpose of cleaning up after themselves at the same time that the table is wet and red wine is running in rivulets on the linoleum!'

'My dear Efraim,' I interposed gently, 'you've just explained how it

38

was the half-conscious Nilsson, and Nilsson alone, who upset the red wine on the table.'

The doctor was momentarily nonplussed but recovered quickly.

'So we have to conclude that the red wine was spilled twice during the evening, but the towel was only used after the first accident.'

'So it seems. Anyway, Gunnar said the towel was stained red.'

'There's too much red wine sloshing around in the damned room.'

The good doctor seemed suddenly upset. It doesn't happen very often.

'How much wine did they manage to down?' he continued. 'And what kind of drunkards are content with only one bottle of wine? By the way, was there only one bottle, Carl?'

'Yes.'

'Would it really be worth breaking the rules of the hotel to smuggle such a small amount of alcohol on the fly? They also made an awful noise, fought and took to the knife. It must have been either an incredibly powerful wine or an incredibly powerful cheese!'

After firing off this round of ammunition the doctor seemed to be extremely happy and rehabilitated. He recuperated the cigar and relit it, sneering at us in a satanic way. There was perspiration on his forehead and his hair, or what was left of it, stood up on his head.

It seemed, all the same, that some sensible points had been made and I developed the idea that the doctor had brought up:

'Didn't they find any corks or bottle caps in the room or outside, under the window?'

'The investigation's not over and it's possible they'll find more evidence. The flower bed is quite wide and there could be more stuff in there.'

'So you think the towel was bloodstained?'

'Think?' sniffed the doctor. 'Not at all: I know! Carl, you said that the towel was wet. Did you really mean that?'

Carl looked puzzled and taken aback.

'Well, it couldn't have been wet all night. I think Gunnar meant it was soiled with dried-up red wine.'

'What colour?'

'Red, of course. Red-coloured spots, Gunnar said.'

'Dark or light? Clearly defined or blurred?'

'I don't know,' replied Carl, distressed.

'Wine spots are not really red. They may possibly be pink but are principally violet. If the spots really were red, it must have been blood. Well?'

The doctor looked around triumphantly. I seized my chance.

'Nilsson didn't bleed anywhere, and there was no wound.'

'True. Continue.'

'But the murderer needed plaster.'

'Right again! If the towel was filled with blood, a plaster wouldn't have gone far. It could at the very most have sealed up the edges of a wound. Suppose the murderer's knife slipped while he was cutting up the cheese, but he didn't think the blood would spurt in such abundance. He patched up the wound and wrapped a towel around it. Then the argument started and they fell out. Nilsson was hit, but they reconciled. Then the murderer, who had not managed to become one as yet, discovered that his wound had opened and that the towel was wet. He became frightened, threw the used and worthless towel in the wastebasket, wound the other towel around his hand and disappeared through the back door before the news broadcast started on the radio.'

'Was there just one towel in the room?'

That was my question. Mostly there are at least two, according to my own experience of hotel visits. That was the case in Las Palmas, where, in spite of my age, I spent a week holidaying a couple of years ago. I would like to take this opportunity to complain about Spanish food. It causes stomach disease. Incidentally, the airplane food was also inferior. It was simply not edible. That was a digression.

'I can't answer that,' Carl replied thoughtfully.

'We'll know soon enough,' said the doctor, still full of himself. 'And where, dear friends, do you think our unsuspecting murderer heads for, since he doesn't think he has anything on his conscience and can still get about on his own two feet.'

'To the hospital!' Carl and I replied in chorus.

'Exactly! At the emergency ward he can get his problem fixed with a couple of simple sutures at any time of day or night.'

So it was as simple as that. We felt very pleased with ourselves and celebrated our success by downing the last drops of punch. The doctor had made the most important contribution, but on the other hand, as I reminded myself, many of the issues fell within his sphere of medical knowledge.

After a while he got to his feet, stretched his legs and put on his jacket.

'May I use the phone, please?'

Carl nodded and the doctor lumbered to the telephone table in the hall and dialled the hospital switchboard.

'Good evening, this is Dr. Nylander, could you put me through to emergency, please?'

He had to wait for thirty seconds.

'This is Nylander. Fine, and you? Were you the sister on duty last night? Excellent. A patient called during the evening and wanted to show me a wound he'd dressed in the ward last night. I directed him back to the hospital. From his description it seemed as if an inflammation may have occurred in the wound. It was itching and painful. I wonder, have you heard from him tonight? No? Nothing? Well, he may turn up tomorrow. His name? No, sorry. If sister checks yesterday's register I am sure that … yes, I can wait.'

The doctor winked meaningfully at us and we were full of admiration. I must admit that he handled it excellently.

'Hello. What time it would have been? Around half past nine, I think. No? Wait, when….? Half past twelve? With a gash in his hand? There we have him! Good, let me write it down. Fritiof Strömlund. Yes, I'll remember it.'

He continued talking about this and that. We stopped paying as much attention to the conversation as we had in the beginning and I began to gather up our files while Carl collected the washing-up on a tray.

Our activities were interrupted by a long, drawn-out: 'No, sister,' and a sigh from the doctor. Then he excused himself, added a few words and put down the receiver in a slow and sorrowful way.

If he had lumbered briskly to the telephone, he now dragged himself from it. We felt a strong sympathy, since we assumed he had learnt something sad which had dampened his spirits. I guessed it was about someone who recently had died at the hospital, perhaps one of his old patients.

'Everything fit so well until the end,' he said, 'when Sister Elsa told me that the putative murderer had not been alone.'

'What do you mean?'

'He was accompanied by his wife. They had been sitting in front of the television and, just before the end of the evening's programme, he had cut himself opening a last bottle of beer.'

Carl left to put on water for the tea.

While the pot was boiling, we all three remembered who Fritiof Strömlund was. He serves as a pastor of the Baptist church. It must have been low-alcohol beer.

The doctor put down his spectacles in front of him on the table and rubbed his eyes. Then he gave a deep sigh and, clearly drained of emotional energy, slumped motionless on the sofa.

A deep gloom settled on our little group.

4

When we began to review the doctor's theory carefully, it didn't take us long to find the weak point in his reasoning. Perhaps it was the spectacles on the table in front of us that put us on the right track. They seemed to be looking at us reproachfully.

In response to a simple routine question, Carl had been embarrassed to admit that he had forgotten an important detail. Nilsson had not been wearing his glasses, and had therefore not been lying "fully dressed" on the floor. He could never have walked across the room from the bed to the radio and back without the light switched on and with his spectacles still on the bedside table. He would have been helpless without them, and would have preferred to remain in bed and call for help if he had felt ill. There was a switch by the bed for just that purpose.

No. Nilsson had been murdered in his room and his killer had not succeeded in making it look like an accident.

'Our killer is smart, but not smart enough,' proclaimed Carl in English. He was probably quoting some author or other.

As I've said before, the name Axel Nilsson sounded vaguely familiar, but I hadn't been able to put my finger on it until now. I may perhaps have already mentioned my cousin, the master-painter Hammarström, who broke his leg last winter due to the negligence of the road maintenance authorities. He is much younger than I, and runs the well-reputed firm of decorators, Hammarström & Son. I had, in fact, heard about Axel Nilsson through the son, Lars-Erik.

Memory can often play tricks on us and many people of my age complain bitterly about how it has failed them. My cousin Hammarström, for example, often forgets what he had for dinner the night before and has not, as yet, succeeded in memorising my new telephone number. On the other hand, my own memory has resisted the ravages of time surprisingly well. I am thankful and proud of that. I can readily recall that my principal meal yesterday consisted of lightly-smoked and boiled Falu sausage with fried potatoes, accompanied by a small bottle of stout. Hammarström's office number is 14693 and his home number is 14007.

So, if my memory isn't playing tricks, Axel Nilsson should be the same Axel Nilsson—and the ages would square—who worked at the railway here ten years ago, and whom Lars-Erik Hammarström talked about. They had been in the navy at the same time, though Nilsson must have been at least a few years older. I myself was in the infantry, where, due to my considerable abilities, I eventually rose to the rank of corporal. Nilsson had been put on jankers several times, due to insubordination. He had drunk on active service and continued to drink after being discharged. My younger relative had, of course, not gone out of his way to maintain contact, but in a town the size of ours it's not possible to avoid chance meetings, and Nilsson quite possibly searched him out to borrow money. Lars-Erik had worked with his father all those years and had always been steady and reliable. Nilsson's visits must have been both awkward and unwelcome, especially since Lars-Erik had married at an early age and was already a father. The mere sight of an intoxicated person could be frightening, even detrimental, to small children.

It was probably in connection with some Christmas party at the master-painter's house that Nilsson had been mentioned and now I decided to tell my friends what little I knew about him, especially as we appeared to have come to a dead-end and the slightest clue was welcome. To my surprise, the doctor picked up where I left off.

'I know most people in this town,' he said, 'and from my years on the local temperance board I remember a person with that name. He was in the pipeline for resolution.'

'Resolution, what's that?'

'It's when a person is ordered to an alcoholism treatment unit. When a person succumbs to alcohol, it is sometimes necessary for society to take care of him. After examination, the doctor is required to give an opinion, which has to determine whether the addiction endangers the individual's health and the patient himself does not understand the consequences.'

'You did this particular check-up?'

'Not of Axel Nilsson. As I said, the temperance board decided that Nilsson should be taken care of, but he refused to commit himself to admission on a voluntary basis. At that time he was about 40 years old and a casual labourer. I think he was a bachelor as well. It was decided that a probation officer would bring him in and I had obtained his papers to read beforehand, but Nilsson and the probation officer never materialised. I waited for an hour, then the officer called to say that Nilsson had disappeared. He had been staying with his mother, but she hadn't seen him for a couple of days.'

'Did Nilsson know about the resolution?'

'He probably suspected something and took the opportunity to run away.'

'Did you hear from him again?'

'No, that's probably why I remember it. The probation officer and I agreed on taking action as soon as Nilsson turned up. Because of that I kept the documents with me for some time while waiting for an examination to be scheduled, but nothing happened.'

It was starting to come together. Nilsson had told Blom that he'd returned from abroad. But had he really been in hiding for ten years, just to escape the alcohol rehab unit? Or did he have other reasons to go underground? What did we know about him? Ten years ago he had been 40 years old and free and independent. A good-for-nothing and a compulsive drinker, a railroad worker and odd-job man. He needed money and he probably didn't just borrow from my young relative. He'd been living in the town for a long time, perhaps his whole life. Why hadn't he left earlier? Had he any other means of support here? Did his mother provide him with money as well as a room? All these questions were buzzing around in my head, but it seemed useless to speculate without more information.

There was a small interruption when Carl's wife came home. She is a charming woman. She came in to greet us and, although she seemed surprised to see us still there, she was her usual kind self and brought us fruit and carbonated drink. Our host then suggested that we air our lungs in the garden.

The apple trees were no longer bearing fruit and the flowers in the well-tended beds were long since gone. In the surrounding houses, partly blocked from view by a dense yew hedge, only a few windows were lit and soon they, too, went dark one by one.

It was a fine autumn evening. I didn't freeze, although I wasn't wearing an overcoat. Thousands of stars twinkled intimately in the magnificent sky. The doctor, less inclined than I to celestial contemplation, observed that they seemed only too inglorious and annoying, reminding him of Axel Nilsson's blinking eye and causing him to wonder if he had any nervous tics.

With that, the mood disappeared and—since the night was now decidedly cool—I thankfully acquiesced to Carl's suggestion to go back inside. As courteous as ever, he enquired whether we were tired and wished to end the meeting, which none of us, of course, wanted to do.

Happily, Mrs. Bergman excused herself and disappeared upstairs to bed.

'I wasn't sure before, but now I've asked Margit and I can therefore contribute another piece of the puzzle,' Carl began. 'I had a feeling that Axel Nilsson's mother, with whom he presumably stayed, could have been the same Mrs. Nilsson who used to clean the book shop a couple of years ago and who died last year, by the way. She was a small, bent-over, humour-haired woman of about seventy who always appeared anxious. She was the widow of a butcher and had settled somewhere down by the creek. We rarely saw each other, since she used to come after the shop was closed and did her duties in the evening.'

'She had a son?'

The doctor could not restrain his curiosity.

'Just a moment! The reason that I didn't think of her right away is because our meetings were occasional and I addressed her by her first name, Agda. I usually dropped formal titles with my colleagues in order to create a more relaxed atmosphere in the workplace.'

He paused. Forgetting he was no longer the owner of Bergman's Books and Stationer's Shop by the bus square, he was starting to wander down Memory Lane.

'Was there a son?' repeated the doctor impatiently.

'Yes. My wife, who kept the accounts and paid the salaries, just reminded me that her name was Agda Nilsson and then it came back to me. There was a small incident which might be of interest. One evening ten years ago, when I was working late filling some orders, I happened to meet Agda—Mrs. Nilsson—in the storage room. She was unhappy and red-eyed and I asked her as discreetly as possible if there was something troubling her. Usually she just said "how do you do" in a polite but simple way, and only replied in shy monosyllables when spoken to. Now she told me that she was alone. I asked if some relative had died and she answered that one could say that. Then she started to cry. I remember it well, for she was ashamed to show it and had no handkerchief. I opened a pack of paper napkins and she wiped away her tears. Later she explained that her son had gone to America, and now she had no relatives left. An elder son had gone there previously and hadn't even sent her a Christmas card.'

'Did she have more children?'

'No, she just kept repeating there was no one left. Not very much more was said. After that I didn't see her for quite a while. I suspect she did her cleaning at a later time to avoid running into me.'

'Didn't she say anything about her son and why he had gone?'

'No, nothing. Neither then nor later.'

'Not much flesh on those bones,' Efraim sighed. 'We already knew most of it. But all right... Nilsson has become a little bit more human now that he has a mother.'

Considering how excited Carl had been just a minute ago, I was afraid that the doctor's disappointment would discourage him, but there were shrewd lines about his mouth that usually promise a surprise.

'But one evening some years later she brought company.'

'A dog?'

'Better than that!'

'A fiancé?'

'Don't be foolish. A child! The girl was a couple of years old. She knocked over a whole pile of paper rolls right under my nose. Agda picked them up straight away and apologised. I took the opportunity to give the girl a colouring-book. She grabbed it from me, hid behind a showcase and refused to come out to say thank you. Agda became very embarrassed. Nevertheless, she was a nice kid and I listened to them from my office. The child babbled quite incomprehensibly and obviously tore the colouring-book in pieces or ate it. Agda gave the girl a good talking-to: "Don't do that with your kind uncle's nice book." They left late that evening and I wondered at what time small children usually go to bed.'

'A two year-old should have at least twelve hours of sleep,' the doctor said.

That remark, which had no actual bearing on our murder case, was probably intended to stop Carl wandering into a comparison with the bedtimes of his own small grandchildren.

'When they left, Agda said: "Now Lillan and granny will go home and sleep."'

'Wait a minute. Didn't you just say...?'

'Yes. One year she was totally alone and the following year she was a grandmother.'

Again the doctor lit another Corona. He was obviously surprised and intrigued.

'Whose child was...Lillan? The eldest son had emigrated many years earlier to America. He could hardly have produced any small children here.'

'Not here perhaps,' I said, brilliantly but rashly, 'but over there.'

'Nonsense. If he's not sending Christmas cards he's hardly going to send children.'

'Could the girl have been Axel's?'

'Why not? A few years after Agda complains about being alone, a two year-old suddenly turns up on the scene. Which must mean that Agda, at the end of the nineteen-fifties just thinks she's alone, whereas in actual fact—.'

'She's a grandmother,' the doctor interjected. 'No more than nine months later.'

The new circumstances were digested for a while. Carl took the floor again.

'The explanation for Axel running away from his homeland could, in other words, be that he not only wanted to get away from his resolution, but also from paternity.'

'What's a poor fellow to do,' the doctor said sarcastically, 'when he finds himself trapped wherever he looks? He goes to sea, naturally. He signs articles on board and sails out to become as free as a lark, while at home the girl walks about grieving ....'

'Do we know anything about the child's mother?'

'No, but we should be able to find out easily enough.'

The case had taken a surprising turn. But again there was something that didn't fit. I opened my mouth.

'But what could cause the runaway father to return after ten years? By that time his alimony debts will have grown considerably and there is a bitter and deceived mother of his child who's been forced to fend for herself, even with the assistance of granny.'

'On the other hand: what chances did Nilsson have of succeeding in America? He probably couldn't live on his brother as he had on his mother. America is the land of the future, for sure, but only for those who can do something.'

It was the doctor who was at it again.

'If Axel Nilsson was a washout here at home, he must have been the same in America. Furthermore, he got older and became sick and totally incapacitated.'

'Now wait a minute,' I put in. 'To begin with, he was not that old and, secondly, there's no proof he was sick.'

48

Carl, who had been quiet for a while, now spoke again.

'Remember, he took drugs and Blom had the impression....'

'Who the devil has said that he took drugs?' roared the doctor.

'Excuse me. I forgot to mention there was a newly opened bottle of Dichiotride-K in the room, on the bedside table.'

'What's that, Efraim?' I asked, for the purpose of pouring oil on troubled waters.

'Diuretic pills, often used in connection with hypertension and heart disease. They drive out bodily fluid.'

'But Blom said that Nilsson was pitifully thin and his clothes were hanging on him. Why did he need to get rid of fluid?'

'He may have taken too many pills!'

The idea came from Carl, and was obviously so stupid that the doctor didn't even bother to respond.

'Maybe it was suicide,' I offered. and the doctor gave me a withering look.

'With diuretic pills? All of a sudden he got tired of living and decided to pee himself to death? Are you serious?'

I laughed rather nervously. It wasn't clear whether the doctor was pulling my leg or in the mood to appreciate my well-known sense of humour, so I decided not to take the opportunity to tell the story of the mystery fan who borrowed the library's phone directory by mistake. I decided to leave it for another occasion.

'How many pillows did Nilsson have under his head during the night?' the doctor asked.

'There was one in the bed and one without its case in the wardrobe.'

'Hmm. Did he have any problems walking up the stairs?'

'No, he seems to have been moving around quite freely despite his wounded leg.'

'Without seeming to be out of breath? That doesn't suggest heart trouble. But who knows?'

The doctor looked simultaneously pleased, concerned and irritated, a difficult feat.

'Why did the limping, blinking, bespectacled, slurring, pill-eating prodigal son come back?' Carl asked. 'Why did he hide himself in a shady little boarding-house? He could hardly have worked his way across the Atlantic, useless as he must have been as a crew member.'

'Axel will be a sailor,' the doctor murmured.

'What?'

'It's a sentence I learned during a grammar lesson in school a long time ago. The meaning shifts depending on which word you stress. *Axel* will be a sailor, not anyone else. He *will* be a sailor, he isn't qualified yet. He will be a *sailor*, not a carpenter or even a tailor. Do you see what I mean?'

Carl and I both nodded. Efraim can sometimes be a little hard to follow.

'Which perhaps is a digression in relation to the problem we are facing,' he continued, 'but I....'

It was at that moment that I found the key to the whole problem, in a literal as well as in a figurative sense.

'Isn't it obvious why he was hiding in the boarding-house?' I interrupted him quietly and unexpectedly.

5

The new information we had just received had made it possible for a startling explanation of the murder riddle to crystallize in my brain. I felt a sense of importance in my friends' eyes similar to when Director Lindquist made his memorable speech upon my retirement from the firm, or when I was entrusted with the responsibility of President of The Watermark Society of Philatelists.

'Don't you find it surprising that Nilsson was staying in a double room?'

'He was disabled,' Carl reminded me.

'Disabled enough to demand a lot of elbow-room and space in room 5, but at the same time capable of running up and down the stairs like a monkey. We know most of the time he was hiding in his room; that he seldom went out and seldom received visitors at the hotel.'

'What are you getting at?'

'That he was not just hiding himself in that room!'

'What else could he have been hiding?'

'Perhaps not something, but someone!'

My little bombshell had the intended effect. My friends looked utterly perplexed, but gradually doubts and objections arose.

'How would that have been possible without the knowledge of the boarding-house owner?' asked the doctor.

'And of the chamber-maid?' added Carl.

'At first sight it does seem impossible,' I admitted, 'but let me get to that later. We must first analyse the situation. According to Nilsson's passport, he landed in Sweden on the twelfth, and on the thirteenth he arrived at *The Little Boarding-House*. Why he returned to his home country we don't yet know, but he did return right now and he did arrive right here. Of all places, his choice was our town. He had every reason to avoid the unpleasantness that the confrontation with certain people would mean, but despite all that he came here. That can only mean that he had everything to gain here and nothing to lose. But for some reason, the time was not quite ripe. He had to stay here to take care of something, but it was still too early to emerge from the shadows, so for the time being he had to lie...

51

down?'

'Lie low.' Carl, who's familiar with detective slang, corrected me.

'Yes, for a couple of weeks. It had been about ten years since he'd lived here, the memories of his indiscretions had probably faded and the resolution had probably expired.'

'That's correct,' the doctor confirmed.

'What's more, he'd changed. He was no longer the small-town Don Juan of the past who had surprised his mother with a grandchild, but a broken, worn-out man, unhealthy before his time. The risk of being recognised was small, but could be made even smaller.'

'How do you mean?'

I shook a little bit in my shoes before my next move, anxious that my comrades should not find it too exaggerated or fabricated.

'Through disguise!'

Quite contrary to what I had expected, this was received with a certain amount of enthusiasm, especially by Carl. The doctor stopped frowning and waited attentively.

'How otherwise can you explain the shapeless clothes, the spectacles, the moustache, the limping gait, the grimaces and so on? Note that he doesn't really put on a mask but is satisfied with a few misleading signs, erasing all connections to the Axel Nilsson who was known in the town, and combining this with his retiring disposition at the boarding-house. All the time he's vigilant and procuring information from Blom. He's biding his time.'

It was now time for a telling pause, letting the idea sink in. After the initial shock, my friends seemed to be thoughtful.

'Let me ask you this: did Blom's description of Nilsson describe him accurately?'

'Are you suggesting Blom's description of him was designed to dupe us and the police?' Carl asked, surprised.

'On the contrary, his description was too good and because of that, misleading!'

Such paradoxical and apparently contradictory statements are what we take pleasure in and excel at. It comes from reading all those detective novels, where similar mystifying remarks are frequently made.

'Just think,' I continued, 'of an individual with very protruding ears! He is easy to describe and recognise. When you meet him you immediately think: "here's that man with the protruding ears." You have then made the mistake of letting a detail become the main feature and with that the description has become inapt. Would you recognise him when he takes off his false ears? It's the same thing with Nilsson. We say: "Aha! He's the one who limps." If the limping is fabricated, then we have less chance of identifying him. Take away a couple of the essential characteristics and he will be completely unrecognisable. In my opinion, the picture of himself that Axel Nilsson has supplied is much more cunningly effective than we suspected, and totally incorrect.'

'You're right. We can't envisage Nilsson without his badly-fitting clothes, the strange blinking and the limping gait.'

'And what's more, it's a disguise which is easy to get rid of and become anonymous again, which made it easier for him when it came to achieving his special purpose.'

'Which was?'

'To look just like his secret room-mate.'

There was a dramatic silence. To avoid looking at my friends during their consternation, I bent down and started fiddling with my bootlaces. They were already quite tight with double knots. It took me some time to untie them and then tie them again, during which the only sound to be heard was the crackling of the fire in the grate. Eventually it was the doctor who broke the silence.

'Do you mean that the person staying with him had a real leg injury?'

'It's quite possible. If two people have to live together for some reason, but only one of them can ever be seen, then why wouldn't the one with the real leg injury be the one to show himself, so that the healthy one is spared the trouble of imitating him? Well, it might in fact be easier for the healthy one to disguise himself as the other. In this case, if the other person was an older man suffering from heart disease, it might well have been easier for Axel Nilsson, 52 years old, to pretend to be older and frailer than he actually was, rather than have the older man try to make himself look younger and healthier.'

'I agree,' said the doctor. 'Do you think that was what decided who the "official" occupant of the room was, so to speak?'

'Not at all, and you'll soon hear why. But it certainly made things easier for Nilsson and reduced the risk of the double occupancy being discovered.'

'Could two people really have stayed in the room without being exposed? After all, we're talking about a period of two weeks.'

'Probably. And they both may not have been there the whole time.'

The doctor looked at me to go on, and I had the feeling that much was at stake before my clever solution would be accepted.

'So Nilsson took the room and could let his double in at any time,' I continued. 'At night there's very little risk in sneaking down the stairs and opening the back door. By the way, Carl, is it true that there are two flights leading up to the first floor, one from the entrance and another from the rear door?'

'Yes. They lead to opposite ends of the first floor corridor.'

'If one of them wanted to leave, he would keep the key after locking his mate in the room instead of handing it in or hanging it up. As you know, Blom had no spare key. If both men wanted to take a walk separately, one of them would leave through the back door and the other would walk out through the main entrance. This would be safe, since Blom could only watch one door at a time. But Nilsson seldom left the room. Probably both of them stayed inside most of the time.'

'What happened when the chamber-maid wanted to come in?'

'Nilsson probably found out when she was expected and let his alter ego leave through the back door and onto the path to Björkstigen in good time before she arrived. Maybe he shut himself in the bathroom or hid somewhere else.'

'But she surely would have suspected mischief if she cleaned the room every day.'

'Possibly, but just think about it. A couple of extra sheets could easily have been hidden in a suitcase, a pair of spare blankets could have been borrowed on the pretext of feeling chilly, and there was already an extra pillow in the closet.'

'It would have been odd to ask for two mattresses because of the cold!'

'Yes, but Nilsson had a double room.'

'The other bedstead had been removed,' Carl pointed out.

'Is that so? Well, maybe Nilsson took the bed and his room-mate made do with an inflatable mattress, which doesn't take much space. If the guest was like Nilsson, he wouldn't have cared much. People of that sort have no great demands when it comes to comfort. Think of the goldsmith in the town park.'

Crona, the goldsmith, is the town eccentric, a habitual drunkard who once had been a skilled craftsman, but who had hit the bottle. On sunny days he stays in the town park, sleeping on a bench with his jacket folded under his head and an old newspaper under his shoes so as not to make things dirty. The park is situated by the church on the other side of the creek. Since he is quite harmless and also serves as a warning to the town youth, he is mostly left alone. Many people consider him to be a colourful contribution to the townscape.

'They took their meals in the room and shared them. After all, they were looking forward to better times ahead.'

'The mystery tenant as well?'

'Maybe. Before I talk about that, let me just go back to what I said earlier. It seems to me quite possible to have carried out this masquerade for a short time. Every time Blom caught a glimpse of his unknown hotel guest, he—.'

'—saw a limping man in baggy clothes!'

'Exactly. What he saw was supposedly Axel Nilsson, and it didn't occur to anyone that the real Nilsson could actually be lurking behind a locked room on the first floor.'

The doctor was starting to become impatient. We had now talked for quite a while about the mysterious double, and now it was time to reveal his identity.

'Johan Lundgren, do you know who that second man was?'

'Yes,' I replied. 'He was the murderer.'

'I guessed as much, but do you know his name?'

'Let me ask a counter-question. What do you know about methanol?'

'Methyl alcohol? I don't see what that's got to—.'

'Is it harmful?'

'Wait!' Carl exclaimed, before the doctor could answer.

A more dramatic writer than I would have been able to depict the reaction in a more graphic way, but my moderation prohibits me from resorting to exaggeration. It would, however, be wrong not to describe his sudden blinding insight as an explosion. Carl stared straight ahead with his hands clapped to his forehead as if he had had a revelation, the sight of which could not be endured.

In novels the detective, in cases like this, usually blurts out that he has been an idiot, which has always irritated me because of the incomparable intelligence of Hercule Poirot, Nero Wolfe and Perry Mason. How can the reader's sense of being at a disadvantage not be strengthened when a commonplace mistake or a natural oversight causes the hero to feel as if he's possessed of a hopelessly feeble intellect?

My secret sense of triumph and the drama of the occasion inspired me to utter the next somewhat blasphemous remark:

'We have been blind to the truth, have we not, gentlemen?'

Hastily, Carl took down a publication from the bookshelf, printed by Lindquist's Printing Office, Ltd. It was entitled *It Happened Here* and was the annual survey of local events for 1946, compiled by Magnus Ekeblad, the former headmaster of the co-educational school.

'You have a good memory, Johan!'

'It was a particularly disturbing event,' I replied modestly.

Then Carl read the following item out loud from Ekeblad's little pamphlet. In my own dedicated copy I had underlined the wording:

"'It was also this year (1946, my remark) that the horrible wood alcohol catastrophe hit several ill-fated citizens. There were more than ten victims, of which many became permanently visually impaired and some totally blind, but there were very likely others who may have been less injured and because of the circumstances found it best not to step forward in the light of the publicity. The matter was taken up in the local papers and the public at large was upset, judging from several aggravated letters to the press and from protests in his own office to the police commissioner in person, calling for a more thorough investigation.

It turned out that one of the town's own sons, who ran a home distilling business, had sold a batch of liquor with an added ingredient of high proof methyl alcohol to his unsuspecting customers. This substance, which is a waste product from our wood-pulp factory, has a potent toxic effect on the optic nerve. However the perpetrator, a former sawmill worker, had succeeded in absconding and was still at liberty.

For the time being negotiations are taking place on behalf of those individuals who are claiming damages. They are represented by the solicitor Lindner and the Health Insurance Office. The case is still dormant with the National Swedish Social Insurance Board.'"

The doctor, Carl and I are not only born and bred in this town, but have always lived here. Therefore, I dare say that no single event over the last fifty years has provoked more pronounced indignation and wrath. Yes, I go so far as to assert that during some weeks of 1946, feelings of hostility prevailed among the population, and I can reveal that behind the signature "Teetotaller" to a letter published by a widely-read and respected local newspaper was yours truly! In it I criticised the slow pace of the machinery of justice and called in question the competence of certain unnamed higher officials. In spite of all the efforts of the police and various individuals, the perpetrator could not be found. In the absence of a formal confession his name was not announced, but it was, of course, a matter of common knowledge and on everybody's lips: Edvin Nilsson, the brother of Axel.

The business had been run out of a ramshackle outhouse in a yard by the creek, where the distillation had taken place and where their mother had lived up to last year. The police found all of the equipment and confiscated it. It was rusty and out of date and had probably not been in good working order ever since the days of their father, the butcher. He had died of alcohol poisoning in the beginning of the 1930s. Edvin had inherited the equipment and he must have been cunning for, in spite of several police raids over the years, they had not previously succeeded in procuring proof.

Many people wondered where Edvin had gone, but few knew, among them the mother. People in general had, in spite of their bitterness, found it difficult not to feel sorry for her. She had passed a deplorable life, starting with her husband's reign of terror and then later as housekeeper and breadwinner for her sons. Her cheerless life, filled with continual disappointments, was nevertheless the only one she had, and we could certainly understand the despair she had revealed to Carl, when Axel in turn had left. She most probably never saw Edvin again. He would not have dared to turn up anywhere near the town. I personally cannot look back at the events that occurred in the mid-1940s without experiencing a wave of loathing for him, and the doctor and Carl, now silent and serious, almost certainly shared the same feeling.

'So you mean that our shadowy figure in room 5 was Edvin Nilsson?'

'Yes, it would seem that he returned.'

'But he would never dare. The period for prosecution may have expired, but....'

'A very apt remark. It would still be imperative for him to keep in hiding!'

'What could possibly have caused him to take the risk of coming back?'

'Exactly, what on earth could have caused two expatriate brothers with that much on their conscience to make that long return journey across the Atlantic? In America they could feel safe, but here it's different. Here, they're coming straight into the lion's den.'

My friends now expected an explanation. I began a little bit lost for words, but Carl put me on the right track.

'Something must have happened that totally changed the situation.'

'For whom? For Edvin?'

'For both of them. They were independent of each other. Brotherhood and loyalty meant nothing to them. If they were together in America, both of them benefitted by that arrangement and, if something important happened, it had to affect them both as much— or be equally urgent to both of them—for them to have decided on joint action. We know nothing of their situation in America. We can only suspect that they were not particularly successful, and didn't have much to leave behind.'

'Maybe things were getting too hot for them over there?'

'Possibly, but the event that decided them must have happened here.'

'And it affected them both?'

'Yes, obviously. Let me just ask you this question: What might constitute something important to these people in life? Something more important than wine, women and fun?'

'Their own security?'

'Which definitely should have discouraged them from coming here!'

'Money? Could there have been money for them to collect here? For both of them?'

'Yes, there was only one event here at home that affected them both, and that was their mother's death last year.'

'In other words, an inheritance?'

'That must be it. They came to collect their inheritance.'

At this Efraim could no longer control himself. He had been listening to our discussion, but now came what I had feared. His outburst, however, gave me a short respite, during which I prepared my defence.

'Money to be inherited? From whom? The mother was their only relative and she had to do cleaning in the evenings to keep body and soul together. Her assets could not have been more than a few hundred crowns. It wouldn't even have covered their travel expenses. We have to do beter than that!'

'How about the house by the creek with the garden?' replied Carl, splendidly doing the best he could to support me.

'A tumbledown hovel and a few square metres of ground? A shed of corrugated iron in the Arizona desert would entice more prospective buyers.'

It was now time for my boldest bid.

'Efraim is right, but what if they *thought* there was something to collect?'

'Aha! They were the illegitimate children of the Wallenberg family, were they? Their bank was up for auction under a writ of execution and they thought that they just had to come with their trucks to the vault. Brilliant! Thank you very much!'

'I'm not kidding. How did their mother feel? All these years she had worked and toiled, but always met ingratitude, and now she wanted to atone for what society had suffered because of her.'

'Not because of her, because of her sons. That's a totally different matter.'

'Perhaps not in her opinion. Before she died she wanted to clear her conscience. The boys were a part of her and their guilt was her guilt. She could not rest until they had been punished, otherwise she would not have paid off her and her offspring's share. All her motherly love had been abortive, and her sons had left her in the lurch when she needed them most. Therefore she called them home.'

'That's impossible. Edvin would never have dared to turn up here!'

'Unless she set a trap and caught them in it.'

'Yes, why not? They rarely heard from their mother and knew almost nothing about her condition. Suppose she wrote a letter and said that she was dying. She understood it was difficult for them to come home, but luckily she could provide for her grandchild through a sum of money....'

'What sum of money?'

'An imaginary one. For example, first prize in the state lottery, which she had deposited in the bank and let a lawyer hold in trust. Furthermore, she could have said that she had bequeathed the sum to the sons but if they did not personally turn up within a certain period of time that would mean that they accepted her decision that Axel's daughter would take over the inheritance. Then she only had to inform the solicitor that her sons could be expected to return home and that the police could apprehend them if necessary.'

I was quite happy with my explanation. Of course I had to base it largely on guesswork, but I was convinced that the brothers had arrived in town together and that an acceptable reason had to be invented. I saw that my friends considered the idea to be plausible.

'If the brothers had been instructed to appear personally, such a letter would have been addressed to Edvin, since he had to inform Axel and needed him as a cover because of his fear about appearing in the town.'

'Did both of them have to travel? Couldn't Axel have got an authorisation from Edvin?'

'How could Edvin guarantee that Axel would actually return with the money? He could have replaced the authorization with a false certificate stating that Edvin was dead and demanded the entire inheritance for himself.'

'But,' Carl objected, 'how could the mother be sure that they wouldn't make sure the inheritance existed while they were still in America and discover the deceit?'

'She gave the name and address of the solicitor and he, for his part, knew of her intention and was willing to join in the game.'

'She gambled that her sons wouldn't dream that she wanted to lead them to destruction. In her farewell letter they were told she had a malignant disease, perhaps the final stages of cancer. How many months would she have left at that point?'

The doctor replied immediately. I'd sought to arouse his enthusiasm for my theories, but it appeared the ice was already broken.

'It depends. Stomach cancer would be quick: a few months at the most.'

'The brothers hadn't much time to act. They had nothing to lose and everything to gain. The personal property they had in America was only a fraction of the supposed inheritance, so they didn't hesitate. But for some reason they postponed the journey.'

'Why?'

'I don't know. One of them could have been serving time in prison and had to wait for his release.'

'Maybe. Anyway, is it really plausible that Edvin would risk returning to the town for the sake of the money?'

'He was still not keen and needed to be sure that the coast was clear, so he sent Axel ahead to get the lie of the land.'

'Now I think you're indulging in fantasies again.'

It was the doctor who expressed his doubts, but it was now time to grasp the nettle.

'Now listen: The brothers were in need of money. As soon as they could pay the tickets they left. When they arrived in Sweden they were cleaned out, and the room arrangement was necessary in order to keep Edvin hidden. Therefore they had to see to it that nobody could get into the room and discover him.'

'How did they arrange it? I mean, how could Edvin be sure—.'

Once again, Carl stopped in mid-sentence and the delight that shone in his eyes meant that another penny had dropped.

'By making the extra key disappear! If Edvin had a duplicate key, he could come and go as he liked, without hindrance. Therefore, gentlemen, Axel actually arrived a month before yesterday's murder and, undisguised, stole the key. We've been told he arrived in the country on the twelfth and came to the hotel on the thirteenth, but what if there were one month and not twenty-four hours in between?'

I turned to Carl, who thought the matter over.

'It's possible. Gunnar didn't say anything about the month of arrival, but in that case why didn't Blom recognize Axel the second time, in the following month?'

'Because the first time he looked different and he probably stayed out of sight as much as possible. His assignment was also over pretty quickly. I suspect all he had to do was to make sure that his mother really was dead and that the name and address of the lawyer were correct.'

'May I ask a few questions?'

It was the doctor again, and I was prepared for the worst.

'Which solicitor was involved and why did the brothers wait a month?'

'It could only have been Lindner, who pleaded the cause of the visually handicapped people in 1946 and is still active as far as I know. Unfortunately, we don't know how the insurance problem was resolved twenty years ago, but what a feather in his cap it would be for him if he could produce the guilty party after all these years! The question of the brother's delay is more difficult. Maybe the lawyer wasn't available in mid-September. That was what Axel discovered during his first visit here and soon told Edvin, wherever he hid himself.'

'Keeping his passport to have a hold over him?'

'Very likely. By the way, it was no problem for him to check in at *The Little Boarding-House* without it. Blom doesn't care about formalities. In any case, Axel's preliminary visit here confirmed that their mother was satisfactorily dead and found no suspicions of a trap.'

'I'm still not satisfied as to why they had to wait until mid-October. They were badly short of money and being in Sweden was risky. And where was Edvin waiting while Axel was doing his research?'

'In Göteborg, at a guess."

'Well, let's assume that, for the time being. But why didn't Blom procure a spare key in the meantime?'

'Maybe due to sheer indolence? Blom wasn't quick on the trigger. The TV in the lounge hadn't been repaired for ages, for example.

'That won't wash!'

'In the meantime, there were guests in room 5, so the only key couldn't be spared.'

'Not good enough. You can get a new key in a few hours.'

'Well, then, maybe he thought he'd be able to get along with one key for a little longer. Or maybe he hoped whoever had taken the key would send it back.'

'I agree the boarding-house was run in a slapdash way, and that Blom wasn't very careful, but it was in his own interest to have a spare key. And note that the longer it took before Axel Nilsson returned—this time in a new shape and with his brother packed away in his luggage—the greater the risk would be that Blom had been able to replenish his store of keys, and the greater the risk would become of Edvin being discovered in the room.'

The silly detail of the key threatened to destroy my whole argument. I was being backed into a corner like a criminal, yet I was convinced that I was right.

It was close to midnight and fatigue began to set in. Carl had opened a window, but the fresh air was not enough to chase away the drowsiness. Efraim appeared almost condescending and didn't seem ready to call it a day. Despite his age and his weight he is surprisingly tireless, probably due to training during many a night as doctor on duty.

'I admit I find Blom's failure to get a spare key to be bewildering,' I said, 'as does the capacity of the brothers to take that into account. Let me see now....'

A moment's pause, a breathing-space, before I continued.

'Perhaps they didn't care whether Blom had a key or not; the important thing being that the brothers had one key each. When it then turned out that Blom had not obtained a new key, it suited them perfectly and—wait a minute!'

Up to this point I had been dreading the lack of explanation of the locked room my friends would demand of me. Now I, too, went to the bathroom. After five minutes I was back. Thanks to the discussion about the keys, I had found the solution.

'When Axel realised that the boarding-house owner could not get into the room, he happily announced the news to Edvin and thereby signed his own warrant.'

'What?!!!'

The doctor and Carl looked at me in astonishment. I permitted myself to insert a pause for effect, during which I sipped at my soda-water, which was lukewarm and flat.

'The brothers installed themselves in the boarding-house around the middle of this month. Nilsson asked for a double room with a view of the passage and he was given, as good luck—or rather bad luck—would have it, room number 5 as planned. Why then did they stay there for almost a fortnight if staying was so fraught with danger? Well, I think that it had to do with the time the lawyer needed to make the financial arrangements. He had his victims in the trap but he waited before acting. Why so? Well, for one thing he didn't know where they were living. All the negotiations went through Axel, who was the only one who dared show up in public and then only in disguise. But Edvin was the key figure—.'

I had made an unintentional joke and did not realize it until my two friends burst out laughing.

'Without a confession from Edvin, the visually handicapped people might not get their just compensation. While the lawyer was trying to discover his address in order to have him arrested, he produced a number of reasons for delaying the inheritance payment, and the atmosphere in room 5 became more and more tense.'

'Why didn't Lindner call the police? Gunnar said nothing about the police keeping Nilsson under observation.'

'No doubt because he wanted to take all the credit for himself. But he never suspected that the individual he was looking for was hiding in plain sight in Axel's hotel room. In any case, he had them where he wanted them, on tenterhooks. After all their efforts to get hold of the inheritance, all they could do now was wait.'

'Then Edvin began to smell a rat.'

Now the doctor had caught on at last.

'Yes. One of them found out somehow that the inheritance didn't exist and that caused a quarrel which left one of the brothers dead.

But before that they had been eating and drinking, someone had cut the cheese carelessly and there had been bloodshed. They had stopped fighting and attempted to obtain plaster for Edvin.'

'What about the glasses?' asked the doctor.

'Edvin must have thought that the accident would seem more convincing if the police could be persuaded that Axel had fallen over while he was intoxicated and in a half-blind state, groping around in the room. So he took the glasses away from the body and placed them on the bedside table to add to that impression. And now we come to the keys. Edvin knew that there were two. He had one of them and Axel had the other. He also knew that Blom believed that only one existed. One corpse, two keys: Edvin suddenly realised he had everything he needed to create a perfect crime and a locked-room mystery to boot.'

'Wait a minute! Maybe he could arrange the technical details, but he couldn't escape. Lindner would know immediately who the murderer was.'

'The fact that the room was locked and sealed during the night gave him enough time to disappear, at least twelve hours. On top of that, nobody would suspect it was murder because the room was locked from the inside. The police would have no reason to look for a murderer. You remember I said that Axel signed his own death warrant when he passed on Blom's information that there was no spare? At the time, Edvin hadn't been thinking about murder. But when it happened he took advantage of the circumstances. By arranging the locked room he was able to make the murder look like an accident, at least for long enough.'

'Are we absolutely sure that Axel Nilsson is the one who's dead?'

The idea was interesting and I welcomed it with open arms. Mistaken identities are a staple fare of mystery literature and it would have been fascinating to be faced with something similar in real life.

'Not completely. The brothers did look alike and it would be difficult to determine precisely the identity of the dead man without clues such as limping, blinking without spectacles and speaking thickly. And Axel could have left his passport behind and become Edvin's double. But, whoever died in that room, the other brother is the murderer.'

Now Carl came to life and proved his alertness with a detail I'd missed.

'The spilled red wine would reinforce the impression that a self-inflicted accident had taken place!'

At that, Efraim must have sensed that his bloodstained towel theory was in danger, for he immediately asked:

'What about the red-coloured towel? How does it fit in the context?'

'The murderer had a lot of things to take care of in the room and he didn't want to leave any clues behind, neither fingerprints nor—.'

'—footprints,' Carl added.

'That's right. He wound the towels around his shoes so as not to leave any footprints in the wine pools, and in order to avoid getting wine from the floor on his clothes. Gunnar Bergman never specified the exact shade of colour of the spots, but he must have meant spots of red wine, although they were not really red in the proper sense.'

'Where did the second towel go?' asked the doctor, with perfect timing.

'It was probably used to wrap up some of the murderer's belongings. He had to collect his goods and chattels and disappear.'

With a sigh, the doctor abandoned defending his theory of a bloody towel and we downgraded the previous theory about the plaster to be about a harmless scratch somewhere on the murderer's miserable body. I continued:

'So how did the murderer get out of the house? He obviously bided his time until the moment when the back door was unguarded while Blom was locking the front door during his round of inspection. If the police haven't already been in touch with lawyer Lindner today, it's quite possible that the culprit has been able to leave the country in peace and quiet. The identity of the victim is less important. The murderer is the stronger and the smarter brother, while the victim had the bad luck to lose.'

'Edvin was suffering from heart disease and was the elder.'

'And, at the same time, he was the more desperate of the two brothers. The identification is a mere formality, and the police will take responsibility for that as they will for capturing the murderer. I myself think that Edvin is the one who's still alive, but I am in agreement that both of them had the same opportunity to arrange the locked-room murder.'

With that, I had returned to the central part of the riddle.

'Yes,' said Efraim, 'we must have an explanation of that before we break up, Johan. How was it done? After all, the room was locked from the inside.'

'No.'

'But, my dear Johan, Blom saw the key in the keyhole, and his testimony is strengthened by the fact that Ivehed's picklock didn't work because the key on the inside was in the way.'

'Gentlemen, I went to the bathroom a few minutes ago.'

The situation was such that I could afford another mystifying clue.

'Stick to the point!'

'I am. Carl, how do you open the door of the garden shed?'

'I use a key, of course. It's hanging on a nail outside.'

'Exactly. When I went to the W.C. just now, I took the liberty of borrowing the bathroom key, which is about the same shape and size as that of the garden shed. I went out and inserted it loosely from inside in the lock of the tool shed door and succeeded in locking the door with the real key from the garden side. After having taken it out with the utmost care, the bathroom key was still in place and visible through the keyhole in the same way as the key of room 5 was visible.'

'You mean it only seemed as though the inner key belonged to the lock?'

'Yes, it had just been inserted far enough to create the impression that it had been used to lock the door. That was the reason the key fell out easily when the police knocked on the door.'

'But in that case Ivehed's picklock would also have fit and unlocked the door, since the key on the other side didn't go in far enough to block it.'

'Not if you put in a small stone or wedge in the keyhole. It can't be seen, but it prevents the key-bit from engaging the locking mechanism. From that, one gets the impression that the key doesn't work because of the presence of another one, but in reality it's not the key that doesn't fit, but the lock that has been disabled in an ingenious way.'

My friends looked suspiciously at me and the doctor even borrowed a flashlight and went out into the garden. Five minutes later he returned, smiling broadly.

'Congratulations, Johan!'

I tried my best to look modest, but inwardly I was swelling with pride.

'But then who turned off the transistor radio in the middle of the night?'

Good heavens, I had totally forgotten the wretched radio. My beautiful construction would collapse like a house of cards if that problem could not be explained. Then I had a brainwave!

'Edvin left the radio switched on in order to make any listeners at the door believe that everything was okay in the room: that Axel was perfectly well after his troublesome visitor had left.'

'But by the morning the radio had been switched off.'

'No, the batteries ran down during the night. It is a complete illusion that Axel or someone else turned the radio off.'

There was an awestruck pause, then the doctor spoke:

'Before we ask Carl to conclude tonight's meeting, which has been the longest in our club's history—I actually heard the church clock striking twelve during my visit to the garden shed—I'd like Johan to call the boarding-house.'

'Why?'

'To find out if Axel Nilsson really signed in there one and a half months ago.'

'But he wouldn't have signed under his own name. Whatever name appears in the hotel register, it won't be Axel Nilsson.'

'So what? How do criminals in our mystery novels proceed?'

'They use a false name.'

'Exactly. Most writers of detective novels write in English. What name do murderers mostly choose when they want to use an alias?'

'Well, anything goes. I don't know.'

'Of course you do! Murderers mostly use the most common name they can think of. John Brown, William Smith and so on.'

'It wouldn't do here.'

'No, of course not. But they would use the same method. I bet the hotel guest who stole the key called himself Erik Andersson or Lars Pettersson. Something like that. Anything but Axel Nilsson. We need to ask Blom about it.'

What Efraim proposed was indeed an exciting experiment.

It was only a quarter past twelve and Blom didn't go to sleep until one, so we wouldn't be disturbing him. We decided for me to say that an acquaintance of mine and his wife might have stayed at the hotel around September 12. Blom would tell me that around that date he didn't have any couples in his double rooms (I counted on it being the off-peak season and the boarding-house being hardly the kind of place where people would stay overnight with their wives) and that my friends must have chosen another accommodation, since his only occupied double room had been held by a single man. After I somehow managed to explain away the wife, I could ask if the name of the guest was Erik Andersson. Using a possible excuse for asking, perhaps by mentioning that my friend had forgotten a valuable item of equipment and had asked me to try to trace it, I would probably be able to get hold of the name Axel Nilsson had been hiding behind.

I reminded myself not to forget to beg my pardon for troubling the establishment and its night porter at this late and inconvenient time.

Our conversation took about one minute. When I replaced the handset and turned to the doctor and Carl, who were scarcely visible in the darkness in front of the almost burned-out fire, they asked me immediately if I had obtained the name.

'Yes,' I replied.

'Erik Andersson?'

'No, Axel Nilsson.'

6

Once we'd recovered from the shock, I had to report the conversation again with scrupulous accuracy. Blom had replied in the negative to the question of whether an acquaintance of mine had put up at the boarding house a month and a half ago and had subsequently returned his room key, which he had taken with him by mistake. After which, Blom had looked in his register and asked me whether Axel Nilsson was the person I was talking about, that being the only name which fit within the period of time I had mentioned.

'Just imagine,' said Carl, suddenly jumping to his feet, 'if Axel wrote from America that he would be returning home and asked for help in getting a—.'

'Please wait,' I asked, but Carl was not to be stopped.

'— commodious hotel room booked. The recipient of the letter suspected complications and misappropriated the key himself when he put up at *The Little Boarding-House* in the name of Axel Nilsson.'

'Why?' the doctor asked incredulously.

'Because the murderer thought that Nilsson himself wanted to put up under an assumed name. With the key, the murderer could perform his trick last night. What do you think?'

Carl looked expectant, but we were just perplexed.

'That's unfortunately impossible,' I pointed out regretfully.

'What's impossible?'

'Everything. The missing key has turned up.'

I hadn't had time to tell them that Blom had also informed me that he'd actually found the key, which had been lost for a long time, on the bottom of a chair in room 5 that very same evening. After which, Blom had begun talking about the weather in a very detailed way, leading me to suspect that our conversation over the telephone was being traced, so I hung up.

The discovery of the missing key had caused everything to collapse. But when we began to pick everything to pieces we found that there were more things that, disquietingly, didn't hold together.

Axel Nilsson couldn't have had any reason to appear at the

boarding house under his correct name on two different occasions, but in two different disguises. If the purpose had been to get hold of the key, he would have had to avoid at all costs being recognized when he returned. Why, then, use the same name? Furthermore, the landlord would already have sensed there was something in the wind during the first visit, if Nilsson at that time had demanded a double room for himself. It would also have been impossible for Edvin to have killed his brother, obliterated every trace of himself from the room, planned his escape, arranged the locked room and exited, all in the space of the mere quarter of an hour he'd had at his disposal.

We had to accept that the radio hadn't been on for the purpose of delaying the suspicions of those who heard the quarrel. Axel Nilsson had indeed actually been listening to the radio.

The doctor also pointed out that there would have been a label on the bottle of pills giving the name of the patient, and had the name been any other than that of Axel Nilsson, the police would have become suspicious.

Concerning the cheese knife, Carl pointed out that it hadn't been recovered. If the knife had indeed played a harmless part, why then didn't the murderer leave it behind?

We even succeeded in demonstrating that the idea of the Nilsson brothers living together was contradicted by Ivar Johanson's knowledge of Selma Lagerlöf.

It had often rained during the night in the week when the readings-out-loud were alleged to have taken place, so it was highly improbable that Edvin would have been turned out of the room in the middle of the night in order for Axel to receive his visitor. Therefore, we reasoned, the travelling salesman must have been lying when he stated that he'd never been inside room 5, since he demonstrably must have caught isolated parts of *The Saga of Gösta Berling* through the wall in room 5. Nilsson himself did not know what book it was. We concluded that Johanson had concealed his dealings with Nilsson for fear of being unnecessarily under suspicion for what happened during that Saturday evening.

No, the hidden brother had never existed. Nilsson had mostly been drinking alone in his room.

I tried to formulate something to the effect that it probably had been wet out of doors as well as inside room 5 during the nights, but I was the only one who laughed.

When we were at last forced to find an explanation for the fact that

Axel Nilsson had put up at the boarding-house around September 12, we were forced to accept that the name is not that uncommon and that a random occurrence was probably the explanation for the key thief being a namesake of our corpse. It was at that moment that the telephone rang. We immediately understood what that implied.

The phone call to the boarding-house must have been traced and Gunnar Bergman wanted an explanation. It was Carl who took the call. People talk about half-choked voices: his was more like strangled.

But even this last phone call ended in anticlimax, this time a rather positive one. It was Kerstin, Carl's daughter-in-law, who wanted to know about the health situation. She apologized for calling so late, but her husband had told her that on this particular night one could call even after midnight. She herself felt fine and she wished us a good night.

I took the opportunity to let Carl convey that I personally was very fit and that I had not noticed any influenza signs.

We all three understood that her call was at the behest of her husband, who was thus communicating his knowledge of our interference in the affairs of the police authorities. It felt like a rebuke.

Before we parted company, the host of the evening was supposed to deliver a comprehensive summary of the evening's events, but given that it had lasted until half past midnight, and therefore far later than usual, Carl was unanimously relieved of that duty.

We thanked him for an exceedingly pleasant evening, perhaps our most successful to date. In spite of our surface cordiality, certain undertones of disappointment, dissatisfaction and general misgivings could be detected with regard to the lingering unsolved questions.

As we were putting on our coats and shaking hands at the door, Carl surprised us by accompanying us in order to get a breath of fresh air. Since during the Sunday evening sessions a small glass of alcohol of some kind is generally served (which is especially welcome during the cold autumn evenings), the doctor had fortunately left his car at home. I can reveal that, although he is an experienced driver, we often have differing opinions about the meaning of certain road signs and traffic signals; and that his chattiness at the wheel, together with his sidelong glances at the passengers, greatly contributes to his diminished attention.

It was a starry night. The wind was blowing quite forcefully, but we were quite sheltered as we walked along the avenue towards the Kungsbron. Just a few night wanderers crossed our path.

Although we were making strenuous efforts to avoid the topic we had spent so many hours discussing, it became abundantly clear that Carl wanted to have the final word.

His home is on the edge of town. Wealthy inhabitants have built their houses in this neighbourhood and the area has an air of stylish and snobbish isolation. Our path naturally took us along Kungsbroallén to the Bus Square and then Centralgatan towards the Old Homestead Museum. After that it was a short walk to Åbrogatan, from which point the doctor had a mere five minutes before reaching home. He would, incidentally, pass by the boarding house if he chose to take Rosenborgsvägen, a considerably longer walk. In that part of town, Centralgatan extends over a kilometre and we had to spend ten minutes to cover the distance.

It took exactly as much time, after we had left the Bus Square, for Carl to solve the problem we had grappled with during the previous four hours.

I had actually thought of buying a hot dog at the stall by the Bus Square, but, out of consideration for Carl, who had been an excellent and generous host, I refrained.

7

'What' wrong with our reasoning up to now,' Carl began, 'is that we've taken for granted that the murderer—either by pure chance or thanks to a casual impulse—succeeded in leaving his victim in a locked room. As a matter of fact, the locked room is the evidence that a murder must have taken place. For various reasons, even Gunnar thought that Nilsson was murdered; although we don't know why. Due to our insufficient knowledge of Axel Nilsson's relationships with different persons in town, we have mostly dwelt upon the technical details of the murder rather than the motive.'

He paused to allow for objections, but when they did not materialise he continued:

'Efraim thought that the murder had been an accident, and that the culprit was unaware of what he had done. Thus Nilsson's death was the unforeseen consequence of the fight, in which even the murderer was wounded. On the other hand, according to Johan, who presented an admirable but quite far-fetched theory, Edvin felt enraged at his brother having duped him, which led—as the result of a violent quarrel—to the manslaughter. And facing *fait accompli*, upset, intoxicated and wounded, the perpetrator was able to devise a clever version of the locked room and implement that plan! But could the murderer's moves and escape have been executed in such a perfect way if it had indeed been a mere accident and a pure happenstance that he was able to recognise and exploit?'

We didn't really understand what Carl was getting at, but his views commanded our outright approval. Something in his pitch and execution suggested that this was merely a beginning.

'Let me put it bluntly! We know from our ... literary experiences that the perfect murder, or even the next-to-perfect one, demands careful planning. Here we have a perfect murder, at least in the sense that it seems to have been committed in the classic locked room, and so I now call for the perfect perpetrator!'

'You mean a murderer who ...?' I asked.

'... who planned everything down to the smallest detail and who, and this is important, had a motive. Find out who had the greatest reason to get rid of Axel Nilsson and then you most probably have your murderer!'

'It sounds simple, but we don't know enough.'

'We can assume and guess once more. Third time lucky! The murderer must have had some kind of relationship to Nilsson. Who has such a connection to him? Do we not have at least one such person?'

'Well, we don't know. No wrong committed ten years ago could still be so topical that it motivates a murder now, and—in contrast to Edvin— Axel had, as far as we know, not been refused admittance here. He could return here and nobody here would mean anything to him, and he himself would mean nothing to anybody.'

'He would to one person!'

'And who might that be?'

'His daughter!'

'Yes, of course. But you can't be suggesting that a—let me see— nine or ten year old girl would be likely to take revenge on her lost father, whom she'd never seen, hardly heard from and perhaps never even heard of?'

I understood of course what Carl meant, but I thought for a moment of *Crooked House* by Agatha Christie, Ellery Queen's *The Tragedy of Y* and *The Bad Seed* by William March, where the writers' speculations about juvenile murderers bestowed the stories with an extra mysterious and macabre character.

'You're thinking of the mother of the child,' I ventured.

'Yes. Whoever she is, it wouldn't be appreciated if the father— especially not this parody of a father—shows up all of a sudden and begins to act.'

'He wouldn't have much to gain. Just think of the child welfare board and all his maintenance advances.'

'That's right, but just because of that, any small amount he could get would be important.'

That was another subtle wording that made us confused.

'He could create a lot of trouble for the mother of the child, and she might try to get rid of him.'

'Do you mean that she might murder him in order to get away from being harassed? But what would he gain from causing her to lead a dog's life?'

'He could threaten her by thrusting himself on her, demanding right of access to the child, revealing spicy details from her past, and generally raising hell in the town with the intention of bringing disgrace down upon the daughter. He could demand compensation to avoid that. What would the poor mother feel if he started visiting the daughter, appealing to her childish compassion, deluding her into believing a lot of lies, waiting for her outside her school, disgracing her in front of her schoolmates, and so on?'

'Carl's right,' the doctor put in. 'Such behaviour would be in line with what we know about Nilsson's personality. He wouldn't hesitate to do something of the kind. Maybe the daughter, if her mother has married, believes that her stepfather is her biological father. A sudden exposure without warning about the fatherhood could be harmful. We could come up with a dozen valid reasons why it would be better to put Axel Nilsson out of the way rather than allow him to encroach on his former girlfriend's life.'

'You mean that if we can identify her, then we have the murderer, or in this case, the murderess?' I asked.

'Yes, or her husband, if she is married. They have created a mutual existence and a common future; they may have children together and a prosperous life. Axel could have known of all this because of letters from his mother before she died. Since he was almost certainly in a state of destitution in America—and, on top of that, suffering from a heart disease—he might decide that a little bloodsucking or blackmailing could lead to a more comfortable life.'

The doctor had been silent during Carl's exposition.

There was no doubt that he had accepted all this. Moreover, he seemed as if he were searching his memory for something. In fact, this something would turn out to be manna from heaven.

We had walked just about half way and, of all coincidences, this one happened just at the right time and place. Centralgatan is, as the name of the street suggests, situated in the central part of town and is our most distinguished shopping street. Here are the big department stores and the banks, and here our lawyers, dentists and doctors have their offices, receptions and consulting-rooms. Even Dr. Efraim Nylander. He stopped outside Centralgatan 47 with the familiar sign advertising that he exercised his doctor's practice upstairs. He fished a bunch of keys from his pocket, unlocked the door, ushered us inside and proceeded to climb the two half-flights of stairs without a word. We followed him and were directed into the small waiting room.

'A moment, gentlemen. I have a surprise for you,' he said

mysteriously, and disappeared into a room which I knew he used for his examinations.

There was a sofa and three Windsor-style chairs in the waiting room. On a table were battered weekly magazines, *Hemmets Journal, Vi, Hoppets Härold* and *Allers*. On the window sill were some drooping begonias. They had not been watered for several days. On the wall was a faded reproduction of the painting *Grindslanten*. It showed some poor children fighting over a coin which had been thrown at their feet from a passing carriage as payment for opening a road gate. The painting could be alluding to the doctor's modest remuneration, or maybe the fight for patients and their symptoms among his colleagues.

After a minute, the doctor appeared with a card in his hand.

'Exactly what I thought,' he said in a satisfied way. 'When I returned the document about Axel Nilsson to the Temperance Board, I made some notes for myself on a case-book card. Obviously, I wanted to have it in readiness if Nilsson resurfaced and the examination ever actually took place. Let's see now!'

He put the card in front of us on the table. The notes were, needless to say, illegible, but with a little bit of good will one could divine that the scrawls in the beginning symbolised the name of Axel Nilsson.

'Born March 2, 1917. Here we have some information of medical interest, but after that we have social circumstances: Unmarried, no children. Fiancée: Rose-Marie Åhlund, dental nurse trainee. Well, that's it.'

'Then we must hope that he didn't make any other girls pregnant before he did a bunk,' Carl objected prudently.

'Yes, of course. What do we do now?'

'Do you have a phone directory?'

The doctor fetched one. Carl took it and turned over the pages with a deft hand to the letter Å.

'We only have three subscribers with that surname. Åhlund, Beata, Mrs.—no, Åhlund, Christer, smith worker—what about that?'

'Who's the third one?' the doctor asked. He was on tenterhooks.

'Åhlund, Sven. Does it say anything?'

'I don't know. Wait a minute.'

The doctor disappeared again and returned after a few seconds with another card. I saw that the name on the new card was Sven Åhlund.

'We must check his address,' he muttered and searched in the directory.

'You've written Jul... Jolin...'

'Johanneslundsvägen 3,' the doctor interrupted me irritably. 'That's right. No, I don't know Sven, but I have a card here for Maja Åhlund.'

The name on the card was Maja and not Sven. The doctor's handwriting made the difference almost indiscernible.

'Maja Åhlund' he read, 'born November 9, 1908. She seems to have come to me about depression in the early 1960's... Phenobarbital tincture, yes, very well. Here: Worse, referred to Saint Katarina hospital. She was obviously in a bad way. No more notes. I assume she recovered.'

'But where do we have Rose-Marie?'

I had hardly been able to hide my impatience during the reading aloud from the journal and my eyes darted to the table, where the cover of a weekly magazine displayed a sickly-sweet Central European royal couple in colour. They were standing embracing each other on the lawn in front of a castle-like building.

'These are her parents!'

I gave a start, hit by the impossibility of Rose-Marie Åhlund being of noble descent. The time was almost one o'clock and an insistent sleepiness might excuse me for my mistake. I had to say something sharp-witted.

'So she's either still living at home, or she's moved.'

No one seemed particularly impressed by my remark.

'She's probably married.'

'Unfortunately, it's rather difficult to call around at this time of night to ask the housewives of the town if their maiden name was Åhlund,' Carl pointed out. 'We must be content with what we have for the moment. If we eliminate Sven and Maja Åhlund as murderers we can ... is there anything else about the siblings of Rose-Marie?'

The doctor picked up the card and looked at the scribble on both sides.

'How fortunate! I don't usually mention anything about the children of my female patients unless they have gynecological problems. In this case, I can see that she consulted me in 1948 for vaginal discharge and ....'

Medical secrecy could be difficult to observe at one o'clock in the morning and after several glasses of punch.

'I noted that she was 2-para,' he continued after a short and embarrassed pause. 'That means two deliveries. Daughter born 1933 and daughter born 1941—the latter could be Rose-Marie.'

'Excellent. Let us exclude the spouses Åhlund and their two daughters as murderers. It should be easy to find the name and address of Rose-Marie's husband in the people registration. He's the guilty one.'

'For the sake of justice, you might at least say a few words about how you can glibly exonerate four of five potential suspects.'

'For the simple reason that nobody except him could reasonably be expected to jump from the first floor.'

Carl didn't give us the opportunity to digest our surprise.

'It's a ten minute walk to the boarding house. I want to do a few small experiments over there. After that I'll explain what it's all about.'

Many mystery stories end with the detective gathering all the suspects, including the LSP—the least suspected person: *den minst misstänkta personen* —in a room, e.g. the drawing room in an English manor. There, the murderer is lulled into security by small talk during one chapter, after which the subsequent unmasking comes as an unpleasant surprise to him or her.

Whereupon the murderer invariably becomes confused, immediately rushing out through the door, only to be captured in the corridor by a superintendent of the police district of the earldom, who has been planted there beforehand.

This kind of cut-and-dried ending has always irritated me, and I was glad that nothing of the kind had to be arranged. As of now, the murderer had been identified and the investigation was moving forward.

Once outside, I noticed in the light of the street lamp that the colouring of the doctor's face had been deepening, a clear manifestation of an approaching explosion.

'Carl Bergman,' he hissed (he always uses the full name of the offender when irritated), 'were we or were we not in agreement that that nobody could have jumped from that infernal window? Have you been leading us on?'

'So truly help me God, no. I meant that a jump across a two metre wide rose bed was impossible to perform from a height of three and a half metres.'

'Well then?'

'Unless you use a trick.'

'What damned trick?'

'I shall disclose that shortly.'

'Well, would you at least be so kind as to reveal the nature of your … what did you call it, experiment? Am I supposed to jump through the window just to confirm that....'

'Absolutely not. But I will ask you to check whether the window shades are down on the lower flat of the short side of the house opening on to Rosenborgsgatan.'

'Then should Johan concentrate on the shades on the first floor of the aforementioned short side?'

'No, and this is not a joke. He is to inspect the ground behind the shrubbery in the garden between the fence and the laundry.'

'Why?'

No reply. Another deafening silence. It lasted as far as Anderberg's fishmonger's shop. Then I broke it.

'Excuse my inquisitiveness,' I said. 'But how could we rule out the other Åhlunds in the phone book as possible parents of Rose-Marie? Carl excluded Beata, and Christer didn't arouse any enthusiasm either.'

'Beata Åhlund is living on Ängbyvägen,' Carl explained. 'It's a short road just beyond the fire station. There's an old people's retreat there, and Rose-Marie's mother would in all likelihood be too young for that kind of care-taking.'

'And Christer is an unusual name among older men,' the doctor added. 'The parents' ages should to be similar to our own, sixty or seventy. Christer is too young. That's what it boils down to.'

Soon we reached Sandstensgatan. In front of the short side of the boarding-house, which has a trellis on the rear corner, Carl stopped, opened the gate carefully, bade me enter and gave me his flashlight in passing. In order not to create any unnecessary noise, I walked on the edge of the gravel path and arrived on the lawn level with the rose bed. There, I turned round and found that the doctor had disappeared and that Carl was standing behind me looking at his watch. I glanced at mine as well. It has luminous hands, which are helpful in the dark. The watch, by the way, is a gift from the staff of my former place of work. It is rare these days that I creep around at night alone and I wonder what my colleagues in the Ornithological Society would say if they could see me now. Bird life is generally sparse around midnight, and in this backyard very few important discoveries would be likely, even at dawn. House sparrows and pigeons lack interest as curiosities.

The house was dark except for the second window of the first floor, counting from the back door. I thought I heard the low sound of a night radio through the open window. I'd reached the farther end of the backyard when I heard half-running steps on the gravel path and saw someone's silhouette outlined against the street lighting. Under the cloak of darkness, as well as the thick bushes, I also caught a glimpse of an individual sneaking in through the back door.

I waited for a couple of minutes without moving, which was quite unnerving. Everything was quiet, but now and then there was a rustle in the branches of the trees. There was a sudden gust of wind, and I pulled my hat far down over my forehead. At one point I discerned a distant mewing, as if from a cat or some other furry animal.

Suddenly the back door opened and a sturdy man came out and stood under the lamp. I couldn't make him out clearly because he was a good ten metres away. After gazing into the darkness for a while he went back inside, shut the door and locked it.

I deduced that it was Blom who had locked the door and that the earlier fleeting figure had been a boarding-house guest returning late. I made a note of the time, which was five minutes to one.

Shortly thereafter, the light went out in the illuminated window, which had been pulled shut. I took out the flashlight, screened it off with my handkerchief—a trick I learned through private studies—and began to examine the ground. I didn't actually know what I was looking for, but in cases like this it is usually footprints, fag-ends—with or without lipstick—smaller articles of clothing and suchlike. Or so I've read.

Nothing of great importance happened after that, except that someone left the house by the back door and silently disappeared. But then I happened to discover what I was presumably supposed to find, in the bushes by the side of the Ekbom laundry. I refrain from describing the rest of my hardship in detail.

Carl and the doctor had been waiting for me for at least a quarter of an hour, and the time was now nearly one thirty. Nobody had any more thoughts of sleep. I proposed that we take refuge in my apartment at Åbrogatan 2 for a final summation, and even promised a glass of warm milk as preparation for sleep.

My friends have often visited me there and, although the situation did not call for any formality, I still put on my smoking-jacket. While they settled themselves in the library, I went to the kitchen to boil some milk for nightcaps, but the doctor shouted that he didn't want any and Carl agreed with him. Maybe they were anxious that it would make them too drowsy. So I postponed the treat until after my guests had left, when I could lace it with a few drops of brandy.

'We can,' began Carl, 'start with any detail and see where it leads. Take Nilsson's transistor radio, for example. We know it was turned on around ten o'clock and that it could still be heard by anyone in the upper corridor at around one o'clock. Now, I ask the following question: What did Blom hear through the door just after ten o'clock?'

He answered his own question.

'He heard a lecture or a recitation, which had just begun. And it wasn't someone reading aloud from *The Saga of Gösta Berling*, for the schoolmistresses did not return to their room until after the picture show, which only began at nine o'clock. According to Efraim, when Axel Nilsson found himself sick a few hours after the departure of the mysterious unknown guest, his first act was to turn off the radio. Now, if he was in such bad condition that he died soon afterwards, and if that change for the worse had developed gradually, why didn't he call the hotel staff for help? Was he too sick to reach the bell right by his bed, but not too sick to turn off the radio by the window at the other end of the room? It doesn't make sense. I've checked the radio programmemes, and at a few minutes after ten on Saturday evening there was an item entitled "Modern Flemish Storytellers" on the P1 channel. That doesn't make sense either, for why would Nilsson listen to that when he was allergic to other forms of reading aloud? Remember that he didn't like listening to a less modern storyteller from Värmland, Selma Lagerlöf. The answer is that he wasn't listening for the pleasure of it. Johan thought that the radio had been turned on in order to make people in the corridor believe that Axel was still alive. But, gentlemen, in that case aren't you surprised that the radio was still on and could still be heard at one o'clock?'

None of us could understand what Carl was driving at.

'Yes, if the radio was on after ten o'clock, when the murderer left—after having been able to produce, as if by magic, the locked room—how could it then be heard three hours later if P1 signs off at half past ten? Even if the transistor batteries were not worn out, the murderer could only have been able to get people to believe that Axel was alive as long as the radio was audible, but not after half past ten. After that time, P1 is silent. But the radio in room number 5 was not silent, which means that the hotel guest must have changed to the music channel, which runs most of the night. So once again we have to ask:

why was the radio turned on? Do you see what I mean?'

I didn't want to appear stupid, so I nodded profoundly.

'I found the solution to the mystery by considering this particular oddity and arrived at the conclusion that the radio was on solely for the purpose of keeping Nilsson awake. The red wine had made him drowsy.'

'But why did he need to stay awake?'

'To keep his part of the agreement.'

'What agreement?'

'The agreement between him and the murderer.'

We didn't understand anything, so Carl abandoned his cat-and-mouse approach and prepared to give us a more coherent account. Before that, however, he presented his own interpretation of yet another minor problem which had bewildered us.

'Let's take another detail and examine it from several different angles. Why was the victim drenched in red wine? Efraim's explanation was that it had spilled over Nilsson when he'd fallen down and slipped into a coma. Johan's was that the wine was there to make the identification difficult. Mine is that the murderer consciously poured it on him in a moment of arranged distraction.'

'What does that mean in plain Swedish?'

'The murderer "happens to" spill the red wine on him. He makes a gesture with his hand but appears to "forget" there's wine in the glass. Nilsson doesn't realise it's deliberate, wipes his face with one hand and ... what does he do next?'

'No idea.'

'Really? Well, he looks down at his soiled shirt and in the next moment the murderer hits him on the head. So there's Axel Nilsson lying on the floor with wine all over him, which seems to have been the result of him falling towards the bedstead. The culprit may have thought of mopping up the wine, but I guess Nilsson had tied the towel around his neck as a napkin. The wine is nevertheless on his shirt and the stains can't be removed. So the wet towel is thrown into the wastebasket and the murderer pours another splash of wine on the man on the floor. Of course, he also arranges the pools on the table and the overturned empty bottle.'

'And before the murderer leaves the room, he turns on the radio?'

'No, no and no again. Don't you understand? The person who quarrelled with Nilsson could not have planned all this—or else why would he have advertised his presence in the room so noisily during the couple of hours before ten o'clock? Forget about him, he's totally irrelevant. But the real murderer, who faced several disadvantages because of the former visitor in room 5, could nevertheless use his visit for his own purposes. He had made preparations for the murder, but, because of the other person's unanticipated visit to the room, it looked as though he had been the one responsible for the crime and the locked room. This complicated things enormously: a murder in a locked room can be impossible to commit at ten o'clock at night, but not at half past one in the morning. Have I made myself clear now?'

Our negative reply was in such perfect unison that one would have thought we were being led by a conductor. The ironic lines at the corners of Carl's eyes proved that he was amusing himself at our expense, and his air of astonishment was worthy of an actor. Troubled wrinkles appeared on his forehead, and his innocent bright blue eyes looked at us in a questioning and helpless way.

'Let's take it from the very beginning. The murderer wants to get at Nilsson, who is threatening his family with blackmail. Call him the son-in-law, since we agree that there's a high probability the perpetrator is married to the daughter of Sven Åhlund. By the way, I can assure you that probability will become even higher shortly, so please listen carefully. Nilsson is aware that blackmail is a crime and wants to avoid being seen in the son-in-law's house. Because of that, the negotiations take place in the boarding-house. The meeting on Saturday evening was supposed to be about agreeing terms, including a lump sum, but the son-in-law has other plans: he's decided to put his tormentor out of the way. While waiting for his benefactor, Nilsson celebrates his anticipated success with a supper of cheese and red wine. It's been agreed that the son-in-law will slip into the boarding-house through the back door at around ten o'clock.'

'Why on earth would such a confirmed alcoholic be drinking Chianti by way of celebration? Wouldn't he be drinking the hard stuff, like any red-blooded Swede?'

Need I say that the interjection came from the doctor?

'Good question. Come to that, the cheese doesn't fit the picture either. But Nilsson hadn't much money and could probably only spend fifteen crowns for supper. We don't know how Nilsson could afford the room, for that matter. Maybe he had received some money in advance and used it to pay for the lodgings.'

We nodded. Carl's explanation sounded reasonable. He noticed our approval and went on.

'What happens next? Round about eight o'clock, or a little bit earlier, there's a discreet knock on the door and his first guest comes in. Nilsson has probably run into a boon companion during his weeks in town and the fellow has turned up, probably with a surprise in liquid form. They get tipsy together. The red wine is set aside but the cheese is consumed, in the course of which the guest cuts himself by mistake and needs plaster. Time goes by, but Nilsson stays sufficiently sober to realize that his visitor has to leave before ten o'clock. His guest doesn't take the hint and Nilsson becomes impatient. A squabble starts. How the unwanted visitor was eventually persuaded to leave is anyone's guess, but during the argument, the son-in-law arrives. He has just entered the boarding-house through the rear door when he hears someone coming down the stairs with Nilsson's curses ringing in his ears. He needs to take cover before Blom comes out from his office. Where does he hide? I think Johan can tell us.'

'Behind the bushes near the laundry.'

'Correct. What did you find there?'

'Footprints.'

'Exactly. Remember that it had recently rained, but had dried up later. The footprints were saved in the sparsely-covered area behind the bushes. And over a period of four hours you get a lot of prints.'

'Four hours?'

'Well, maybe three. For, after the son-in-law has waited for a couple of minutes and sticks his nose out, what happens?'

'Blom installs himself by the backyard lookout!'

'That's precisely what he does, and the murderer realises he can't get inside without being seen. Neither can he use the front entrance, for in that case Blom would hear the doorbell. Nilsson, who understands what has happened, shows himself at the window. He spots the son-in-law behind the hedge, but he can't do anything except point at the illuminated window in the floor below. After that he keeps himself awake and waits. The son-in-law is forced to remain in his hiding-place whether he wants to or not. He has plenty of time to go over his plan during the three hour wait, and the details he was unsure about at ten o'clock are fully worked out by midnight. Eventually Blom goes to bed, so Nilsson can let the son-in-law in and be murdered.'

'With what?'

'They used to call it a "blunt instrument," perhaps a Chianti bottle wrapped in a towel to avoid breaking the victim's skin.'

'And then the perpetrator locks the door and jumps through the window?'

'Yes.'

'But that's impossible!'

'Why so?'

'To begin with, it's too high up.'

'How high?'

'Good grief, do we have to go through that again?'

The doctor took out his notebook and drew a triangle.

'Here we have the height,' he said, 'three and a half metres, as you have stated. Here is the base, the rose bed, two metres. Finally the third side that will be, let me see now: the square of the hypotenuse, according to Pythagoras' theorem....'

He scribbled down some numbers.

'The length of the jump would be four metres.'

'That's not much. The only problem is the take-off. He has to land two metres away from the house so as to avoid the roses. But that's easy for a fit man in ... his thirties, or whatever.'

'Then he would end up on the gravel with a great deal of noise, waking Blom, who's sleeping within earshot. Furthermore, he might sprain his ankle.'

'Not if he throws out something soft to land on! Some spare blankets from the store, for example.'

'What store?'

'The boarding-house store on the first floor, where Blom keeps beds, mattresses and blankets. The murderer could move about freely and undisturbed at that time.

'But what he takes will be missed whenever Blom or anyone....'

'No, the son-in-law puts them back in the closet when he goes back inside again.'

'Goes back inside ... are you serious?'

Now it was my turn to object. I tried my best, but had as little success as the doctor.

'Yes, wait a minute and I'll tell you. Do we agree on the jump?'

'No, far from it.'

My reply was vocally supported by Efraim.

'Why not?'

'The jump was impossible for the simple reason there was nowhere to take off from.'

'Don't forget the window-sill. It was covered by a smooth and clean cloth, which would first have to be pushed aside before the jump— otherwise there would be dirt on it. Remember that he had been standing in damp soil for three hours.'

'He could have moved the cloth a few decimetres, in order to make room for his feet on the support.'

'Did the police find the cloth displaced and....'

'No. It was stretched out. The murderer went back into the house again and put it in order.'

When Carl uttered those words, my mind went totally blank again, but not so blank that I couldn't pull myself together and ask two vital questions:

'How could he get inside through the rear door, and how could he enter the room he had locked from the inside before jumping out? That's what I would very much like to know.'

'Me too,' echoed the doctor.

'The back door was no problem. He had left it unlocked when he was let in a short while earlier. The other matter is rather tricky. Here we go: the window was still open after his jump and one of the rooms next to his was empty, right?'

'Hell no! The schoolmistresses occupied numbers 4 and 6! Besides, which room are you talking about?'

'Either the one to the right or the one to the left of Nilsson's.'

'The same thing. None of them was accessible.'

'Yes, but the son-in-law didn't know that.'

'So what? All the same, the murderer couldn't use any of them!'

Carl offered us a smile of combined pride and modesty.

'Johan and Efraim, dear friends, do you remember that Nilsson had asked Blom when the schoolmistresses would leave? He wanted to know it because he was constantly being disturbed when they carried on reading aloud during the night. When he complained, he was told that they would be leaving on Saturday afternoon. That was what he had wanted to know, for next evening he wished to speak undisturbed with the son-in-law. The poor insulation of the walls troubled him. However, the answer was reassuring, for it was not likely that many new guests would arrive during the seasonal lull. He knew the chambermaid worked weekday mornings, so he calculated that the schoolmistresses' rooms would still be empty when his meeting with the son-in-law was to take place. (That is, assuming they left as they had promised, *nota bene*.) So Nilsson knew that the rooms on both sides would in all likelihood be empty, and that was what he had told his visitor, for whom the information was a prerequisite for the locked room set-up.'

'But the rooms weren't empty, so his plan should have come to naught.'

'Yes. Just imagine his disappointment when he was lurking in the dark garden and saw the two ladies entering the house round about eleven o'clock and, shortly thereafter, lights in the rooms on either side of Nilsson's!'

'So why didn't he abandon his plan?'

'Maybe he did think of it at first, but he couldn't give up his visit to room 5 because of Nilsson's threat. However, once he was inside, he must have learnt something which told him that one of the rooms was indeed empty. When he rebuked his presumed murder victim for the false information about the neighbours, he learned that one of them was down with the flu. Because of that, she as well as her friend had decided to stay an extra night at the hotel. Towards the evening she had felt better and had even dared to go to the cinema, trusting the ladies' lavatory. Perhaps also Nilsson and his guest heard sounds of wailing or even vomiting from one of the adjacent rooms—proving that the patient had got worse—and the voice of her colleague promising not to leave her alone. Women have a tendency to become distraught in cases like this, don't they, Efraim?'

'That's right.'

I remembered my own flu in 1958. Both the chief physician and the nurse Astrid on that occasion had had reason to admire my physique and powers of resistance.

'Well, one of the schoolmistresses' rooms was empty and the murderer entered it.'

'How?' the doctor asked.

'With the key that the Good Samaritan had dutifully hung up on the hook outside her door, when she'd left the room to stay with her friend. During my own visit to the hotel....'

All of a sudden I realized that the one who had gone in and out through the back door during my stay in the garden must have been Carl, and I now demanded an explanation.

'You obviously wanted to check that there was an easily accessible store at the hotel during your intrusion tonight, but how did you avoid Blom's watch?'

'You sneaked in through the back door, of course, after enticing

87

him to the front by using the night bell. Blom must have thought that some joker had passed by and pulled his leg. Nevertheless, I heard the females cackling upstairs in room 4. The sick woman was obviously still sick. I could hear them quite clearly, so our supposition that Johanson must have been within close enough earshot in order to identify *The Saga of Gösta Berling* seems to be plausible.'

'Couldn't the son-in-law have acted in a similar way when he was about to sneak into the house?'

'I think that the idea may have struck him after a while, but if he went to the front door for that purpose, he would have noticed a sign saying guests were referred to the garden door and been discouraged by it.'

All three of us looked at the clock, which now showed a quarter past two.

'So the murderer went into the hotel twice in the middle of the night,' Carl resumed. 'The second time was without Nilsson's help. He put the blankets back into the store, entered the empty room 6 and opened the window. After that it was easy for him to put out a two metres long object with a hook at one end and, with the help of this device, reach the cloth on the sill of the murdered man's room and draw it back to its original position.'

Carl paid no attention to our loud protests. Instead he waved his arms, raised his voice and concluded his speech.

'Then he closed Nilsson's window with the same object he had used to restore order to his take-off point in the crime scene. The distance from the wall to the window in both rooms is half a metre, and the whole window is one and a half metres wide altogether. The object was exactly two metres long and the outstretched arm added some seventy-five centimetres, which was longer than needed. After that, he only had to close the window through which he had performed his simple manipulation, lock the door, hang the key back up on the hook and go home to sleep. He had locked the back door from the inside, unlike me when I took the same way one hour ago. Finally, he probably left the house by jumping out of a window in the ground floor, where several rooms can be used for that purpose, the kitchen and the breakfast parlour, among others. The police certainly didn't check any of them for indications of foul play.'

During Carl's explanation, the doctor had slowly risen to his feet and was now standing with his legs wide apart and his hands ominously on his hips. The last part of the summary had been performed at a furious pace. It was as if Carl had been afraid of being interrupted before he'd finished it.

'What bloody object is two metres long and hooked on one end?'

'Did I say that? Sorry, that was wrong.'

'I hope so.'

'It was formed like a hook on both ends.'

'And is easily accessible to anyone?'

'Yes.'

'Well, then show us yours.'

'I haven't got one on me. But, on the other hand, I do have several at home.'

Carl stared innocently out of the window and up towards the star-studded sky as if seeking appreciation from higher and more powerful authorities.

'Johan has lots of them, I suspect.'

'He has at least one.'

'Two metres long?'

'A folding ruler,' I tried, forgetting in my haste that such an object is rarely supplied with hooks at any end.

'Efraim,' said Carl, 'can you please tell me if the blinds are down, here in Johan's living room?'

'No, they aren't. In fact, there aren't any blinds, only ordinary curtains.'

'Exactly. They are attached to rods of the same kind many people have. Each is two metres long and supplied with hooks at both ends.'

The doctor asked for a glass of milk. I heated it in the kitchen.

8

Our meeting came to an end well after two o'clock this morning. We experienced a powerful sense of kinship when we said goodbye. Carl was pale and could hardly keep his eyes open. While the taxi I had called waited outside, swallowing one crown after another, I helped him to put on his overcoat. He almost stumbled down the stairs after we shook hands for the last time.

The doctor preferred to walk home. He said that the fresh air would be good for him and help clear his head. Otherwise he might not be able to sleep with all the thoughts ticking over in his mind. We wished each other goodnight and he closed the door behind him.

At this time the murderer would be sleeping peacefully somewhere in town, unaware that we had identified him and that capturing him was now a mere formality.

It's difficult to say why I used the door-chain on this particular night. While I was emptying the ashtray I heard the doorbell ring.

'Who is it?' I asked through the door and opened the flap of the letterbox, but even though I stooped down and peered through the slot I couldn't see anything in the darkness outside.

'It's just me,' I heard the doctor say.

He had forgotten his spectacles. I handed them to him and was once again alone.

My sleep was troubled, even though I'd had two glasses of milk before I went to bed. I dreamt that I was hiding behind a rose bush. The flowers smelt like red wine and I fanned myself with a cloth! All of a sudden I was holding a radio antenna in my hand and playing on a xylophone hanging from some branches. Keys of different sizes were fastened to a curtain rod. It was a very strange dream and it scared me quite a bit.

Oddly enough, I was awake and alert at eight o'clock and seated at my desk shortly thereafter, having enjoyed a breakfast consisting of sour milk, two cups of coffee and a cheese sandwich.

My friends, who most possibly were resting during the day, had not said anything about when my report was due. As soon as I started to write, a string of essential questions crossed my mind, but I didn't feel like calling the doctor or Carl.

For example, we had not asked ourselves if any of the parties involved happened to be right-handed or not, a rather serious oversight. It's surprising how many people, especially murderers, are left-handed in mystery novels.

Neither had we discussed an important aspect of most murder cases—the condition of the victim's watch. How often has a murderer been unlucky enough to have aimed a staggering blow towards his adversary and smashed his wrist-watch at the same time as his temporal bone, thus establishing the time of death?

And were there any fingerprints on the glasses in the murder room?

Were there, perhaps, textile fragments under the corpse's nails which would, after further analysis, turn out to originate from a cheviot suit bought at Molander's haberdashery on Drottningatan?

And did Nilsson, at the moment of death, while summoning all his last physical strength, succeed in writing some secret message on the piece of linoleum with a finger dipped in red wine, thereby exposing the perpetrator—as so many dying individuals have done before him in the literature?

Soon my fingers began to dance speedily across the keyboard. In the 1930's, I attended a course in typewriting at the Workers' Educational Association, in order to be able to use all ten fingers when typing, and I still make a considerable amount of strokes per minute.

After a short break in the afternoon and dinner at six o'clock—Falu sausage with fried potatoes and a glass of milk—I have, after working the whole day long, at last reached the end of my report.

I shall shortly post it to Detective Sergeant Gunnar Bergman, Polishuset, Rådhustorget 9, as agreed. We're convinced that our conclusions will considerably shorten his investigatory work.

A copy of my elaborate notations is meant to be saved for our little club and attached to the blue file. Maybe we'll have to buy a new one for the coming year. I'll bring the question up, together with the question of my expenses for stamps, typing-paper and a fresh ribbon, on our next gathering, which takes place at the doctor's home.

I don't know which mystery novel he will select. I'm very much looking forward to the event.

PART TWO

Town Hall Square, Friday, October 31

1

My wife Kerstin insists that I have an even temperament. In fact, I am always in a bad mood. On Saturday evening I could hardly contain myself when I saw Pelle Ramsten calmly staring at her cards, whereupon she abruptly decided to serve the sandwiches, even though we'd all agreed beforehand not to eat before the German mini-series *Babeck* was on TV. I'd just about calmed down when the children started squealing. First they wanted to go to the toilet, then they said they were thirsty. And every time they got up they made a point of running into the living room, when they were supposed to use the hallway. It was when my daughter Lillan took it into her head to sing a silly song about a chimney-sweep that I decided I'd had enough and carted her and her brother up to their beds. Needless to say, they immediately started caterwauling and I had to send Kerstin up to calm them down.

After everyone had finished watching television and we were desperately wanting to call it a night, those annoying Ramstens decided they wanted another round of cards. Kerstin, however, was thankfully unable to find the pack. When Pelle announced he was thirsty I put a glass of sparkling lemonade on the table, but when Kerstin didn't feel very well and almost vomited, he pointed out that whisky was the best thing to have under the circumstances. After a while it finally dawned on the dimwitted Inga-Lill that it was time for them to go. By that time Kerstin was in such a bad condition that I almost had to carry her upstairs.

In the morning she couldn't get out of bed. By eight o'clock, the children had already started clamouring. The boy had reopened a wound and it had to be bandaged again. Usually he wants to become some kind of missionary when he grows up, tending to the Negroes in Africa, but just this morning he'd decided he should become a high pole artist instead, using the floor mop for training purposes. He'd probably seen some nonsense on a children's TV programme the day before. So I had to go upstairs to look for a plaster in the bathroom cabinet and stepped into a pool on the glazed tile floor. It was from Lillan's potty, which had been overturned. We'd taught her to sit on the toilet like ordinary people, but she hadn't done so because her brother had forgotten to flush.

There was no way to go back to bed after all this, so I gave the children cornflakes and read to them about Mister Hedgehog and his cheerless family. When we called their paternal grandmother and told her that we couldn't come over for dinner because Kerstin was sick, granny was sad but she promised to come over with bilberry soup for the patient so that the rest of us could go on a picnic or something.

Kerstin tried to get up to clean the children's room, but I packed her back to bed and Lillan played nurse. The boy disappeared into the garden on some secret assignment. It was good to get rid of him.

It was in the middle of all this mess when that idiot Blom called.

Our town is full of idiots. In fact, it's amazing that so many have succeeded in congregating in one small Swedish town. But after a week filled with insanity, stupidity and incompetence, the question is whether the biggest idiot of all isn't your humble servant, Gunnar Bergman.

So it was that, at five minutes to eleven, I flung myself into the car and headed for Sandstensgatan and *The Little Boarding-House*. Kerstin was still tucked up in bed and the children had promised to behave until their granny arrived. I'd promised to take care of the washing up later, if nobody else volunteered. Granny, for example.

All the guests made difficulties of course, but Blom was, as expected, the worst one. He had the nerve to tell me he had to go to a handball match and I had to explain to him that it was suspended, at least as far as he was concerned. We've had our eye on him for quite a while and now I intended to show him who was the boss. Once it dawned on him that I was serious he shut up—luckily for him, otherwise I would have set Ivehed on him. By the time the reinforcements from the station arrived and some kind of order was restored, it was already after one o'clock. How time flies.

I posted Melin to keep strict watch on the first floor and Gustavsson in the reception area. He'd already called for a photographer, but he'd had all kinds of trouble convincing a Danish doctor at the hospital that we had a corpse on our hands. After clearing up some language difficulties, it dawned on him that we were talking about murder and not someone's mother, whereupon he agreed to store the stiff in his refrigerator and we finally called an ambulance.

By the time I got home, the children had been waiting for me in their outdoor clothes for an hour. Kerstin had been up vomiting again and my mother refused to leave her. The new district medical officer was on a sick-call and Nylander didn't answer the phone at home or at the surgery. Even if we'd reached him he would probably have told us to pick stinging nettles for a soup. I was relieved when granny sent us packing. She said we were in the way and Kerstin seemed to agree.

At the playground by Rådhustorget square the children started to argue over one particular swing although they had three others to choose from. Then I dragged them along Drottninggatan to the book shop. As we stood in front of the window, I had to explain for the hundredth time that their paternal grandfather was old and could no longer work. They immediately assumed he was about to die. Without thinking about Axel Nilsson, I said "nobody dies here," which started Lillan crying, whereupon the boy demanded we immediately drive to grandfather's place and check that he hadn't caught cold. Needless to say, I drove them there and grandfather was somewhat surprised when the children climbed on him and touched him to check his temperature. We sent both of them out into the garden.

The old man was reading one of his eternal mystery novels. He almost seemed to be vexed by our visit, so I left him alone for a while. I had not eaten and was wolfing down an old piece of pie I'd found in the refrigerator when granny called to say they'd been trying to reach me at home several times. It didn't seem to be urgent. Then grandfather came over and asked what it was all about and it was then that I proved my foolishness.

He listened with great interest and asked several questions which *per se* were not too bad. And I unsuspectingly kept talking. Now, I did know about the Sunday meetings with him and his friends, but I still thought it was safe to have a few words with my own father in private. Private, indeed!

Anyway, he pumped me dry in less than an hour. He became very excited, too. It was almost as if I needed to ask the children to check his temperature once again.

I managed to drop in at home before I returned to *The Little Boarding-House*. Kerstin was feeling better and seemed to have caught some sleep while grandmother was preparing the food. The ironing-board happened to be open and the flat-iron was warm. Kerstin was in bed reading *Femina* magazine. The children were given their Sunday sweets for good behaviour and grandmother promised to read to them about Mister Hedgehog at bedtime. I frankly didn't care what happened to that tiresome character, but the boy promised to wake me up early the next morning before I went to work to let me know.

It wasn't until around midnight that I discovered who the biggest idiot in town really was. We were in the process of discussing the situation in the boarding-house dining room and, since it was very late, we were not expecting to be disturbed. Well, there was always the press of course, but the reporters had probably gone to cover the handball match earlier that afternoon.

Blom came running in. He said that there had been an anonymous phone call. Someone had wanted to know who had been the occupant of room number 5. I rushed to the telephone upstairs and tried to get the call tracked. The female operator wanted us to wait until eight o'clock in the morning because she had to call the telegraph director and so on. It took me ten minutes of arguing before I finally got the number. Gustavsson kept his side of the line open all the time.

From which number had the call been made? Believe me, it was the last one I had expected. The one in my father's—Carl Bergman's—house. It wasn't difficult to imagine that the three old boys were seriously at it. I became very upset. They didn't even know the name of the murdered man. Kerstin and I used to joke about their little mystery club. She calls them the Three Wise Men. For my father to have spilled the beans was bad enough, but if we weren't going to be able to work without interference, I was going to have to give them all a piece of my mind. Especially Lundgren, Lord Peter Volatile, as Kerstin calls him.

I dialled Kerstin and asked her to call grandfather and tell the whole pensioners' meeting to go to blazes. I explained the incident as vaguely as possible to the others waiting patiently in the dining room, but I really felt embarrassed. And my troubles had only just begun.

We had to be thankful for being left in peace all the way to one o'clock, when we were able to get some pilsner beer and sandwiches. They were ordered from the station. Vivianne at the switch board fixed it in no time at all. We preferred that to anything that Blom could serve us; his rubbish is not for me.

As we were sitting there, Gustavsson thought he heard someone sneaking past on the gravel outside. He went out and was soon back with a small, pitiful figure, who was trembling all over but trying to appear natural. Johan Lundgren, of course.

'I found him in the garden,' Gustavsson reported. 'He was creeping about in the bushes. Take care, he has a flashlight and it's loaded!'

'You were looking for angling-worms, of course?' I asked Lundgren.

He remained silent, so I was mercifully spared the sound of his voice. It has a whining, querulous quality which indicates that—centuries ago—he must have been brought up in the western part of Mälardalen, perhaps in Eskilstuna or Örebro.

'Have you been with a girl and now you can't find your way home? Well, what's it all about?'

He looked offended but preferred to smile in embarrassment. It was really laughable.

'We haven't got the whole night. Say something, Lundgren!'

As luck would have it, he was paralysed with surprise and fear and couldn't speak. It would have looked bad if he had begun to babble about the doctor, and above all about my old man, so I asked the others to leave us alone for a moment, while I grilled him.

'OK, Lundgren, I understand what you've been up to. However, we don't want any assistance from you or your geriatric friends. Get that into your head and clear out!'

He stammered something which sounded like thanks and raised his hat. I should have knocked him about really hard, considering all his stupid visits to the station. He has pestered us about his old rusty bike for years. Some discerning person cut the tyres to pieces several years ago. We regarded it as striking a blow for road safety, but Lundgren saw it as the greatest crime of the century, even worse than the Public Road Association's attack on his cousin. I've forgotten the man's name. It seems that one winter they failed to grit Åbrogatan and the cousin fell and sprained his ankle. Lundgren reported the matter to the office of the Public Prosecutor and got some senile old people in his building to sign it. He's not quite right in the head, believe me. And then you have his interest in detective stories! He reads everything he can get hold of, just like my old man. Once I bumped into Lundgren outside the library and, before I was able to escape, he had pressed me into a corner and told me that tedious joke about the fellow who borrowed the phone directory at the library. I couldn't even raise a weak smile.

Personally, I don't mind reading a book or two on vacation or during a long train ride or suchlike, but it doesn't mean that I wax lyrical when a murder occurs. I have my work and when I'm free I play with the children or read the newspaper *Expressen* while Kerstin prepares dinner. What else I do in my spare time is my business.

Be that as it may, I got rid of Lundgren, but I felt bad when the lads asked me what it had all been about. I can't remember what I came up with.

Everyone except Melin was permitted to go home and turn in. Kerstin woke up when I sneaked into the bedroom. We talked for a while in the darkness. I told her everything, with the exception of the old men's contribution. I had to put it out of my mind, otherwise I'd have become excited and then it would've been impossible to sleep.

The next time I heard from The Three Wise Men was on the following Tuesday. I got a big envelope in the mail containing some kind of report. I had no time to read the tripe, for we were in the midst of the investigation, so I took it home with me to the hornet's nest. That day, Lillan and the boy were arguing about whom granny liked best and Kerstin had unplugged the phone so that they couldn't call and ask her. Luckily enough they didn't know her number, but they had nevertheless started dialling at random and had reached three destinations. None of those answering seemed to appreciate the calls, according to the boy.

I forgot the document on the hat rack, and it was not until Kerstin was bathing the children that I found it again. At first I thought of throwing the whole report in the wastebasket, but then I thought better of it and began to read. My Leica camera, which I had looked for the day before, was also up there.

Kerstin came in and asked what I was laughing at. She read a few lines over my shoulder and didn't understand a word. I asked her to put the children to bed as fast as possible, and when that was done an hour later we read aloud to each other. We have never had so much fun. In the midst of it all the telephone rang. Kerstin picked up. 'It's your father!'

She left the room discreetly while I answered. My old man sounded innocent but the eagerness in his voice was not to be mistaken.

'Did you receive anything special in the post today?'

'Yes, I'm reading it at this very moment.'

'What do you think?'

'Well, there's quite a lot. It's ... interesting.'

Of course, I didn't want to disappoint the poor man. The situation was awkward enough as it was. In the end I said something about the children. He promised to call back later and I said that we would probably be going to bed very soon. I don't know how we got through it. I thought it was the worst nonsense I had ever read. Kerstin, who had kept herself up to speed about the real investigation, agreed that the whole thing was highly speculative, but in a way she appreciated the old men's efforts.

Personally I thought that the report proved their brains had become addled, but I had to admit that certain details were accurate, such as some of the street addresses and the weather conditions.

She thought that I was being unfair since they'd only had the facts that were known as of Sunday afternoon to work on. The next day she planned to take the papers to school and read them once more when she had a gap between lessons. I don't think I've mentioned before that Kerstin teaches twenty hours of English and Swedish at the intermediate level. The children have a child minder, costing fifteen crowns per hour, and they keep her busy. The money is well earned— she is already a shadow of her former self.

I didn't have the heart to tell Kerstin how far from the truth the old men were. It's embarrassing. Not only was the jump from the window impossible, with or without a trampoline, but the hooks for the curtain rods were held in place with rusty nails and had not been taken down for years. Åhlund's son-in-law, whom we interviewed, had been down with the flu the whole weekend with a temperature of 40 degrees Celsius. In other words, a cast-iron alibi.

I'll skip the rest of the details, but we did indeed find a note in Nilsson's wallet with Åhlund's telephone number, so there was a connection. But the number has not answered for a whole week. As for the son-in-law, Rose-Marie's husband, his name is Göran Eriksson. Apart from a few parking fines and one speeding offence, we have nothing on him.

When we went to bed that night, Kerstin was looking thoughtful. She probably pities my old man. I wondered what I would say if he called again. Maybe I'd say we'd had some tip-offs but that we'd had to scrub the idea of a murderer. Indeed, by then we already knew who had been in the room. The fact that the confession had not come until Thursday, yesterday, was beside the point.

By the time he was caught, I had actually become tired of the whole case. The last interrogation had been hard on all concerned, even though nothing sensational had emerged. Besides, I was furious at everyone involved.

I was angry at Gustavsson for volunteering a warning conversation with that damned milksop Blom which had ended with a punch on the nose, which was not very polite; at the newspaper journalist

Mårtenson, who wanted to use a picture of me on the first page of the Friday edition; and at the post mortem examiner, who couldn't cough up his report in time; and at Big Boss Bengtsson for having had the gall to choose this very week for sick leave.

But there's no point in getting upset over cretins in this town. They're in the majority here.

If I hadn't been one myself, I'd have called it a day after my lower certificate examination and started behind the bookseller counter. Then I could have stood there for fifty years, selling a lot of pretentious trash, weekly magazines and other bumf. And if I'd had enough money, I would have bought a croft far away and moved there with Kerstin and the children. At least with … no, the children too.

I don't know where I got the idea of joining the police from. I mean, what kind of profession is it, when all's said and done? Most of the day is spent typewriting or trying to find something to typewrite. Down at the station, old hags complain about being robbed of half-rotten bananas, alcoholics wander in and out, and there are still a few imbeciles who haven't grasped the principle of driving on the right. I take the opportunity for the last time to remind everyone that Stationsgatan has been a one way street since January 1, 1963. We even put up a sign about it.

And in the midst of all the thieves, parking offenders, missing persons, runaway cats and riders without tail lamps on their mopeds, one has to put up with madmen like Lundgren. I was calmer when I was on patrol duty; at least I got fresh air. What's more, it's not possible to bring a typewriter along. I never found a pocket for that in my uniform.

OK, it's become better since I came over to the criminal investigation department this spring. We have a small and pitiable district and Bengtsson, our first criminal inspector, was in need of reinforcements. He's on sick leave again because of his bronchitis and my colleague Sandén has gone away. That's how I became the chief all of a sudden and have a few boys from the department of law and order at my disposal.

But this is not the same job as I thought it would be when I was a young lad. I thought there'd be shoulder belts and billy-clubs, ID-tags, brass knuckles and suchlike. I'd probably seen too many gangster movies.

Instead there were parking fines in the daytime and Mister Hedgehog in the evenings.

Anyway, all that's behind me. When I got home yesterday evening –it was late and I was sour and grumpy—Kerstin wanted to know the result straight away. She uncorked a bottle of wine and had bought shrimps. I seemed to become more sociable after a while and we actually had quite a nice time together, until she finally dared to tell me that Inga-Lill had called and invited us to come over the following evening. We had ruined too many Saturday nights at their place, so I wondered if it was not a little bit too early after her bad sickness. She reminded me that she had been working since the day before yesterday, which left me without an argument. So I had to give it the green light and promised to call Pelle. That was fine, Kerstin said, for granny had already promised to take care of the children.

I don't know what prompted me to write all this. I suppose I wanted to get a true version of the facts down on paper. There's a world of difference between the grim reality, as we call it, and the old men's speculation. Their galloping imaginations played tricks on them.

I haven't looked at their document for a couple of days. That's just as well. It's good to be able to escape Lundgren's drivel in this house.

Vivianne at the switch board has promised to copy this out tomorrow, in spite of it being Saturday. She's cute, but not to my taste. I prefer brunettes.

2

Blom was waiting for me outside *The Little Boarding-House*. He is an uncommonly disgusting man, obsequious, pasty-faced and sweaty, with a squeaky voice and an averted gaze.

He began by saying how very sorry he was for having to disturb the inspector—me—on a Sunday. I said that it remained to be seen who was to be pitied. Then I tramped past him through the reception and up the stairs.

Ivehed was standing outside the caved-in door.

'We thought something was amiss, chief. Nobody answered in the room and when I couldn't open the door, I battered it down. He's inside, dead.'

'Has anyone except you been inside yet?'

'No. I only felt the pulse, which was quite unnecessary. He was as stiff as a board and the *livor mortis* was already visible.'

'In that case, he must have been dead for some time. Was it necessary to break the door down?'

'I tried the picklock at first, but it didn't work.'

'Keep everyone out while I go in and take a look.'

The room was a total mess. To begin with, there was the dead man, of course. He was lying on his back and had fallen in a rather peculiar way, for his left hand was pinned under his body. His head was near the foot of the bed and his feet were under the table. The body formed an angle of 60 degrees with the bed, with an overturned chair next to it. When I took a look at the corpse I became a little bewildered: Ivehed hadn't said anything about the red wine. I assume he wanted me to fall into the same trap as he had and think that it was blood, which I would have done but for the stench of old booze. Come over to the station one Saturday morning and put your nose into one of our cells—"single rooms" we call them—and you'll understand what I mean. Of course, I noticed the red wine bottle on the table as well. The liquid had splashed over the dead man's face and stained his shirt front and pants as well. He had been wearing a white shirt, open at the neck. No tie. The jacket was hanging on a chair by the window. Ivehed came in immediately when I called.

'You haven't moved anything here?'

'For heaven's sake, no!'

We squatted on either side of the corpse.

'Not much point in trying a heart massage,' I said, attempting to lighten the atmosphere.

'I don't think so. How long could he have been lying like this?'

'No idea. The medics will find out, taking samples of visceral contents and such. His watch shows a quarter past eleven, the same as mine. What are we doing to do now?'

Ivehed was wise enough not to say anything. He shouldn't, of course, advise me what to do.

'Do you know his identity?' I asked him.

'He answered to the name of Axel Nilsson.'

'Very well.'

At the sight of the messy stiff, Ivehed grew paler.

'Do you feel sick? Drink a glass of water.'

He didn't dare contradict me and slithered away to the wash-stand.

'Chief, there are three glasses here.'

'What about it?'

'Usually there are two glasses in every room. These three are all different and they've been washed.'

'Let me see!'

He was right. There was one with ribbed glass, another was a plastic mug and the third the kind of glass you get when buying mustard. They were totally clean, hardly any finger prints.

'Let's look around and see if we can find something.'

Ivehed checked the door, while I scrutinized the windows. They were firmly locked; the right one even had the window-catch attached. On the window-sill stood Blom's horrible flowers, and repulsive keepsakes ranged along a narrow cloth embroidered with an Art Nouveau design.

'Here's the key Nilsson used to lock the door. It's lying here on the carpet and it blocked the view when Blom tried to look through the keyhole before he called us.'

'Good. Make a note of it.'

A few moments later Ivehed found the towel in the wastebasket, wrapped in a bundle and smelling awful.

'Anything else?'

'Yes, bits of paper and…wait … there's some cheese!'

'Cheese? What the hell do you mean? Did he keep food in there?'

It was a wedge of cheese, which someone had hacked away at, so that there were a lot of irregular cuts in it. Kerstin used to scold me because I did toboggan-runs of the wedges. In this case, it was more like a downhill race.

We put everything on the carpet, which was the least dirty spot.

We continued to take inventory. In the wardrobe there were socks, frayed underpants and faded shirts which had been folded carelessly. There was also a pullover and a pair of unused handkerchiefs. A threadbare suit was suspended from a hanger. On the floor was a pair of unpolished shoes. The left shoe was worn-down on one side and the shoestrings had snapped a couple of times. They'd been tied back together again and the result was like the upper side of a Christmas gift when the sales clerk has rippled the pieces of tape.

I found a wallet and a passport in the inside pocket of Nilsson's coat. In another pocket there were a few small coins, a beer-bottle opener and a matchbox. The others were empty; likewise, there was nothing in his trouser pockets, except for a bandanna.

The passport had been issued this year at the Swedish consulate in Washington. The immigration officer in Göteborg had put a neat stamp in it: Entry October 12, 1969. Mr. Axel Leonard Nilsson, born March 3, 1917, was 179 centimetres tall, had fair hair, humour eyes and was unmarried. A non-descript face smiled stupidly out from the photograph.

In his wallet there were a few creased ten crown bills, a page from a diary; a few newspaper cuttings in English, a guarantee certificate for a shaver, an old Swedish driving license, a handwritten prescription for some kind of hair pomade and a few slips of paper with sundry scrawl and numerals, which could be telephone numbers. That was all.

The findings were not too illuminating, I thought. We put the rubbish on the carpet, next to a medicine jar Ivehed had just found. According to the label it contained 100 Dichlotride-K-pills, sold at Uttern, the pharmacy, with instructions to take two pills twice daily. The box was almost full.

'I found it on the bedside table together with a pair of spectacles and a few issues of the porno magazine *Lektyr*,' Ivehed said.

I sent him over to the window to check the view. I suggested he should try to estimate the distance from the window sill to the ground below, rather than peep at the naked girls in Nilsson's paper.

'At least four metres,' he said. 'I wouldn't try to jump down.'

If Ivehed couldn't jump that, then nobody could. He plays soccer and hockey and is incredibly fit and fast. I myself am swiftest when it comes to talking and using my fingers. I am trained in typewriting and playing poker at the station. At home it's mostly bridge. I'm a very good dummy and I'm afraid that's what I'll be proving at the Ramsten's tomorrow. What I mean to say is that people lose their shape after they're married. While I was doing physical training at the Police Academy I could run the steeplechase course in four minutes. Or maybe it was ten. Anyway, it was fast.

From above, the jump really looked impossible. We opened the windows and looked at either side.

'How did he get out?' Ivehed asked.

'Who?'

'The murderer.'

'What damned murderer? I haven't said anything about murder.'

Ivehed looked surprised, but said nothing. I myself was at my wit's end. The dead man was lying on the floor bathed in red wine, there had been a piece of mouldy old cheese in the wastebasket and the room was locked from the inside. I became angry at Ivehed.

'Let me handle this. If it's murder I'll let you know. Understood?'

Then I sent him off to question Blom about the boarding-house guests, especially Nilsson.

For a while I stood at the window and tried to collect my thoughts.

It was a matter of trying to make head or tail of things, and it had to be done fast, for at home the situation was critical due to Kerstin's illness and the children's fidgetiness. I looked around the room, from the sagging bed to the table streaked with wine and to the spot where the bottle stood. The bottle was wrapped in twined straws and contained some Italian slop.

My next thought was that a doctor had to be called. One couldn't say anything for sure before a thorough medical examination had been carried out. Surely it was an accident, but what if it wasn't? I mean, the room was locked from the inside, no doubt about that. That's why I really got angry when I thought of Ivehed yelling about murder! He who couldn't even handle a picklock!

I must get Gustavsson to come here, I decided. He can take care of this. I called out to Ivehed again and asked him to dial the station and summon some sensible people. Notice that I used the word "sensible"!

That left me with a breathing space for mental activity. I walked out of Nilsson's room and settled down in the sparsely furnished reception area. In addition to the two armchairs, there was a sagging plush-covered sofa and a table with full ashtrays. The TV was next to the staircase banisters and had to be fed with coins. Underneath the window was a bookcase with a few issues of the annual volumes of the Swedish Tourist Association, the local elementary school song-book, a few pulp novels from the turn of last century and a couple of battered cheap detective stories: *Lawless Desperado* and *Fair-Haired Women Are Dangerous*. At the very bottom of the case I found some party games. The ludo board had been used as a combined ashtray and cuspidor. There was also a chess set with many of the pieces missing. I've never been very interested in chess. It's all about luck and manual dexterity.

For a while I sat there, staring into the distance. I tried to look intelligent in case someone happened by. A thought was nagging at my mind. I freely admit I'm not a big thinker, but I do usually get somewhere. Except now. My mind was a blank.

After a quarter of an hour I went back to number 5. Sometimes you get fresh ideas when your initial impressions are dispersed and you return to the scene of crime a second time.

I walked slowly around the room and regarded the body from different angles. Then I turned on the radio by the window. A mass was being broadcast, so I turned it off at once. On reflection, the music did fit the environment, but I kept it off anyway.

I nearly tripped over the towel with the almost-rose-coloured stains of red wine on it as I left the room and headed for the reception area.

My mind was superficially blank, but there was definitely something there gnawing at me. In such circumstances, the best thing was to wait and see. There was no point in forcing anything.

At this point I shall permit myself to squeeze in a few lines for literary effect. When gazing out through the window, one could see a blue sky and a yellow sun. As the sunbeams filtered through the dirty curtains, well … there was a lot of dust in the rays of light. When I was a boy I thought that the dust particles were vitamins. I used to stand there breathing deeply to become fresh and strong. I was obviously an idiot from the very beginning.

It had been windy during Saturday evening with plenty of rain. I remember it because I had felt an incredible need to go outside and cool down when Pelle's cheating was at its worst. Now it was calm. I'm not usually one for physical culture, but I am able to determine whether it's raining or not. We do have quite a lot of rainfall in the town at this time of year.

Gustavsson surfaced as I was sitting there in a philosophical mood. I sent him away to do a reconnaissance of the place. The numbskull Melin was with him. We used to engage him for particularly sensitive operations. He's particularly well equipped to order and pick up sandwiches from Modin's café. We used to vary between meat with cheese and salami-type sausage, so that he would not find police work too monotonous. In that way he could learn to focus his attention and follow instructions to the letter, important things for a policeman. Otherwise he is utterly useless. I told him to walk around and knock on the room doors, making a note of each room number and the names of the guests. If Melin managed to survive that ordeal by fire, he could maybe rise up in the world. He could, for example, have a sandwich with liver pâté next time.

I had just got him out of the way when Ivehed emerged and told me what Blom had had to say about Nilsson. I was also informed about the hullaballoo last evening, about the plaster at half past eight, about the turned-on transistor radio and about the key which had vanished.

It wasn't until he mentioned Blom's surveillance of the house that I pricked up my ears. Ivehed carefully described the host's room at the rear and how the back door could be monitored. I got to know the approximate times of Blom's activities, how he locked the back door at one o'clock and how it was opened again by the maid in the morning. Just as the room keys were deposited on their hooks behind the reception desk, the back door key was similarly hung up in the same place.

It was not until I got the report from Gustavsson that an idea finally took shape. He gave me a detailed description of the house with entrances and rooms, including the basement and the attic. Gustavsson had also been snooping in the garden. He showed me a neatly executed sketch.

Then Melin reported that there were three guest rooms on the ground floor. For some reason none of them was occupied, perhaps because of their proximity to the dining rooms. Blom served beer and various salads at "reasonable prices." He also had a "Today's Special." According to the menu the special on Sunday consisted of boiled sausage and mashed potatoes. The reasonable price was three crowns and seventy-five öre, inclusive of VAT and service, the latter probably provided by Blom himself. He was not fully licensed and could only serve light beer. Let me add that the dining-rooms (notice the plural form) of *The Little Boarding-House* enjoy a deservedly bad reputation. If, against all expectations and wishes, I had to eat there I would gladly pay a five crown bill in order to avoid service.

Be that as it may, Melin supplied a list of the rooms and guests on the first floor:

No 4. Schoolmistress Berta Söderström, Stockholm. She had been there since October 20.

No 5. Mr. Axel Nilsson, moved in October 13.

No 6. Schoolmistress Sylvia Hurtig-Olofsson, Stockholm. The same arrival date as her companion Söderström.

No 7. Vacant.

No 8. Travelling salesman Ivar Johanson, Malmö, arrived October 23.

No 9. Vacant.

No 10. Warrant Officer Sten Renqvist, Boden, arrived October 24.

Melin had discovered that the schoolmistresses had checked in together and were attending a conference on some esoteric subject of no interest whatsoever to anyone outside their profession, an event which would last the whole week. They had jabbered a lot in their rooms and on Friday Nilsson had asked if no younger women would come soon. He had been told that the conference would be ending the following day.

One of the ladies was built like a rugby forward; the other one was more mousy and ran around with a bag over her shoulder, attempting to look ambitious and busy.

Johanson was a frequent guest at the hotel. He was a heavy drinker and was in possession of several empty bottles when Melin examined the room. He said there had been a lot of noise during Sunday evening from room number 5 on the opposite side of the corridor. He'd knocked on the door at around nine o'clock and caused at least a temporary silence.

The warrant officer Renqvist had stayed at the hotel for a couple of days because he had been called up as an instructor by the nearby regiment. He had an expense allowance which made it possible for him to live outside the barracks. He'd run into Johanson in the upstairs corridor on his way to the loo at nine o'clock. Gastric flu had caused him to spend half the night there.

Such was the information I assembled, which was quite enough for my purposes.

The last thing I did was to scrutinise the stiff a little more closely without changing its position, of course. I carefully tucked up the shirt-sleeves, turned up the trousers from the ankles, examined the face and the neck and looked carefully at the scalp. There was not a single scratch anywhere, much less any plaster.

There was a rose tattooed on the right forearm. Utterly charming.

It was at that point that I realised how the case should be handled. All the problems were now over and done with.

Before I dismissed everyone, I announced that we would resume the hearings in the dining room at six that evening. I told them I'd have a surprise for them.

When it came to my subordinate colleagues, it was a question of giving them something to think about. Had I dreamt of what a row there would be amongst them after my conversation with my old man, I would of course have remained silent. All the same, I didn't hoodwink them. All the details were absolutely right, although I did keep it secret that murder had never been on the agenda, at least not on mine! Is it my fault that they made a muddle of it?

As far as I was concerned, everything was as plain as the nose on my face from the very beginning. Nilsson had got drunk during the evening of Saturday and when his visitor had gone, he had locked the door, washed the glasses and closed the window. He was intoxicated and slipped or stumbled and his head hit the bed and he died. When he fell he got red wine all over him, and that was it.

Can I be responsible for the lads getting hold of the wrong end of the stick, raving about a locked room? And making a great feature of the wine spots on the towel? Don't you think that I can see the difference between blood and red wine? Had there been something fishy about the towel, we would have analysed the spots. But because there was nothing notable about it, the maid could dispose of the rag.

Then there's the business of the damned transistor radio. Nilsson was listening to it before he died. Nobody but he turned it off.

In fact, the investigation had come at a good time. Now I would at last get the opportunity to take a closer look at Blom. On the pretext of investigating the circumstances surrounding the death, I'd be able to poke into his affairs undisturbed. That the old men in the detective club would be the losers, so to speak, was icing on the cake.

I'd been thinking about this—and the joyful prospect of grilling Blom really hard—while I was driving the children over earlier to see my old man. I was feeling very pleased with myself, and it was probably for that reason I was foolish enough to bare my soul about official business. My father took it without blinking and a few hours later the doctor and Lundgren had both been brought in.

However, before my third-degree interrogation with Blom,-I — hardworking as I am—took the time to visit another person for a less dramatic chat.

After her cleaning duties, Blom's maid had already gone home to her husband by twelve o'clock, but it was necessary, in my opinion, to ask her about one or two things. Ivehed had spent some time with her during the morning, but that examination was probably not worth very much, seen from a police point of view.

She lived a couple of floors up in a housing co-operative. The name on the door was Svensson.

A teenage girl opened the door. She just stood there, her mouth open, and stared. I said who I was and her chin dropped even more. It was as if she'd never seen a policeman in her life.

Her mother came hurrying over to ask me in. The girl left and I hung up my trench-coat. I had bought one with flaps and a belt and stuff, just like all the cops in the movies wear. You have to stay up-to-date.

Loud pop music was streaming out of a nearby room. The door was open and I understood that it was Miss Svensson's room, for there were a lot of horse pictures on the walls. Among the gee-gees there was some with unusually long manes and a few others that looked somewhat human. I recognized one. Paul Anka was his name.

As I entered the living-room her mother steered me in the direction of a rocking-chair, in which sat a toothless old hag with watery eyes and a red, runny nose. She grabbed hold of my tie with a bony hand.

'Are you Hadar?' she asked.

'No, mother,' said Mrs. Svensson. 'Hadar is dead.'

'Mum is here for a cup of coffee,' she explained to me. 'She lives in the old people's home at Ängsbyvägen.'

'Ekgården,' her mother whimpered.

Mrs. Svensson and I sat down at the other end of the room.

'You do cleaning at *The Little Boarding-House*,' I began.

'Yes, for the past fifteen years.'

'Have you ever suspected that Blom could be … how should I say … a little bit imprudent?'

She looked at me in an unappreciative way.

'Dishonest,' I blurted out.

A negative look crept into her eyes and she fell silent. When I raised my eyebrows and smiled encouragingly in order to appear nice, she muttered something about motes and beams in the eyes, which I vaguely recalled from our school Bible class.

We plodded through the subject for a while but got nowhere. At last I realised she was quoting stuff from the Bible. Just to keep up with her I began to search for quotations from my own memory.

It turned out that I wasn't well versed in the Scriptures, and when it came to hymns, I only remembered *Den blomstertid nu kommer.* It deals with the time flowers arrive in the summer and we used to sing it at the end of school term, but I found no reason to recite it then.

It was obvious that Mrs. Svensson didn't want to talk about anything to do with her employer. I began to ask her a little bit about Nilsson.

'At what time did you arrive at the hotel this morning?'

'Seven o'clock.'

'And the back door was locked?'

'Yes, as usual. I have my own key. The other one was hanging on its hook inside the door. I told the constable all that this morning. I started to wonder when Nilsson didn't let me into room number 5.'

'Why?'

'Because he was very particular about getting the room cleaned. He knew that it had to be done before twelve, because that's when I leave.'

'Ekgården,' said a voice from the rocking-chair.

'Did he say anything about expecting you this morning?'

'No....'

Suddenly she stopped speaking and turned red. She looked over at the old woman and then started talking with small syllables.

'He was quite impertinent,' she whispered. 'Yesterday he was shameless enough to propose that on Sunday, which is the day of rest, we could....'

'What?' I wondered, most interested.

'But the Lord's judgment fell on him and he was called hence!' she announced triumphantly.

'Ekgården,' cackled the old woman.

'How was he otherwise?'

'Not very nice, I must admit. But he kept his things in order. He was very careful with his medicines as well.'

'What were his pills for?'

'I don't know.'

I didn't get any more out of her. She hadn't noticed anything suspicious at the hotel during the morning hours. All the windows on the ground floor had been locked.

I didn't get anything more about Nilsson, either, but I hadn't expected to. The only thing I had hoped for was perhaps a cup of coffee.

When I left the room I had to shake hands with the old crone again.

'Bye, bye, Hadar,' she croaked.

From the girl's room came gramophone music blasting at full volume.

'Children will be children,' her mother said in a spiritual way.

'*Tryggare kan ingen vara*,' I quoted a hymn about how safe the children of God are, in an attempt to be clever. I shut the door as fast as I could. It's always good to have the last word.

That was that. The visit was a total waste of time.

We were due to gather, as agreed, in the dining room at six o'clock.

During the afternoon, the ambulance had taken Nilsson's body to the morgue. Photos had been developed, though I don't know for what purpose, and our fingerprint expert had gone over the room. We would hear from him shortly. Nilsson's personal belongings had been collected in a big plastic bag and sent after him to the morgue. Since that part of the case had been concluded, I saved the meeting with the medical examiner for the following day.

Melin arrived first. I turned up at the same time as Ivehed, and Gustavsson emerged from a closet, where he had been rummaging among a lot of spare beds.

All the guests were in the boarding-house and Blom was walking about in his felt slippers. It's an understatement to say that he looked uncomfortable. I took the opportunity to prepare him on the way in.

'The performance will soon begin, just a few short minutes to go!'

He grinned anxiously and obsequiously and opened the door to the dinner room for me. Unfortunately, I happened to tread on his foot as I walked past him. Just bad luck, it wasn't really intentional. The contact was unpleasant for me as well.

'I'm sorry, Superintendent.'

'Detective Sergeant!'

When the four of us were gathered and had lit our cigarettes, I gave a short speech.

'Well, this is quite a nasty incident. We can't exclude a serious crime, so we must apply all our resources as fast as possible.'

I spoke in a loud voice and at the same time I gave Gustavsson a sign. While I was talking, he sneaked over to the door and when I nodded he opened it. Needless to say, Blom was standing there eavesdropping. He tried to compose his flabby features and looked very embarrassed.

'If we need anything, we'll call you,' I roared.

He slouched away and Gustavsson shut the door again. I continued.

'Now listen!' I continued. 'A man died here tonight, but it's not a question of murder. Some of the masterminds here have demonstrated their total inability to comprehend this and so I repeat: Nilsson's death was an accident. Does anyone need it in writing? Ivehed?'

'No, chief.'

'Melin?'

He shook his head. Afterwards I came to thinking that maybe he couldn't read.

'Good! We've had our eyes on this third-class boarding-house for a couple of years and this situation gives us the opportunity to find out about Blom. Do you understand what I'm saying? In plain language: under the pretext of a murder investigation we will observe this place, so you will all shut up and not talk about our real intention. The public at large and the press must be kept out of it as much as possible. I'm through with the Nilsson case, but it doesn't mean I'm not interested in who he was drinking with in the room yesterday evening. Gustavsson is to collect information about Nilsson and his contacts in the town, find out why he was here, check those telephone numbers, investigate why he needed the medicine and so on. Ivehed is to enquire in the area about witnesses who may have seen or heard something. He is to do it as discreetly and tactfully as possible. If people don't answer when he knocks, he's free to smash the door down, just to keep his hand in. There may be new stiffs piling up in the garden, beginning at the western corner. Melin and I constitute the brains trust. Any clever questions?'

Gustavsson was the only one who had anything to say.

'Why are you so interested in the visitor now, if there's no crime?'

'We've got to have someone to hunt, for heaven's sake. The show must go on.'

3

I've been stuck in this hole now for seven years. Since I joined the police, that is. I was born and bred here and I know the town like the back of my hand. Most of what happens here is totally without interest. No action. It became more tolerable when we got TV. Not many new things happen at the office either, but it's strange that we haven't been able to catch Blom up till now. We've long suspected that he's mixed up in unlawful bootlegging and possibly other dubious activity. This Sunday I decided the time was ripe for putting the screws on him.

He was unsteady and anxious when he entered, and that was what I had hoped for. He was sweaty as usual and was continually wiping his forehead with the back of his hand. He claimed he'd been running a temperature since a day ago and that he thought that he'd caught pneumonia. He coughed in an artificial way.

'It's about time we got a clearer picture of one or two things, Blom. Do you prefer it to be here or at the station?'

'Whatever the superintendent wants. I have nothing to hide.'

'We can turn a blind eye to some things, but what's just happened is the last straw. Now I want answers to my questions and the answers have to please me. Is that understood?'

'You'll be satisfied.'

'I've been dissatisfied for a long time.'

'Without any cause whatever, I can assure the superintendent.'

'I'm a detective sergeant. Well, let's start with why you watch your back door every night until one o'clock in the morning? Why have you put a twenty centimetre layer of gravel on the pathway? Why have you put up a window-mirror? What purpose does the espalier serve?'

'I don't want anyone to get into the house. Nobody unauthorized, that is.'

'Horseshit!'

'That's the truth. Why would I go to great pains to keep a strict watch, if it wasn't for the benefit of the guests?'

'I'll ask the questions. How does it benefit the guests if you hang out of the window in the back of the house halfway through the night?'

'My goodness, a murderer slipped inside yesterday evening and you doubt my intentions.'

'The truth at last! That I doubt your intentions. Very well worded, Blom! Maybe the watch is deliberately intended to be ineffective!'

'Would I keep the doors wide open and allow a lot of riff-raff to come and go as they like?'

'Isn't that exactly what you're doing?'

He didn't reply. I think he understood what I meant. He wet his lips with his tongue and his eyes avoided my steady gaze. They shifted and roamed about the room like a billiard-ball bouncing around until it hit a pocket.

'Do you know what Melin is doing right now?'

'No idea.'

'Listen!'

I opened the window and at first he looked relieved when the clean, fresh air streamed into the room. Then we both heard the clatter of gravel. Blom turned pale.

'This is a murder investigation, Blom, and because of that we have to go over your house with a fine-tooth comb from the basement to the attic. Right now we're turning the garden upside down, starting with the gravel path.'

'I have nothing to do with Axel Nilsson.'

'Perhaps not, but we can't turn a blind eye to whatever turns up during our investigation. Have I made myself clear?'

Now he really was on the defensive. It was a bluff on my part but it could work. He was thinking frantically and I was helping him to do it in my own way....

'It could take quite a while before we find the connection under the gravel. That's where we're starting. Perhaps we could avoid a lot of inconvenience and not have to excavate the whole path and ruin the lawn if you ... my lads are careful, but quite ruthless. I've had quite a few complaints about that.'

'It's nothing criminal.'

'Excavating the backyard? No, but installing a burglar alarm in a particular way could be, perhaps. I don't really know. I must ask the public prosecutor tomorrow.'

'Well, before I gravelled the path a couple of years ago, I put a few contact plates down. They're connected to an electric bell wiring system. When anyone treads on them I hear a signal in my room. How did you find out?'

'We know almost everything at this point, Blom. It was wise of you to remember a little bit more, it is about time.'

The surveillance had seemed to be suspicious from the very beginning. It seemed to be preposterous to watch the back door for hours at a time through the window, even if possible disturbers of the peace did enter the field of vision when they rounded the espalier and even if the window-mirror made it a little bit easier. Furthermore, I had been sceptical about the supernatural hearing ability that could catch footsteps on the incredibly well-raked gravel path outside, with or without an open window, and with a radio blaring. Why had Blom been so anxious to arrange such inconvenient methods, when it was so much simpler to have fixed an alarm device? Hadn't Blom let the cat out of the bag when he explained that no murderer could have avoided his watch the past evening? With that he had to explain how such a watch was performed and it turned out to be so complicated that we suspected mischief. Why go to that much trouble?

'How about taking it another step further, Blom? Why is it so important to control everybody who comes in? I guess that nobody slips out without your knowledge either. The stairs are creaking, aren't they? Your door is ajar and you have good hearing.'

'As I told you, I want to keep my house in good order.'

'Isn't it more like the other way round: you want extra visitors here?'

'Why would I want that?'

'To boost your income a little bit. How many rooms have you got?'

'Ten.'

'How many double rooms?'

'Two. Number 1 and number 5.'

'Disregarding the prices, isn't it strange that there is such a small difference between single and double rooms here?'

'The double rooms are bigger.'

'Just a few square centimetres. Strictly speaking there are just ten single rooms, isn't that the case?'

'Not true. There are two double rooms, but all right, they are not very big. The guests don't mind. On the contrary most of them are very contented with all my facilities.'

'I am glad to hear that. And if the double rooms are occupied and another couple who want a double room overnight arrives?'

'In such a case, I must direct them to the *Private Hotel* or to

Videll's Lodgings for Visitors.'

'But you don't do that?'

'Of course I do. Once in a while I may put in an additional bed.'

'Does it fit?'

'If the guests put up with it, yes.'

'How many extra beds are there?'

'I don't know exactly. A couple of them.'

'You have six extra beds in a space inside the TV room.'

'Yes, that's possible.'

Now was the time to make a decisive thrust. Blom had recovered from the exposure of the alarm system and seemed to be relieved when I rapidly dropped the subject.

'This place has a bad reputation, Blom.'

I raised a warning hand when he started to object.

'You're keen on keeping the bad reputation alive. It's here that the men in town put up when they've got a playmate and need a *chambre separée* for some entertainment exercises. In reality you don't have any double rooms, and you put up signs prohibiting visitors to the rooms after ten o'clock. So they pick a single room and smuggle the partner into the hotel through the rear door. Nothing prevents them from entering that way after nightfall. That's what they think. But you know it, because you're the one who's admitted them into the trap.'

Now he was seriously frightened. Beads of perspiration stood out on his forehead and there was a twitch round the corner of his mouth. There was no point in wasting this opportunity. It was just piling it on.

'Then you knock at the door and enter, but not until they have undressed and it's after ten o'clock. The man has hardly been able to button his flies and the woman hasn't had time to cover her charms with the sheet.'

I gave him a few seconds to digest my words and went on:

'Damned if I know what you threaten them with, perhaps the police. You show them your damned sign on the inside of the door—where, by the way, there's a hook so that the sign is usually covered by clothes. To begin with, you talk about the reputation of the hotel and about scandal and corruption of morals, which unfortunately is true. After some discussion you make an exception. You put in an extra bed and charge for a double room. Am I right?'

I was right. It was obvious.

'For heaven's sake, I'm only trying to help them. What's wrong with that?'

'OK, you substitute one lack of morals for another. I'll find out if that's unlawful. You just need to know that I know. We also know that you're selling alcohol on the sly, and my lads are right now looking for the stock. It means profits on the side, and when the assessment authority has taken a look at your income tax returns of the last few years, we'll see what happens to your right to run a hotel. We'll keep an eye on you. Our investigation into the murder will continue the whole week and we will be right here. You mustn't leave the hotel and we may at any time have to interrogate you about Nilsson's death. Any questions?'

He got to his feet uncertainly and went towards the door. I saw that he was shaken and, in a way, sort of relieved. He'd expected worse, but it wasn't yet time for the final round.

'You're a big zero, Blom. Let me say it with the best of intentions, for your information.'

He didn't answer. I took his silence for an admission. After he'd gone I called in Melin, who had been walking about on the gravel outside.

'It worked like a charm! Now dial the telephone company and make arrangements to monitor all outgoing calls. We could send Vivianne over to them for a couple of days. You'll be responsible for Blom not leaving the house.'

My plan was to obtain permission for wire-tapping later on. The idea was that Blom be allowed to fall into the trap. To be sure, it wasn't about these small matters but about much bigger things. But, as I said, those would have to wait.

We would strike on Wednesday, but already a lot of things had happened. For example, we'd discovered the name of Axel Nilsson's visitor. Just fancy that!

4

In order to avoid any misunderstandings, I want to be clear that all our methods within the police department are very humane. We go for a soft line, as it were, and I myself am a weak person, primarily emotional. If I have to take strong measures it's always most regrettable. Ever since I became a chief I occasionally let Gustavsson sit at the table during interrogations—as a kind of insurance, in case I should lose my temper. His confident presence is very comforting to have, sitting there with pen and pad. He can adopt an expression of regret or reproach as required and that is very efficient. At regular intervals, he interferes in the conversation and puts in his cues with great precision.

No specific tactics are laid down for routine questioning. Normally Melin is the secretary. His expression is just stupid enough to put people at their ease. On Sunday evening he was watching Blom, so I had to run the show on my own.

First I called in the schoolmistresses, one at a time.

Sylvia Hurtig-Olofsson was a thin, nervous type. She had a bun at the back of her head, which spoiled her appearance even more. Her upper teeth protruded and, when she dropped what little amount of chin she had, they looked like two icicles hanging from a roof. She twisted her hands non-stop and blushed easily.

'Mrs. or Miss?' I began, politely but unnecessarily.

'Miss.'

'We regret that you and your woman friend have been kept here.'

'It's quite all right. Miss Söderström fell ill yesterday, so we had to stay over the weekend anyway. There's been a conference for home economics teachers here and we're on leave of absence from our schools in Stockholm. I myself work at Östertorpsskolan in the Bandhagen suburb.'

'Do you mind giving me your age and address?'

'July 18, 1924. Ringvägen 88, Stockholm SÖ.'

'Thank you. I assume you know why we're talking right now?'

'Of course. Iit has to do with Mr.Nilsson's death.'

'Did you know him?'

She didn't reply immediately. It was as if she was trying to find suitable wording.

'He was not an acquaintance. We exchanged a few remarks in the lounge. One should not speak ill of the dead, but he was quite uncouth.'

'How so?'

We're used to putting small conjunctions of this kind in the conversation. It conveys the sense of a real dialogue to the other person. One can also use "really?" or "is that so?" for the purpose of stressing surprise.

'He was rude. He swore.'

'Sorry to hear that.'

'Once he told my friend that male persons were prohibited in the rooms.'

'Really?'

'Oh yes. And there was more! He drank! There was always a smell of alcohol about him.'

'How unfortunate, Miss Hurtig-Olofsson. Did you notice anything else?'

'We rarely saw him. Usually we were in our rooms. The TV set in the lounge was out of order.'

'I see. Could you tell me about yesterday?'

'Well, it was like this. The work week ended with a big luncheon at *The People's House* and we had counted on packing our things in the afternoon in order to take the eight o'clock train, but then Berta became ill and got....'

'Gastric flu?'

'Exactly. I put her to bed and rushed to the greengrocer's and bought apples. Did you know that grated apples are an infallible remedy when it comes to loose bowels?'

'I had no idea. I'll make a mental note of it.'

'They should be finely shredded.'

'I understand. Please continue.'

'Round about eight o'clock she felt better, thanks to the apples, and we decided to go to the cinema. They were showing *Rio Bravo*. We sat at the end of the row, but didn't need to leave early, and returned back to the hotel just after eleven.'

'Did you hear anything from room number 5 when you went out or returned? Did you meet anyone?'

'N-No. We were together for a while in Berta's room. By the way, have you read *The Saga of Gösta Berling*?'

I remembered that my schoolmistress in Swedish pestered us with that drivel in junior secondary school. It's about a priest who gets fired because of alcoholism and begins monkeying about with broads. Pure rubbish, if I remember it rightly.

'*The Saga of Gösta Berling*? Of course, a lovely book.'

'You like it? Oh, that makes me so happy. We read aloud from it.'

It was meant to be a grandiose declaration. She thought that I would clap my hands and roll up my eyes to heaven. I couldn't bring myself to do it.

'Yes, we had reached that wonderful chapter about the home of Lilliecrona. ...'

She made a telling pause and I managed to smile in a melancholy way.

'... and could not fall asleep. All of a sudden Berta got sick again and had to run to the lavatory. She had a high temperature. 38,7 Celsius. Do you know what we did?'

I took a wild guess.

'Grated apples?'

'Right you are! I gave her a double dose of it but did not dare to leave her alone. She was very weak and her pulse was 112. We were at our wits' end. Well, after some time her poor stomach calmed down and when the pulse went down below 100 we could at last fall asleep. I hauled my mattress over to her room, laid it down on the floor and stayed the night there. She's much better today. No fever.'

'And her pulse?'

'78 in the evening, a little bit too much but not dangerous, thank goodness!'

'Are you sure that you didn't hear anything during the night?'

'No. The house was quiet, that I can swear.'

'No radio music, no footsteps, no other sounds?'

'Absolutely nothing.'

'In that case, I won't detain you any further. Thank you very much for your help.'

We shook hands. Hers was small and bony with many bracelets that rattled against each other. She turned back at the door.

'Can we leave the hotel tonight? There's a train before midnight. Poor Berta won't sleep if she has to be in the room next to the dead man's.'

'I quite understand. Yes, you can leave.'

She curtseyed in an affected way and disappeared.

On the scratch pad, where I'd scribbled a little bit for the sake of appearances, I'd written about twenty dollar signs in a row, quite decorative.

The next person was another hag, big and clumsy. If you've seen a female Russian discus-thrower, you know what I mean. If such a person gets diarrhoea it takes quite some time to empty the bowels. She pushed the door open in the same brutal way as Ivehed probably had in the morning.

'Here I am,' she boomed cheerfully.

'Please come in and sit down. How are you? I heard that your health has been rather delicate?'

'Thank you, I'm fine. One is wise enough to cure oneself.'

'Grated apples are a blessing,' I tried, having decided to go ahead in the partly pious style.

'Nonsense. That's what Sylvia thought. I had to put away a lot of it yesterday and even more during the night. No, constable, I took Enterovioform pills, but I hadn't got the heart to tell Sylvia.'

'I heard that you were here by virtue of your profession.'

'That's right. If one gets an opportunity, one takes it. I am a domestic science teacher. Do you understand what that means?'

'My wife is a teacher.'

Here I took the opportunity to be a little bit personal. Sometimes it relaxes them.

'I pity her. Most girls are tolerable, but the boys, constable... But I'm quite accustomed to it and know how to command respect. Between the two of us, they call me the Big Terror.'

'I understand—I mean ... what about the boys?'

'Eat potatoes that have got burnt five days a week and clean the saucepans with steel wool afterwards, then ask!'

'You should have returned home yesterday?'

'Yes, but thank goodness I became sick and was spared the usual Sunday visit to my old aunt. Sylvia began to lament exaggeratedly when the flu broke out, but I can tell you that I was not in any danger. At eight I felt better. You see, that was the time when the train left. We were able to go to the cinema show at nine. Sylvia wanted to see *Dreams of Happiness* or some such nonsense, but I took her to a western. I recommend it.'

'You got worse during the night?'

'Not really. I had a slight fever of course, but that was nothing. When we returned from the cinema, Sylvia read aloud from her book.'

Now seemed a good time to go on a charm offensive, I thought.

'*The Saga of Gösta Berling*? A lovely book.'

'Does the constable really think so? Sickly in my opinion. Well tastes differ. Anyway, Sylvia persisted in reading aloud, but around one o'clock I couldn't stand it any longer. I went to the lavatory but when I returned, there she was grating apples like anything. I just had to say thank you and swallow them. After that she dragged her mattress into my room and I didn't get a moment's peace, because she felt my pulse every other minute. We didn't fall asleep until three.'

'Did you notice anything unusual yesterday, during the day or the night?'

'No.'

It wasn't so much her replies as her attitude that bothered me. All the time she regarded me in a patronizing way. This person was a nightmare.

'Miss Söderström....'

'Mrs., if you please.'

'Sorry, but I got the impression that you were unmarried.'

'Widow. My husband was with the streetcar line.'

She had probably eaten him up. That Miss Hurtig used her title on her woman friend was probably something to do with their common profession.

'May I ask when you were born and what address you have?'

'Ask as much as you like. February 11, 1912. If you want to visit me, I live at Stagneliusgatan 17 in the Fredhäll suburb. Bring *The Saga of Gösta Berling*.'

'Just a moment. This is a murder investigation and no joking matter.'

'Is that so? I've said I don't have anything of interest to tell you. Regarding the murdered man, I saw him a couple of times. It seems that he had accosted Sylvia, so I stared him in the eye and he disappeared into his room in a flash. That's how disabled he was. May I go now? We have a train we don't want to miss.'

She got to her feet and walked out. I thought that my scratch pad was empty. But no, in a corner at the bottom of the page I found a flat fish without scales.

The next day I learnt that they had not gone off until the morning train. Melin had met them in the corridor while they were dragging their luggage downstairs. Obviously there must have been some hundred pages still unread in the book and Miss Hurtig-Olofsson had not been able to stop reading. They had simply missed the train. Melin had politely asked where they were headed. "To Stockholm," the Söderström woman had screamed, while the other one acted as if in a trance, whispering something about Jerusalem. He thought that they were planning some kind of conducted tour together.

The next person was a small round man with a ruddy complexion and a good-natured appearance. He was dressed in a faultless business suit and there was a smell of hair lotion about him.

'You are Ivar Johanson?'

'At your service.'

'Why are you in town at the present time?'

'I have the pleasure of representing Ström & Söderlund, the well-known textile company. I specialise in furnishing fabrics. Business brings me here every couple of months. I'm responsible for this sector and now and then I make contact with businessmen in order to show them our new products. I have many friends in town. I'm always welcome. May I offer you a small advertising handout? Compliments of the company.'

He put a ball-point pen on the table in front of me. On one side was printed: "Ström & Söderlund, sells for all the fabric is worth." I nodded but left the pen on the table.

'Do you have anything to tell me about yesterday evening?'

'Very little, actually. I came to town on Thursday. Since I was alone, I asked Nilsson to accompany me in the evening. I thought of the annex of the *Grand Hotel*. Maybe a cocktail or two. But he hadn't got the time for that.'

'How did you get acquainted with him?'

'I didn't! We met briefly in the corridor and I got the impression he might be thirsty. In this business you become a little bit of a psychologist. You see what sort of person people are. I am known for that talent.'

'What kind of person was Nilsson?'

'Difficult to say. He was a complicated person. Ivar, I immediately said to myself, there's a man with problems, a human being in need. Something within me exhorted me to stand by his side. One day you yourself may need consolation and support, officer. Then it could be me who comes to look after you, saying "Ivar Johanson, here I am!"'

He made a dramatic pause to allow me to applaud or burst into tears. The man was drunk, there was no doubt about it. He had moved nearer during his statement, and the smell of menthol from the Thule lozenges could not disguise the brandy.

'What did he say about himself?'

'Nothing. I didn't see him again. Last Saturday in the evening, I mean yesterday, he had a row in his room with some person unknown to me and I went there in order to hush them up. Nilsson didn't respond to my knock on the door and didn't open.'

'Did you hear anything else?'

'Oh, yes. As I said, I was alone. When they became silent at last, I knocked again at half past ten, hoping for a brief chat with him and perhaps a drink. But he didn't respond. The radio was on, though. I could hear it through the door. Then I came to think about the other male guest.'

'Renqvist?'

'Yes. I had only exchanged a few words with him. Ivar, I said to myself, that man has problems. You must share his struggles. So I knocked. Nobody opened there either, so I went to bed and fell asleep.'

'So you don't have any more to add?'

'Yes, I have. I woke up again. It was then that I heard someone crying.'

'Crying?'

'Yes, crying. It sounded heart-rending but it was not very strong, more like a whimpering. I dressed rapidly and went into the corridor, but by then it had stopped. It was nearly two o'clock. Nilsson's room was silent and he didn't react to my knocking. Oh damn it! I forgot to tell you! I had heard the radio just before one o'clock when I went to the lavatory but not an hour later. Anyway, I was standing there while someone nearby needed solace for his or her despair. But where? I heard the monotonous sound of voices talking from one of the women's rooms, so they were ruled out. That left Renqvist, so I knocked at his door and this time he replied: "Come in." He was in bed and I sat down at the end. "I hear that you have problems," I said. "What can I do for you?"'

'And what was his answer?'

'He said "Clear off,"' Johanson replied. 'At that, I gave him a pen and went back to bed. Then I heard nothing more. In the morning, when I had washed and shaved, I went out to call my mother in Malmö and happened to see Blom in the corridor, outside room number 5. Just think if Nilsson had been able to talk to me in a timely manner before his death and unburden his soul!'

'And are you sure that the radio in Nilsson's room was off at two o'clock?'

'That's God's truth.'

'Will you be here tomorrow?'

'Yes, you can count on me if need be. Keep the ball pen.'

He walked out in a dignified and careful way, but in the doorway he gave a slight lurch as he met Renqvist, our last witness. He was a thin, upright man of medium height dressed in an unbuttoned Crowns humour uniform and a most tidy leave-of-absence tie on the slant.

He inspected me critically with clear, sharp eyes under shaggy eyebrows.

'You wanted to see me.'

'Yes, please. Just a few formalities. Your name is?'

'Sten Renqvist, warrant officer, Infantry 19. What do you want to know?'

'Everything that could shed light upon the death at this hotel.'

'OK, I'm innocent. That's the only thing that's important to me.'

'We don't suspect you of anything. We just want some information.'

'Fine with me. I'm here as instructor at test shootings with some old pieces of ordnance. There are not many people who can handle them any longer, and there are a lot of damned regulations to observe when the tests begin tomorrow morning and continue until Tuesday. Then there will be inspections and care of arms, and I will return home to Boden that same evening. I never saw Nilsson.'

'You were in the hotel yesterday evening?'

'Unfortunately, yes. I should have been at a mess party, but I caught your damned flu and was confined to bed. Had to run to the loo a couple of times every hour. It was hell.'

'Then you must have been in a position to notice things.'

'So it may seem, but I had enough of my own problems.'

'Did you hear any strange sounds?'

'No.'

'Mister Johanson maintains that you were unhappy yesterday.'

'I'm never unhappy.'

'He said that you were crying.'

'I never cry, but I understand what you mean. There was somebody squealing and whining on and off between midnight and one thirty. I thought that it was that thin hag.'

'Did Johanson visit your room during the night?'

'Yes, he rushed in just when I'd finally been able to fall asleep. He was drunk as a lord and tumbled on to my bed with a bottle of brandy. He said that he felt alone. He had a lot of problems he wanted to tell me about. I told him to go to hell. It was two o'clock in the morning.'

'How can you be so sure that the crying, or whatever it was, ended at exactly half past one?'

'I hadn't been able to get to sleep, so in order to kill time I counted the number of stitches in the curtain. I began at eleven o'clock with breaks for visits to the loo. Then I heard that whining noise. It went on non-stop after midnight. Was it Nilsson?'

'So it would seem.'

'I was in bed counting but my position was very uncomfortable. I turned over at about half past one and I noticed that the sound had stopped. Since my position was now more comfortable, I fell asleep. But of course I woke up a couple of times after that damned nuisance Johanson had disturbed me, but then it was quiet. That's all I have to say.'

On his way out he picked up the ball pen and gave me a meaningful look. I had drawn a row of stars in the form of a spiral. It could have symbolized the brandy, or a military badge of rank. The biggest and centrally placed one could have been a representation of me, Gunnar Bergman. In that case, it seemed to be somewhat exaggerated.

It was nine o'clock, time for my and Gustavsson's little game of cards. He dealt them at his usual lightning speed and we both had our stakes ready—we play for coins, not matches. It takes him about fifteen seconds from start to finish.

Then Melin insisted on spoiling everything by playing the master detective. He ran in claiming there was a drinking-glass missing from room number 9, which was vacant.

We had just got him into a chair, given him a hand of cards and explained to him that his fiancée would have to sacrifice herself for the sake of law and order and forgo his awkward company that evening, when Ivehed came in to tell me he had found a couple more witnesses. At that point the game was already afoot and we were rather grumpy because of all the unnecessary interruptions. I had to give it a break.

A man and a woman were standing in the reception area. I recognised the man. He's a pork butcher at Metro.

The woman's name was Ekbom and she runs a laundry. She

introduced the man as her fiancé. From what I hear, he's only part-time, but I don't like to disillusion people, so I pretended to believe her. His name was Odestam. It sounded as if he had chosen a new surname. I prefer fine old family names. Like Ivehed.

'Carl-Henrik has something to tell you,' said the woman.

'Yes,' Carl-Henrik said, 'my fiancée and I ... last night at twelve o'clock....'

'Go on,' I said, encouraging him.

'As a matter of fact, I had to pass water, and since the rain had stopped, I went outside to do it.'

'Well, thank you very much for the information. I understand what a load off your mind it must be to have told us this. However, we won't need you anymore. Good night.'

'But that wasn't all.'

'Really?' I said, making it sound as if I was quite surprised.

'There were two rooms brightly lit on the upstairs floor. They were side by side on the same side as the back door, so to speak. The left one was open.'

It is possible that these were important things, but right then I was in a hurry, so I asked if I could take down the information and contact him later if need be.

Finally, we sat down for our game. That's when we got the shock.

Ivehed's wife had taken all his small coins. I know that she does it to punish him. It's happened before and it cannot go on like this. I shall have to talk to the commissioner about it. While Ivehed drove to the railway station to get small change, I called Kerstin to ask if anyone had called. 'No,' she replied, 'not here.' The children were asleep and mother had returned home in a taxi.

At the same time Gustavsson, who can sound very authoritative, especially when he lowers his voice one octave, called Mrs. Ivehed from the other telephone and said that her husband was on official business and should not be expected home before midnight.

At half past ten we could at last begin. We extracted all of Melin's pocket-money in short order, so he was obliged to borrow a five crown note from Gustavsson at 25% interest.

Just before twelve, the fingerprint guy called. He'd found a lot of gorgeous prints on the wine bottle. It shouldn't take long to check them in the archive. He promised to get back to me quickly.

We sent Melin, who was already broke, over to the station to pick up beer and sandwiches and then we could start again. We hung up a sign with the words "Private" outside the door. Gustavsson had found it on the premises. He's fantastic.

After that, when we'd finished eating and were about to shuffle and deal again while Melin washed up, Gustavsson heard something outside the window and ran outside. That was how we caught that imbecile Lundgren.

After he had left us, it was time again. Not for poker, since everything seemed to be going wrong for that, but once more for Carl-Henrik. As he knocked at the window I opened it and whispered that he didn't have to notify us whenever he took a piss. He said he wanted to report a Peeping Tom, an old man, who was creeping around outside. I explained that it was an extra policeman from the vice squad, charged with observing morals at night, but that Odestam had nothing to worry about because in his case there wasn't much to see. Then I shut the window.

Next it was the turn of Stissler, our fingerprint expert. He's a foreigner, German I think. Nothing wrong with that, most of them are very ambitious and methodical. He said he could give us the name of Nilsson's mysterious visitor. *Nota bene* that this was long before The Three Wise Men came up with their nonsensical theory.

Stissler started toying with us by making us wait whilst he lit a cigarette, but the effect was spoiled because he couldn't get his lighter to work. He fiddled with it for a while until Gustavsson took over and found that the flint had worn down.

'It's a very well-known person in this town,' Stissler began.

'One of our talented colleagues?' I wondered, remembering that Ivehed had been the first one to enter room number 5 in the morning and was quite capable of contaminating any crime scene in my precinct.

'No.'

Stissler shook his head triumphantly.

'One of our popular and colourful repeat offenders?' I asked.

'The most colourful one!'

At that point we didn't have to guess who it was. When you work as a policeman you know who the regulars are. They come and go. Or, rather, they stagger in and are kicked out. Our regular habitué, number one for many years, has been Algot Emanuel Cronlund, nicknamed Crona the Goldsmith.

And he is indeed our oldest customer, take my word for it.

It was not until I was in bed back home that it dawned on me we had actually forgotten to take the fingerprints of the guests at the hotel. It was our good luck that these particular prints happened to be in our archives. Otherwise we would have been standing there with egg all over our faces.

Strangely enough, we had also forgotten to check potential plasters or wounds on the guests. That, too, was embarrassing, since I had actually sworn that nobody was wounded when my old man had asked me. If pressed, we would have to say that we simply hadn't had the time. Other things kept cropping up and one can't do everything. After all, honesty is the best policy, as the saying goes.

Nevertheless, as I was lying there trying to fall asleep, I did begin to feel like the biggest idiot in town.

5

On Monday morning my typewriter broke down. The ribbon got stuck. What a shame! I was actually preparing to do some of the paperwork which had piled up over the last couple of days. Now I would have had to postpone it again. One learns to accept that kind of setback philosophically. The police profession is fraught with such challenges.

Now that I had a moment to spare, I could work out a brilliant theory about the events at *The Little Boarding-House*. Here goes:

Nilsson and Crona are old buddies and they're going to have a good time in a big way on Saturday evening. Since Blom is busy with the accounts that particular evening, Crona can steal up around eight o'clock without being seen. For a while they kick up their heels, but then there is a quarrel and Crona leaves just before the newscast, just when Blom's surveillance begins. When Nilsson is alone, he locks the door and opens the window in order to air the room. Then he lies down on the bed with the intention of listening to the radio. After a while he falls asleep, but wakes up a few hours later, around two o'clock, because the window is squeaking in the wind. Then he drinks some wine, turns off the radio and shuts the window. The three old men made a mistake when they thought that Nilsson had been unable to get to his feet without his glasses. The light was actually on when he woke up! We know that thanks to Odestam. On his way from the switch at the door he stumbles in the darkness, hits his head and falls to the floor. He hits the chair as well as the table with the wine bottle on it, and the result is what we found.

I take back what I said about the mystical whining reported by Ivar Johanson. It could not have been the result of Nilsson's death struggle ending at half past one or two o'clock, for if he lay there moaning from midnight on, how on earth could he then get to his feet and shut the radio after an hour, in the middle of everything?

What do you think? I ran this past the lads at coffee and they thought that it was super. Except Gustavsson, who asked what they had been drinking in the room if they had been satisfied with one Chianti Ruffino between them and there was still wine left over. I said we could search the rose bushes below the window and find out.

At Gustavsson's question about who had washed the glass that Nilsson drank from before he died, I replied that the glass had been washed earlier that evening at the same time that the wine was mopped up with the towel. After that, in the middle of the night, Nilsson did what other normal citizens do. He swigged it, if he was drinking at all. The farewell drink was my own little addition that would give my theory an added credibility. When Gustavsson still looked questioningly at me, I informed him that swigging means drinking straight from the bottle. Then he kept silent. For five seconds.

Why did they have three glasses in the room when there were only two people celebrating, one of whom one was used to drinking straight from the bottle? That was his next shrewd question.

I replied that both of them could have been swigging, because then they didn't have to wash anything at all, if that would be better, and the borrowed extra glass could have been for flowers. That was my theory. If I had interpreted his tattooing rightly, Nilsson was a lover of flowers.

At last we bet on it. I guessed that we would find the two bottles among the roses. Ivehed bet on one and Gustavsson refused to take part unless we put five crown notes in a pool.

We clinched the deal and he took out a paper and wrote down our guesses, plus his own solution. Melin still had no money and he passed. We sent him over to *The Little Boarding-House*, after which we cleared up some routine measures and felt that we had worked very hard.

We gathered again in my stylish office, supplied with every imaginable modern convenience: a letter-opener, a pencil-sharpener, a hole-puncher and who knows what else. There is an enormous sense of comfort and well-being: King Gustav VI Adolf is hanging on the wall and Kerstin Bergman is sitting on the table.

Constable Birger Melin brought in the results of his painstaking investigation: five paper bags containing four bottles and seven empty half-bottles of spirits, a bottle of wine and at least twice as many beer cans, all empty. It was Gustavsson who had guessed there would be twelve and he pocketed his booty of five-crown bills. Things got even more interesting when Melin said that he'd been into the room and opened the window, and the hinges squeaked like nobody's business. Well done, detective Melin!

Since we were in discussion mode, the question of the time of death arose. We had two versions of when the noise from the room ended. According to Renqvist it was at half past one, but according to Johanson it was closer to two o'clock. It was curious that the two hags hadn't heard anything. Maybe the home of Lilliecrona had been too distracting, or maybe they didn't care about being disturbed, because they weren't able to sleep anyway. Otherwise they should have heard the sound better than anyone else, since the squeaking window was so close to theirs.

Ivehed was of the opinion that Johanson was right about the time and that Renqvist simply fell asleep when he changed position. For my part, I thought that the warrant officer seemed to be reliable. While you're asleep, sounds can be unconsciously registered; sounds which are recalled when you awaken and are assumed to have happened then. That was the explanation of Johanson's wrong estimate of the time.

Melin shared my opinion, but Gustavsson felt that it wasn't important and it was enough to establish that the window was shut just before two o'clock, that Nilsson was still alive at that time, and that he died soon after.

At this point, it occurred to me I should call the medical examiner. When I called the switchboard, I first got no answer and then I was disconnected. When I called again, Nyegaard's associate, who was the one who should know where he was, had gone for lunch. In a tone that did not sound promising, I was requested to call back in the afternoon.

I drove home to the ranch. Kerstin had fully recovered and the children were healthier than ever. We got hot dogs with creamed spinach, which Lillan refused to eat because she was afraid of getting the same kind of knobs that Popeye has on his elbows. At last she promised to eat if Kerstin fed her, but only one bite for every Donald Duck figure I could remember. Just to be bloody-minded, she replaced the tablespoon I had produced with a slender egg-spoon of plastic. It went well until I ran out of names for those damned annoying animal specimens. I had to go through a pile of comic books before she finally finished, thanks to Gyro Gearloose and a cur called Tramp.

I fled before the dessert.

When I finally reached the associate who should have known where Nyegaard could be reached in the afternoon, she told me he had gone out. I left a message asking him to call me.

Then there was a down-period until two o'clock, when the afternoon tabloids arrived. Gustavsson appeared just as I was leaving for the day. He left a short and concise account of what he had dug out about Axel Nilsson.

Nilsson was born on March 12, 1917, the youngest son of Valentin Nilsson, a butcher, born in 1895, and his wife Agda, born Lindgren, in 1899. The father died in 1937 and the mother in 1968. The brother Edvin left the country in 1946 and was heard from for the last time four years ago, when he was in San Francisco, USA. Axel Leonard Nilsson enjoyed six years of elementary school with modest results, after which he held a couple of jobs of short duration and in different trades. He was probably jobless much of the time. He left town in 1959, his last recorded home address being Torggatan 10.

He did compulsory military service with the Swedish Naval Forces in a low position on fatigue-duty, on account of alleged nervous difficulties. Contact with the temperance authorities since 1948 and with the police a number of times in connection with drunkenness, disorderly conduct, unlawful assault and insulting a civil servant. He had been fined and had had three jail sentences for a total of 14 months. Several sojourns at the detoxification centres at Ryboholm and Ramsättra. Strangely enough his driving license had never been revoked. No weapons. Was charged for non-payment of maintenance in 1960-63 for Yvonne Linnéa, daughter of Rose-Marie Viktoria Åhlund, born 1941, since 1963 married to foreman Göran Eriksson, Tallåsvägen 19.

'It seems as though Yvonne Linnéa is his only surviving family,' observed Gustavsson. 'May I suggest that the chief mercifully inform her of the man's death.'

It had to be done sooner or later.

There's no big drama when one is travelling on official police business of this sort. If anyone thinks we have police sirens on and two screaming wheels when we take the curves, while people stand two-deep waving Swedish flags, they are mistaken, at least in our precinct. My old Volkswagen has a leak in the gear box which leaves a trail. There's some damned gasket loose, but I can't afford to send it for repair. They say that the brake-light doesn't work either, because of a loose contact, but I've not been caught as yet. Ivehed once stopped me at the corner of Västra Långgatan and Kungsbroallén and asked to see my driving license, which I had forgotten at home. He was so droll, leaning into the car to smell me. I just love policemen with a sense of humour.

Tallåsvägen is situated on the fringe of the town, almost down by the marina. There are mostly one-storied houses there, with fences and hedges. Number 19 was quite a new building, low and stained brown, with a separate garage on the site. There was a set of white stained furniture on the lawn and a flagpole in front of a children's playhouse. Behind the building, through a screen of birch-trees, one could glimpse the waterfront.

Nobody opened when I rang the door-bell. I knocked at the back door but got no answer there, either. Not until I was back inside the car did he come out on the porch in pyjamas and dressing gown.

'Are you Göran Eriksson?' I asked.

'Yes, what's it about?'

'Sorry to disturb you. I am from the CID.' CID has a nice ring to it when one wants to be a bit official.

'Is something wrong?'

'No, I just want some information. Can you spare a moment?'

He gazed anxiously in all directions to see if his neighbours had seen or heard me. Out of sheer decency I tried to make myself small and entered quickly. It would be unfortunate if his wife could no longer borrow sugar from her neighbors because she was married to a criminal lunatic.

I recognized the fellow. He was in his mid-thirties and seemed pleasant enough. I was directed into some kind of living-room which was covered in dust. She who did not clean grinned out from inside a silver frame on the bookcase. Another photo showed a lass seated at a school desk with a map of Sweden on the wall behind her. There were shots of other uninteresting, smaller children with and without front teeth, an older couple standing arm in arm in front of a tourist bus, an elderly gentleman with his hair plastered down with water and a white shirt that was sagging around his neck as a result of his tie being pulled too tight, and, lastly, an old woman seated with a flower pot on her stomach and ten bouquets in vases around her. She had perhaps been hiding from the photographer in the greenhouse, but had nevertheless been found.

'Is this the family?' I asked.

'Absolutely. My wife and children.'

'Where is your wife now?'

'She's away. Back this week. She's been with the smaller children on a holiday for needy housewives in Mamaia. Yvonne, the oldest, is staying with her cousins because it's closer to school. I work most evenings and am very bad at cooking.'

'I see. How old is Yvonne?'

'She turned nine this summer. I hope she hasn't done anything wrong?'

'Not at all. May I ask, Mister Eriksson, if she is your daughter?'

'I regard her as such.'

'Does she know… I mean… who her real father is …?'

'No. We've talked a lot about it, Rose Marie and I. It's not easy to know what to do for the best. We have two other children, Lisbeth and Kennet. Rose-Marie has told me a lot, but, honestly, I'm not that interested. I've never met the father and I'm not from these parts. I came here in the beginning of the 1960's. Is he in trouble?'

'In a manner of speaking. He's dead.'

Eriksson looked out of the window. There were worried wrinkles on his forehead and he was biting his nails in an absent-minded manner. He turned and looked questioningly at me.

'He died yesterday night,' I said. 'He seems to have been here in town a couple of weeks already. You've had no contact with him?'

'No.'

'What were you doing last Saturday?'

'To be honest, I've no idea. I fell sick before Saturday and have been in bed. I was so sick on Saturday evening that the new district medical officer had to come over. I'm on the sick-list for this week. The flu. I'm better now.'

'Good. How is it that you don't know what you were doing last Saturday?'

'I was delirious and practically unconscious. My brother-in-law had to stay with me the whole night.'

'OK. Given that Nilsson has no other known relatives, I had to notify you. What you do with the information is your business.'

'I may just forget it.'

I understood him. The situation was awkward, but I had to go through the formalities.

'Do you know what Nilsson was doing here?'

'No.'

'Do you think that someone else might know something? Your wife? Your parents-in-law?'

'Rose-Marie hardly knows anything. She would have told me. And her mother died … let me see … seven years ago. Why do you want to know that?'

'We wonder why Nilsson came here. I think I'm going to have to ask your father-in-law'

Eriksson got to his feet and paced a few steps on the carpet. Then he went over to the bookcase and looked at the photos.

When he turned to me there was resolution as well as fear in his eyes.

'Is that necessary?'

'What?'

'To ask Sven. He'll only become agitated. Let the whole thing rest! Nilsson has caused enough trouble. Do you know about his brother?'

I nodded. I didn't want to interrupt him. We—that is Gustavsson—had dug up that old story about Edvin Nilsson that afternoon.

'Maja, my mother-in-law, had weak nerves. She frequently took anti-depressants. When Rose-Marie became pregnant with Yvonne, Maja had a relapse. She would lie in her room and say nothing. Sven didn't dare take responsibility for her. Dr. Nylander had to call St. Katarina's hospital to arrange for a bed there. She was given electrotherapy and recovered enough to return home again. She went back and forth to the hospital many times. The medical treatment didn't seem to work very well in her case. She hanged herself in the hospital. I never met her. They say that she was a hopeless case. Nobody could have done anything for her. That's called melancholic depression or something and it runs in my wife's side of the family.'

'You mean....'

'I only want to say Sven has got over it now. His wife would perhaps have been ill regardless of what had happened, who knows? That's what the doctors thought. Please don't remind Sven. Has the newspaper written anything about the incident?'

'No, unless someone has paid for an obituary notice, but who would do that?'

'None of us would. Sven went to Stockholm last Friday. He's supposed to visit his sisters and return home together with Rose-Marie when he arrives from Mamaia. My brother-in-law called him in Stockholm yesterday to tell him I was sick. Sven can't possibly have heard anything about Nilsson's death and he has said nothing to me about being in touch with him during the past weeks. I would have known it if Sven had.'

The whole conversation was very difficult. It was obvious that nobody in this family had anything to do with the case, but someone had to ask the questions. A policeman's lot is not a happy one.

'It'll be all right,' I said. 'Trust us.'

Then I slunk away. The Volkswagen didn't start. It was just standing there coughing and gathering a lot of children around, making fun of me. Eriksson came out and opened the engine hood. He had some knowledge about cars and screwed and pottered about for a while until the damned thing started. There'd been some moisture in the distributor cap. I almost asked him to fix the gear box while he was at it.

Outside the station I let the motor run while I ran to my office.

There were a couple of messages for me.

One was from Vivianne and had been placed on my typewriter. For some reason she had changed the ribbon.

"Nyegaard's assistant called after you'd gone. He asked you to call. V."

The other message was from Gustavsson. I don't know his first name, but on the other hand we've only known each other for seven years.

"Nilsson's medicine, Dichlotride-K, prescribed by Doctor Halling, Göteborg (unavailable). Purchased October 13."

His information didn't make me any the wiser. That takes more powerful messages. Below I read "p.t.o." That's shorthand for " look at the other side of the page." During one's training days one learns this kind of thing.

I turned the paper and read what he had scrawled down.

"Who will bring Crona in before it's too late? Or has that detail been overlooked? He hasn't been seen since Friday night, according to his fiancée Elvy. If we wait too long, he'll be heading for America. That's where they all go nowadays. Many loyal and personal greetings. Gustavsson."

I came up with many new and original swearwords on my way back to the car. I came up with a few more when I found that the car had stalled. I had given it a little too much throttle, I suppose. Then it wouldn't start again, no doubt because of moisture in the distributor cap.

It was pouring with rain. I should have waited until it stopped.

I hailed a taxi and was home in ten minutes. The children were waiting with the book.

6

The hunt for the adventurer Algot Emanuel Crona went on for three days. During that time some pretty sensational events occurred.

On Tuesday evening I had a good laugh reading The Three Wise Men's report. I found this brief moment of hilarity most relaxing.

The following day we arrested Blom. That was another agreeable moment. We'd tapped his phones while Melin saw to it that he didn't leave the hotel and the result was not long in coming. Our reward came in the form of a series of phone calls from Blom to a number of his blackmail victims in and around town. They were gentlemen who had used the facilities of the hotel for extra-marital entertainment. Under pressure from our threats, our favourite boarding-house owner had taken the opportunity to squeeze more out of them before the well ran dry. The list of victims was quite long, but unfortunately didn't include any of my friends. It would have been great fun if Pelle Ramsten's name had been on the list. Then maybe he would stop cheating at bridge. But that would have been too much to ask.

Another surprise was that we were actually able to get hold of Nyegaard on Tuesday afternoon. Needless to say, he groused about us not calling him earlier because by now the stiff would be half rotten, and if we weren't that interested we may as well leave it at that. He went on digging at me in like vein, but he nevertheless promised to come over as soon as he could.

I was sick and tired of the whole business, which had ruined several days for me. Not that it was a conspiracy directed at me personally, but it was a hell of a coincidence that there had been swimming competitions in the sports hall twice this week. Kerstin comforted me by stressing that I'm not the least interested in sports, but how is it possible to become interested when stuff like this is going on?

I kept wondering why Crona had made himself scarce. He's obviously keeping something to himself which he doesn't want to come out. I know someone who could drag it out of him in less time than it takes to tell. Myself.

We went to Crona's spot in order to locate his fiancée. I call it a spot. There's no other word for it. "House" is wrong, for it's in the back of another building. "Residence" sounds too solemn and "apartment" makes one think of wallpaper, flowerpots in the windows and carpets. It's possible that what was draped over the threshold and made me stumble was a carpet, but I don't want to commit myself. It could have been a cat.

Elvy is a small, wizened woman with frizzled hair. She sometimes picks Crona up when he's spent the night with us. She drops coins into the coffee cash box from time to time in order to help us forget the incidents. Last year we even got a Christmas card in the mail: A Merry Christmas and a Happy New Year from Elvy and Crona.

'Where is he?' I began.

'Who?'

She peered at me with innocent eyes.

'Guess.'

'That will be difficult. Wait a second... Crona?'

She called him plain "Crona," just as everyone did. They may be engaged, but they haven't got around to dropping titles. For he's seldom at home.

'Bull's-eye. Where is he?'

'I don't know. I've no idea. Why do you want to see him?'

'His single-room has been a little bit empty for a couple of days. We got worried.'

'Now you mention it, it's been quite peaceful here for a while.'

'Where has he gone?'

'Are you sure he's not somewhere in the station?'

'Yes.'

'Have you tried Bussparken?'

'Of course. That was the first place we looked.'

'Then I am afraid I don't have any more suggestions.'

When she saw how disappointed we were, she made some coffee to cheer us up. Gustavsson went out and bought some buns. The coffee had no taste, but one has to be polite, so I didn't complain. At the second cup Gustavsson recalled something.

'Does he have any relatives?'

'No, not anyone alive.'

She was actually serious. Unlike me she has no sense of humour.

'We'll find out.'

We thanked her and she promised to come over if she got an idea. When we walked across the garden she sat in the window and waved. We issued a description of him that afternoon. It said that the former goldsmith Algot Emanuel Cronlund, 58 years old and 1.67 metres tall, with humour hair and a humour moustache, brown eyes and a tattoo of a shipwreck (appropriately enough) on his chest, had been missing from his home since October 26.

Originally I had written "missing from his cell," but Gustavsson didn't agree. When last seen he was wearing a humourish-brown striped suit and a blue shirt. We were quite sure about his clothes. He was always dressed like that. They were a gift from The Salvation Army. Otherwise he's not very religious. Anyone who's seen him or has any other information about him should get in touch with us or the nearest police station.

Nothing happened during the first twenty-four hours. Elvy came over a couple of times and asked if we had made any headway. She advised us to work in a calm and methodical way. As far as she was concerned there was no hurry to find him. Afterwards I heard that her life had never been better.

Ivehed got a list of those people who had spent time at Ramsättra at the same time as Crona in the summer of 1966. That had been his last institutional care. Ivehed found thirty-two names, twenty of which were unavailable, six back at the institution again, while some had moved to Stockholm and Norrköping. One was at an old people's resort and two were at their homes.

After twenty-four hours he gave up. One positive thing about the investigation is that Ivehed himself was out of the way while he was on meaningless assignments.

Gustavsson sorted the WANTED tip-offs. One was that Crona had been seen in the town park of Sundsvall, sleeping on a park bench with an issue of the daily *Västerbottens-Kuriren* under his head. That was a false lead, since Crona would never put *Västerbottens-Kuriren* under his head. He always puts it under his boots.

Another brilliant idea came from a reader of the daily *Dagens Nyheter*, who thought he'd identified Crona at the head of a student demonstration in a telex picture from Paris.

Further tip-offs indicated that our friend had been seen simultaneously at Umeå, Stockholm, Bredvik and Bulltofta. In the last case, he had been dressed in a brown-humour suit, as in the description, but had been accompanied by two female private secretaries. Gustavsson couldn't resist telling Elvy this, and her face turned totally dark before she understood that it was a case of mistaken identity. And she has no sense of humour.

We checked with taxi drivers, we asked at booking-office windows in railway station and talked with drivers at bus-companies. Nobody had seen Crona.

At last we got a break from someone calling himself Roger, but that was an alias. He refused to give his real name, address and age and he wore a black mask. We assumed he was about ten years old. On his birthday he'd been given a bike. It had been stolen since Sunday and now he wanted to report the loss.

In the absence of anything else we decided to suspect Crona as the bicycle thief. We thanked Roger for his assistance and he asked if we could do him a favour. He wanted to be locked up for a while, only a quarter of an hour or so, in a real cell. Of course, of course, Gustavsson said and dragged him into cell number thirteen, which was empty. After one minute he began to scream that he wanted bread and water, so we had to buy another bun. Roger was disappointed, for he had expected an old dry one or a rusk, and not something with almond paste. After fifteen minutes he went away. He had written "Magnus 1969" on the wall.

That evening we held an important team meeting. Ivehed surprised us by winning four times in a row and suggesting upgrading the stakes to half a crown. We had just been paid, so even Melin could keep up with things and had enough courage to be decisive over the phone, when his fiancée wanted him to go out dancing.

At eleven o'clock, Gustavsson got an idea all of a sudden and left the room in order to check something. When he returned he looked unusually smug.

'It occurred to me that Crona has lived here in the town all his life.'

'So what?'

'So maybe he was born somewhere in the vicinity.'

'And what difference would that make?'

'Listen to me. This is from an old pre-sentence investigation. Born in the rural district of Vallersberga in Stora Hede, 1901. Parents: The crofter Petter Cron—.'

'Get to the point, Gustavsson.'

He is expert at slowing down investigations with meaningless pieces of information. He can go on endlessly with factual information about names and dates. The older things are, the more excited he gets.

He should have been an antiquarian.

'It says here that he was at school in Modhult. That school was shut down ages ago. Assume that his parental home was somewhere in the neighborhood.'

'Do you mean that he wanted to brush up on his past scholastic achievements?'

'Hell no, but he could have gone into hiding in the crofter's cottage.'

'How far away is the school?'

'About 30-40 kilometres northwards. Do we have a map?'

Reluctantly I rummaged out an old ordnance map issued by the general staff. We leant over it and looked between lines and dots. It took us a hell of a long time. Here and there it was impossible to read the text; it was indistinct and faded. Bengtsson, my superior on sick leave, had probably spilled a considerable amount of beer and cough mixture on it over the years.

'Here's the school.'

It was Melin who lent forward. He had his spectacles on.

Gustavsson pushed him away and blocked the view with his fore finger.

'Stora Hede,' he said triumphantly.

He pointed to a black square. Beside it one could read "S...a Hede." It was far away and on the edge of a wood.

'There's a pine forest here and some broken ground.'

Ivehed is an orienteer and wanted to parade his knowledge.

In that pine forest and on that broken ground there were some small dots that could represent cottages. Gustavsson suggested that we should go and get Crona that same night, and Ivehed was very happy. I guess that he wanted to go at it like a steam-roller, causing the police authorities to become liable for damage to the land owners. He would readily have jumped into his track suit and run straight away with a compass in his hand.

My opinion was that, if we were going to follow idiotic leads of this kind, it should at least be done in the daytime. We had downed a lot of beer, and I was neither prepared to drive 30-40 kilometres in the middle of the night, nor look after the others in the darkness. It would be difficult to fine-comb the area, and since it was pitch-black, Crona could easily hide as soon as he saw the beams of our flashlights. And one or two of us would perhaps be afraid of the dark.

After a lot of ifs and buts, it was decided that Gustavsson and I would drive over there the next day—as of yesterday, that is to say. The others could do whatever the devil they wanted to do. Play cards if they wanted—one is after all a liberal and modern employer.

147

I told Kerstin about our trip. It was in the middle of the night. Now, it doesn't concern anybody what we do in the night, but she was uneasy and thought that we were after some kind of desperado. She had heard that Crona sometimes is troublesome, and he had grown to an enormous size in her imagination. In the end, I had to promise to bring my service pistol.

In the morning I overslept. Gustavsson called at a quarter past nine and sounded rather angry. Kerstin had packed an enormous box lunch in a knapsack. I refused to put the damned thing on, for it was not a scout excursion. At last she became reasonable and packed the sandwiches and the Thermos flask in my briefcase.

We took the patrol car. Gustavsson drove.

For the record it was a truly fine day. The sun was shining and so forth. There are many charming colours in nature at this autumn time of the year. Red, yellow, violet and who knows what else.

We kept fairly good time while we turned around the southern traffic circle of our nice little town and sped through the outskirts. Then the houses thinned out on both sides, the speed limits were eased and we were in the back of beyond.

Farmers were standing around in the fields looking bucolic. They would take a few steps forward and then a few to the side, as if they were on a chessboard. There were cows scattered here and there, red barns and whatnot....

Just as you would expect in the country.

Gustavsson turned on the car radio. There was a worthless information programmeme for foreigners about our beautiful country, followed by the mushy singer Lasse Lönndahl rattling off a song, followed by a lot of greetings to sweet grandmothers sitting around beaming all over the country.

Half an hour later he slowed down opposite a yellow two-storied wooden house. In front of it was a gravel spot. I guessed this was the school.

There was nobody in sight, so we looked at the map. Gustavsson had entertained me with a lot of information about the environment, ancient monuments and such, so I thought it was about time for some action.

We drove for a few more kilometres and stopped to consult the map again. We twisted and turned it a few times, looked at the sun—which according to the hymn-book, rises in the east—and at the road which, according to the general staff, rose in the direction of the north-west.

In front of the car, on the left-hand side, a path led straight into the forest. It seemed we should follow it for about five hundred metres to reach a clearing. And there we would find Stora Hede. There were many small cottages and Crona was to be found in one of them, if Gustavsson was to be believed.

After just a few metres we found the bicycle. It was a new, blue one, a boy's bike. One has to be tipsy or really frightened to steal such a thing and ride forty kilometres on it in the middle of the night. On the handlebars was a sign: "Property of Magnus Rask."

Gustavsson was humming a monotonous melody as he walked forwards. He seemed to be very pleased, but had no reason to be, considering the quality of his singing. I told him to shut up.

Everything went fine on the way to the house. The route had been abandoned long ago. Those who left have my full understanding.

Gustavsson began to wax lyrical about animal life. He pointed at some gnawed-off twigs which had been attacked by roe deer, birds' nests in the trees and rabbit droppings along the path. I cannot understand how anyone can be happy about things like that. The rabbit droppings looked just like common dung, I thought, though smaller and rounder.

There was swampy terrain and branches hanging down for the purpose of pricking and scratching. One had to shut one's eyes and keep one's mouth closed. Gustavsson had to do the same, so there was a positive side as well.

We fumbled our way towards a bare hillock a few hundred metres ahead. When we reached the top we could see the first cottage. It was a poor, small, dilapidated thing, crouching beneath a few firs.

There was no one inside and there hadn't been anyone in my lifetime, I swear. So we went on to the next place.

We'd selected five spots in the forest and were prepared to spend the whole afternoon looking for him, but it was actually there that we found him.

We saw the cottage at about the same time that we almost hit our noses against the timber wall. The forest had sort of grown together with the house or vice versa; the changeover was hardly perceptible.

Now, some people might think it would be very dramatic, but not so: it was all very calm and orderly. The wounds I would show when I returned home were caused by the branches in the copses and the result of a sprain I got when I stumbled upon a damned stone.

His snoring could be heard through the walls. Even though the door creaked, he didn't even wake up when we went inside. The bed he slept in was more or less the only piece of furniture, apart from a broken Windsor-style chair. It seemed obvious he'd come into this place in a hurry. We saw no belongings anywhere.

Crona was sound asleep. From time to time, strange guttural noises emerged from his mouth. He was dirty and his clothes were torn and his hair was in wild disorder, but the jacket was neatly folded up underneath him and his feet were placed on a yellowed Sunday supplement of the daily *Aftonbladet.*

Gustavsson shook him gently and Crona probably thought that he was down at the station and it was time to leave again. He slowly sat up, fell back again and looked around in a surprised fashion. One could see that he was totally consumed by hunger and fatigue. Fear surged over him. He opened his eyes wide and his pupils dilated. His body stiffened and his hands twitched convulsively. Maybe his pupils contracted instead—anyway, they changed in one way or another, if that's any interest.

'What is it? I didn't do it, I didn't—.'

'What is it you didn't do, Crona?'

'Nothing.'

Then he was silent, refusing to answer.

We walked back in a line. First Gustavsson, then Crona. It's not really true to say he walked. Rather he stumbled along.

Gustavsson insisted on sitting with Crona in the back seat. He tried to talk with him now and then but he never got an answer. On one occasion he flew into a temper and I heard a thud behind my back. I saw in the driving mirror that Crona disappeared for a moment and after that he looked as confused as he'd looked before the smack, but now with a red spot on his cheek. It became darker and his right eye became swollen.

Gustavsson is a decent man deep down but he has some problems with his temperament, perhaps because of some difficult childhood experience--what do I know? Things like this shouldn't happen, but, on the other hand, the swelling could have been something allergic. That's possible. Anyway, I didn't see anything. After some time, Gustavsson took the Thermos flask out from my brief case and offered Crona hot chocolate. Most of it got spilt, but we're used to wiping up after Crona.

He ate all the sandwiches except the one with meat. Gustavsson ate that one. Anyhow, Crona became more attentive and at least murmured some kind of answers to Gustavsson's questions. Then he asked for Elvy, but when we had said that she felt very fine he fell silent again.

I did manage to grab a cup of coffee before the interrogation, but I didn't get to eat a single one of my sandwiches.

By now I was quite pissed off, frankly. Gustavsson noticed it and seemed to be embarrassed. The only one who was fairly calm and collected was Crona. That would soon change, I thought, when I screwed in the lamp in the interrogation room. I mean the ceiling lamp. We have no spotlights for the third degree. We would never be able to afford the electricity.

7

Crona was placed in a chair on the other side of the desk. There he shrank down, and from where I was I could see most of his head, which stuck up above the table-top. Gustavsson had put an ashtray in front of him, and if one squinted a little bit it was as though his skull was in it. It looked quite funny, and you need to take your entertainment when you can in this profession.

'We don't think that we got an answer to the question of what you claimed not to be guilty of, back at the cottage.'

And we didn't get it now, either.

Gustavsson, who was sitting at the short side of the table, leant towards Crona and patted him on the shoulder.

'The detective sergeant hates it when he doesn't get answers, Crona. He becomes upset and impatient, which you will not find at all funny. And, by the way, I don't like it either.'

'I haven't done anything.'

'Why did you stay at the cottage?' I asked.

No reply.

'I don't understand why this man won't answer,' I continued. 'It doesn't create a good impression.'

'It's bothering me too, chief,' said Gustavsson.

'Do you want a lawyer, Crona?'

The goldsmith looked up. He looked completely helpless. On the table was a packet of John Silver cigarettes. Gustavsson had put it there. With trembling hands Crona took one of them, but he was shaking so much that he needed assistance to light it. Then he put his head in the ashtray again and let the cigarette stay in his mouth.

'Should we call a lawyer? We're trying to help you, Crona.'

'The detective sergeant is trying to help you,' Gustavsson clarified. 'He has served you sandwiches and hot chocolate, he has given you cigarettes and he is promising to arrange a lawyer for you. He's being as considerate towards you as he can possibly be. But you're just sitting there silently, not even saying thank you.'

'Thank you.'

'That's the spirit. We like civility here, answering when spoken to, for example. What were you doing in the cottage?'

'I was in hiding.'

'From what?'

'I don't know. What am I accused of?'

'You know perfectly well,' boomed Gustavsson. 'And it's not up to us to answer your questions.'

He was sounding really indignant.

'Should the detective sergeant really have to answer all your questions?' he continued. 'This is not an information centre. So listen carefully to me! Why did you disappear from town Sunday night? Quit stalling!'

Crona was certainly frightened, but still he didn't say a word.

Gustavsson, who looked like a mountain by his side, got to his feet and, with a deft hand, seized Crona's upper arm. It created a most threatening impression, exactly as in the gangster movies. Then he turned his head a half-turn, so that it caused deep wrinkles in his bull-neck, and hissed sinisterly at me:

'Could I take care of him for a while, chief?'

I nodded and left the room. In a situation like this a short nod is more definitive and terrifying than answers like "Do as you like!" I've tried different methods but have settled on the nodding. It's performed with a slightly protruding lower jaw after a short inhalation through a half-open mouth.

I listened for a while outside the door, but it was totally silent in the room. Gustavsson is reliable and effective, so I wasn't concerned. The incident in the car was a pure exception. An accident at work.

When I called home I found out that the boy had spread Selukos, a dandruff medication, on Lillan's sandwich. It looks exactly like Kalles kaviar and it was pure luck that Kerstin suspected mischief, because he was acting in an uncharacteristically friendly manner.

Strictly speaking it was my fault. I hadn't put the tube away properly in the bathroom cabinet.

I promised to come home as soon as possible. Food was waiting for me, she pointed out, it just had to be warmed.

Vivianne at the switchboard came in and wondered if there was anything more to do. There wasn't, but I remembered that Nyegaard should have performed the autopsy the day before. No report had arrived in the mail and we had not heard anything from him. At forensics I was connected to a secretary who regretted that the post-mortem protocol hadn't been written out until the afternoon. She explained that it was on its way. She didn't remember anything of its contents and Nyegaard wasn't there. She worked overtime and it was already half past five. I was just as wise as I was before.

Gustavsson came out of the room after half an hour. He said we could go on and appeared very pleased. His sleeves were rolled down, exactly as they should be according to the regulations. I was prepared for the worst.

Crona looked calm and almost exhilarated.

'Well, Crona. Why did you leave town?'

'I don't know. It's true, I swear.'

'Shall we begin all over again? What the devil do you mean you don't know?'

'It's my memory. I've lost my memory.'

Gustavsson jumped into the conversation.

'He said the same thing to me, chief. Loss of memory. Black out.'

'Okay, I don't believe it. A damned coincidence, eh? If his faculty of speech has returned, then his faculty to remember also should return. Immediately.'

'I swear. It's true. You know I have problems with alcohol.'

'We noticed.'

'Sometimes I get blackouts like that. At two o'clock on Sunday morning there was a click in my head as though a switch had been turned on. And do you know what? I found myself running along Björkstigen. I wasn't sober either. I must have downed a few.'

'That wouldn't entirely surprise me.'

'The strange thing is that I can't for the life of me remember what I'd done. I was scared and I was running, right there in the middle of the night. I was in a great hurry and I had the feeling that something horrible had happened. I had to get away but I didn't know what from!'

'Did you see anybody?'

'No. Well, perhaps. A dog with slobbering jaws, sir. And bats, thousands of them. I jumped on to a bike and fled.'

'Do you recall anything before the time you fled?'

'Well, I was at Bussparken in the afternoon, but everything after that is black.'

'That doesn't hold water.'

'No, you're absolutely right. I must stop drinking, otherwise I'll be ruined.'

He began to cry. We left him and went into the corridor.

'How the devil did you do it?'

155

'Do what?'

'How did you persuade him to open up?'

Gustavsson looked very innocent, which usually means mischief. He looked down at the floor and squirmed, adjusting his tie and so forth. All of sudden I understood. I went back into the office and opened the lowest desk drawer. It was empty. I mean the bottle of gin was empty. Holding it in my hand, I went out to my associate and kicked the door with my foot. The bang released new screams in the room.

'Where's the alcohol?'

'Oh my, is the bottle empty? He must have found it when I went out to wash my hands.'

'There's a washbowl in the room.'

'I would never think of borrowing your personal soap.'

Well, that was how it happened. Gustavsson had, as if unintentionally, let Crona take a look into the drawer and then he'd announced he had to leave for a moment. Crona had yielded to temptation. But it was my alcohol. I had relieved some kids of it last week.

'That was most irresponsible on my part, chief. It won't happen again.'

'I hope not,' I growled.

After that we continued with Crona for some time, but with no result. He was very pleased with his version of the delirium and decked it out with even more fantasies. There had been a lot of snakes and rats after him and on his way to the cottage he had seen an unbelievable crowd of animals lurking in the forest. Gustavsson smiled tactfully and I almost thought of sending him out to search for droppings.

Crona had, in fact, suffered from real deliriums in the past and we'd once assisted when he was transported to St. Katarina's, the lunatic asylum in this region. That was after he tried to cut Elvy's throat. It had taken three men to hold him until the ambulance arrived.

We didn't believe Crona, of course, but it was impossible to pursue the interrogation. He stuck rigidly to his claim of memory loss and when we put pressure on him, he cried.

Loss of memory is a common phenomenon among our customers, but mostly it can be solved. This time we were not successful. A most embarrassing situation.

Gustavsson suggested that we should call the mental hospital and try to get a shrink to talk with Crona. The psychiatrist on duty answered our call but refused to accept us. I asked what kind of authority he had to hinder a sick human being from coming to him, and was told that we first had to produce a lot of documents from the district medical officer.

At last, I had the idea to call Nylander. At the sound of the name, Crona became happy.

'Just call him. He's a friend of mine. He'll help me stop drinking.'

We called and the doctor promised to be with us within a quarter of an hour.

When he arrived I told him about the case. I explained that Crona was suspected of withholding information about the death at *The Little Boarding-House*. To begin with Crona had referred to loss of memory, and then to *delirium tremens*.

Nylander dropped into my visitor's chair. He is a thickly-built old man with a very small brain, but decent enough. I've gone with Kerstin to see him a couple of times. To begin with, he looked sheepish, since he probably realized he'd made a fool of himself with those stupid amateur detective activities of him and his friends.

He said that he'd treated Crona for many years. No results have ever been observed and the devil knows what the treatment actually consisted of; the laying on of hands, I expect.

I pointed out that Nilsson had probably died as the result of a self-inflicted accident, but we were interested to hear what state he'd been in when Crona had left him. He had a lot to tell us, no doubt.

Nylander lit a cigarette and looked at me over his spectacles.

'Is he intoxicated?'

'Yes, but he's capable of talking.'

'What do you want me to do?'

'We want you to find out whether he's really suffering from memory loss and whether he in that case can use it to avoid giving evidence.'

He stared hard at the glowing tip of the cigarette and flicked the ash off absent-mindedly into the wastebasket.

'How did Nilsson die?'

'We don't know. The post-mortem was performed yesterday, but the protocol hasn't arrived yet.'

'Was there blood on the towel?'

'No, it was red wine.'

'I see, so Crona didn't cut himself?'

He didn't wait for my reply but stamped off through the door.

There I sat looking through the window. Dark rain clouds had gathered in the sky during the afternoon and it was only a matter of time before it came down heavily. There were a few documents on the table. I flipped them over three or four times, but they all looked the same: uninteresting. After a while I remembered that Magnus's bike had been left in the forest and, because of that, I told Gustavsson off. What had he been thinking? He would have to pick it up next day, this time with his own packed lunch. At last I succeeded in getting down to work methodically, but I didn't feel better for all that.

We called out for some food and a waitress from Rådhusbaren came over with a basket. None of us said anything while we ate.

Nothing could be heard from the nearby bathroom. Time passed slowly.

After an hour the doctor came out. He gave me a look I couldn't interpret.

'What's happening?'

'We're all done. It went quite well. The delirium is not a topic anymore.'

'Has his memory returned?'

'It seems Crona suffers from an amnesia, a loss of memory covering a couple of hours before wakening up. It occurs with alcoholics. I think it depends on some kind of brain damage. Popularly called "blackout."'

'Do you mean we won't be able to get any more out of him?'

'He has a lot to tell you. He'll give you some valuable information. You'll be surprised.'

'But you said that he doesn't remember anything.'

'I didn't say that. I said that he has a memory loss covering several hours.'

This is a typical example of how people make fun of the police. We have to appear in a well-pressed uniform and be of service no matter what, whereas the public gives us no respect. He was trying to make a fool of me.

'Ask him what he remembers from the time he woke up,' the doctor said in an encouraging way. 'That waking up happened long before he was at Björkstigen. It happened in Axel Nilsson's room.'

'How did you get him to talk?'

'I just said that it wasn't necessary to lie about the delirium.'

'So he made up all that stuff about dogs and snakes?'

'Not at all. He saw animals, but not that many.'

The doctor looked mysterious.

'How is it that he was willing to give up his cock-and-bull story about mental derangement?'

'Because I told him that he's innocent.'

'How do you know? Excuse me for asking.'

'Because Nilsson didn't die of any mistreatment on the part of Crona.'

'How do you know that?'

'It's in the post mortem report. You'll see.'

He buttoned his coat and put on his hat. He pulled his gloves on slowly and carefully walked to the door.

'May I ask a question?' he said. 'What kind of cheese was in Nilsson's wastebasket?'

'I don't know. It doesn't make any difference, does it?'

'Doesn't it?'

The doctor laughed heartily and noisily.

'I think that the red wine was Chianti Ruffino.'

'But you can't say anything about the cheese?'

'No. It doesn't matter what kind of cheese it was!'

'On the contrary, it could be the most important question. Let me give you a piece of good advice. Try to find out. Good afternoon.'

We watched him through the window. When he reached the parking lot, he turned around and came back. Without knocking he opened the door and walked over to the desk.

'My glasses,' he said apologetically.

He'd left them behind the portrait of Kerstin.

8

Inside the interrogation room we found a highly excited Crona. The ruddiness of his face had returned, and the swelling framing his right eye was much smaller, so that the bloodshot white of the eye peeped out. He radiated comfort, well-being and good-naturedness. This version of Crona often occurs in the town at different times around the clock. Our professional experience of him when taken into custody is usually limited to the loud-voiced, somewhat reluctant version, and a downhearted, apologetic and remorseful one after using our sleeping accommodation. We were welcomed with a smile.

'Come in, gentlemen.'

'There's no reason to be particularly joyful, Crona.'

Gustavsson's voice was harsh.

'But what the hell, Gustavsson.'

'Don't swear when the detective sergeant is present. He doesn't like it.'

The reproach didn't put much of a damper on Crona.

'I'm sorry. I'm not well, simply suffering from amnesia, difficult case.'

I wanted to get things done and banged the lead pencil on the table-top. It was one of the government's yellow pencils, degree of hardness No. 2, just recently equipped with a sharp point.

'Now your account has to be detailed and truthful. Understood?'

He sighed and an unmistakable scent of gin permeated the room. Gordon's Dry Gin lingers a long time on the palate. Gustavsson sharpened his pencil discreetly and turned to an empty page in his notebook. Then he gave his cross-examination victim a laser-like stare.

'Come on!'

'Where am I supposed to begin?'

'Tell me everything you remember. How was it in Bussparken that afternoon?'

'It was nice. I sat there talking with a few friends. They were Olle Asp, Tinsmith and Vilhelmsson. You may know them?'

'Only too well.'

'We discussed some domestic policy problems, commodity taxes, the principles of price fixing and similar things. The debate was animated. Tinsmith had the pleasure of offering us a small pick-me-up and....'

'Consumption of spirits within the green open spaces of the town is strictly prohibited.'

Gustavsson never misses an opportunity to rebuke the public.

'Is that so? Anyway, after that we were invited to Mr. Asp's quarters, but I declined, for I had a prior engagement.'

'Axel Nilsson?'

'Yes. The day before, we had agreed on an appointment. We had met by chance outside the State Liquor Store.'

'Did you know Nilsson?'

'Yes, he was a close friend of mine. He had returned from abroad some time ago and now he thought of settling down in our beautiful town for the rest of his life.'

'What did he tell you about himself?'

'Almost nothing, besides his affirmation of our meeting at eight o'clock. But I don't remember anything after I left Bussparken.'

In a regretful way, Crona flung his hands about, leaned expectantly backwards in his chair and readily accepted a cigarette. Gustavsson had to retrieve his lighter.

'I must have fallen asleep in the room. I don't know how I got there or what happened. I was woken up just before two o'clock by a knock at the door, and there was Nilsson dead on the floor. Outside the door was someone called Ivar. He wanted to come in, but he disappeared soon enough, and in the next room there was someone who seemed to be praying. It was a horrible situation. What was I to think, with Nilsson bleeding and my pocket knife on the table? I've thrown it away now, too dull to be of any use at all.'

'What the hell are you saying? Was Nilsson bleeding?'

'Of course. His face was covered with blood. I thought I'd cut him somewhere with the knife.'

It didn't make any sense. Nilsson hadn't been bleeding. He was covered in wine. There wasn't any doubt about it.

'Take us through that again. You woke up and found Nilsson dead and you thought that you were the guilty party?'

'Yes. I was terrified. I had to get away, but I had to remove any evidence I'd been there, for I reckoned I was a murderer. And he really was dead, cold and stiff.'

In that case Nilsson must have been dead for several hours, I thought.

'In front of me on the table there was a bottle of red wine and a piece of cheese, which we probably had feasted on, but also a bottle of pure schnapps. I threw it out of the window into a flower bed, then I tidied up a little, picked up the knife and washed the glasses.'

'… and you wiped up the red wine with a towel?'

'What red wine? No, first I wiped the blood off Nilsson's face. After that I poured red wine over him.'

Gustavsson and I looked at each other in utter bewilderment.

'But don't you see? When I wiped blood off his face, I found that there were drops of blood on the shirt as well. The intention was that it should look as if Nilsson had been killed by a concussion of the brain when he fell and hit the back of his head against the bedstead. I thought that's what everyone would believe if there was no blood.'

'But where did the blood come from if you didn't knife him?'

'I didn't fully understand it myself until I asked Nylander a few minutes ago. He told me that Nilsson may well have been killed by a fracture at the base of the skull, and in such a case. blood could indeed run from the brain through the nose.'

We had never thought of that explanation. I still didn't understand all the business about the red wine. Crona saw how puzzled I was and tried to explain.

'If I'd left him with blood stains on the shirt, the police would later have looked for the origin of that blood, found out where it came from, and wondered why he didn't also have blood in his face. That's why I poured red wine on his face as well as on his shirt. The red wine spots concealed the real blood stains.

'And the towel was …'

'It was stained by the nasal discharge. Afterwards I washed it in the sink, but the blood stains didn't really disappear, so I poured some red wine on it as well.'

It was childishly simple. Anxiously, I wondered if Nylander had worked out that I'd lied about investigating the towel. At the same time I got a bright idea but it didn't help much. I still felt unusually cheap, because the week had been a long failure as far as I was concerned and nothing could change my realisation of that.

Crona had been able to reach room number 5 from the garden because Nilsson had detained Blom for a moment in the reception by asking for a plaster! Here we had the explanation of the plaster—it was never needed!

163

Even if my little reconstruction didn't restore my self-esteem, it reassured me to see that Gustavsson was still looking confused.

In a flash, it struck me that the piece of plaster had to be somewhere. Why hadn't we found it? I was going to turn the town upside-down to get it! The next moment, I decided not to. Why should I bother? It was probably lying somewhere in the rose bushes, making them extra untidy.

Then I thought of another clue.

'Wait a minute!' I said. 'You threw the bottle of schnapps through the window. Was it empty?'

Crona looked indignant. His face became noticeably redder and he gathered himself up before he spoke.

'Would I, Algot Emanuel Cronlund, have let a half-empty bottle go to waste? I take that as a personal insult. The bottle was totally empty.'

'So you and Nilsson emptied it together?'

'Naturally, although I admit there might still have been some nectar left in there for Nilsson after I fell asleep.'

'And there was some red wine left as well?'

'A drop at the bottom, yes. Not much, a few decilitres perhaps. I used the last of it for my—camouflage.'

I wondered how sober Crona could have been after a half bottle of schnapps and an almost half-filled bottle of wine. He'd slept himself sober during four hours, of course, but he wasn't so befuddled that he couldn't pull himself together long enough to give the room an overhaul and perform a few cunning manoeuvres.

'And there was also wine on the table?'

'Absolutely! I left the bottle lying there, but I washed the glasses.'

'Why did you use three glasses—was there someone else at the party?'

'We were the only ones in the room when I woke up. If there had been three at the beginning, Axel must have let the third one out before I woke up. In any case, the door was locked and the key was in the keyhole. Are you suggesting that someone killed Nilsson, who then, just to be kind, rose from the dead to let his murderer out and lock the door behind him? The idea appeals to me.'

It didn't appeal to me.

'I don't know why we used three glasses. I had to wash all three to remove my fingerprints. I didn't know which one I had touched. It was the same thing with Nilsson's spectacles.

'They'd fallen off and were by his side. I put them back on his nose so the stiff would look nicer, but then I realised that there was a risk my fingerprints might be on them, so I polished them and put them on the bedside table.'

Crona looked crafty and pleased with himself. Nevertheless, he'd left his fingerprints all over the wine bottle. I didn't have the heart to tell him that. He'd really done everything to make it seem as if Nilsson had been alone in the room.

'If you made so much noise that the neighbors complained, how would anyone believe that Nilsson alone was responsible for the disturbance?'

'Were we that rowdy? I'm sorry to hear that. But how could I know that when I woke up at two o'clock that morning? I didn't remember anything. Or do you mean that Ivar knocked on the door because I'd disturbed him with my snoring?'

Crona had been able to avoid even that pitfall. At that very moment another thought appeared, as if I had ordered it. There must have been more money than the ten-crown bills in Nilsson's wallet. There was enough room for big notes in a billfold. I decided that Crona had stolen them and launched a frontal attack.

'Crona, I want you to put your cards on the table. Confess that you stole something when you disappeared on Sunday morning!'

The goldsmith's reaction was immediate and very revealing. I realised I'd scored a direct hit! He reddened and chewed on his moustache.

'That was bad of me, but it was there and it seemed to me that nobody needed it for the time being.'

'But it didn't belong to you.'

'Who did it belong to, then?'

'Are you kidding, Crona? To Nilsson of course.'

From his expression, Crona seemed genuinely surprised.

'Good God, I never suspected that. But why would he keep his bike at almost the other end of the town?'

Gustavsson turned away and coughed tactfully.

'I'm talking about Nilsson's money! What did you do with it?'

'I didn't see any money.'

A flock of birds chirped in a provocative manner outside the window. I suspect that some idiot had fed them with bread crumbs. Maybe Vivianne at the switchboard. I will take up the matter with the commissioner.

'Well, Crona, what did happen, then?'

'As I said, I thought that I'd been guilty of at least manslaughter under the influence of drink. That was when I made up my mind.'

'You decided to escape and let us believe that it was all an accident behind locked doors?'

'No, I decided, once and for all, not to touch another drop for the rest of my life.'

This dramatic announcement failed to have its desired effect, not least because of his present state of intoxication.

When he saw us looking doubtful he hastened to elaborate.

'I admit that tonight I submitted to temptation, but that only strengthens my determination to become a sober man. Chastened and liberated, I am now standing in front of you offering my hand. Let us seal my promise!'

He extended the said hand and Gustavsson, who loves any kind of futile gesture, clasped it with warmth. He used to stand outside the drunks' cells in the morning, clasping our guests' hands, just like a clergyman on the church steps after the service.

'Steady now. We're not through yet. How did you get out of the room?'

'It wasn't difficult. I walked out.'

'No, it can't have been that simple, can it? How the devil did you arrange for Nilsson to be locked up from the inside when you walked away?'

He looked flabbergasted, his eyes wide open, even the right one.

'The hell he was locked up from the inside!'

'Well, he was when we arrived.'

'If he was locked up, it was from the outside. I locked him up and then I ran away.'

'What about the key?'

'I put it in my pocket.'

'Where is it now?'

He felt in his pocket. An expression of comprehension spread across his face.

'I put it back where it belonged.'

'You put it back?'

'Stop repeating what I say. It was cold and there was a cutting wind in the backyard. I put my hands into my trouser pockets and there, of course, was the key. I threw it through Nilsson's open window.'

So this was the solution to the riddle of the locked room. I didn't know whether to laugh or cry. For a moment I thought of getting angry, but I couldn't think of a fitting scapegoat. Wait, there was one: Blom. How the hell could he maintain that he'd seen the key through the keyhole in the morning? The man told us nothing but lies. He is totally unreliable.

Perhaps he had been too lazy even to bend down and look through the key-hole, and therefore gave his false evidence in this matter when the key was found on the doormat, presumably having fallen down when Ivehed forced the door open and....

Well, we will never know for certain and, frankly, I don't give a damn. The less I think about Blom, the better I feel.

'But how did you manage to close the window?'

'If you're asking me,' Crona replied pitifully, 'then you must be tolerant with a man with such a difficult handicap. I mean my amnesia, of course. In any case, I don't understand what you mean. What window should I have shut?'

'Nilsson's!'

'It was open. Nobody could have shut it from the yard, if that's what you mean.'

All the same, the confounded window was locked in the morning.

'Chief,' said Gustavsson, 'isn't it possible that the wind slammed the window shut? It seems to have been open during the night. Isn't that so, Crona?'

'That's right. In any case, one half of the window was open when I woke up. I remember it well, since I was near it when I threw the bottle out. There were also a few very nice fancy goods on the window-sill.'

I lit a cigarette and recalled in my mind the window as it had looked that morning. The left half of the window had not been fixed with the window-latch. Regarding the bric-a-brac, I didn't exactly see eye-to-eye with Crona. I remember a small Ölandish windmill made of birch bark, a miniature of a sailing boat with the word Smögen painted on it and an ashtray with a dreadful Dalecarlian picture and a crude inscription, obviously put there for the purpose of deterring tourists from ever visiting Tällberg.

'Why didn't you shut the window while you were in the room?'

'I don't know. Should I have done?'

'No, perhaps not. Did you want to let the smoke out?'

'Neither of us had been smoking. Tobacco is unhygienic and unhealthy. Just think of the risk of getting cancer!'

167

It was true. Neither ashes nor fag-ends had been found in the room. The ashtray had been stowed away in a drawer of the bedside-table, together with the Bible.

I stubbed my cigarette out discreetly.

Regarding the window, it's certainly not impossible that the wind might have slammed it shut. It was blowing hard that night, but Crona had obviously been both blind and deaf to the outer world when he slept leaning against the table-top. After the wind's assault on the window just before two o'clock—when Johanson had been woken up by the creaking—it had probably died down for a while, and when it rose again the window had been slammed shut. By that time Crona had gone, and the key had been tossed in through it and landed on the doormat.

I couldn't understand why Renqvist, who made a point of insisting that the sound was heard exactly at one thirty, hadn't been awakened when the squeaking concerto came to an end half an hour later. Neither did I understand why the school mistresses said that they hadn't heard anything.

Or had the wind somehow pushed the window shut without making much noise?

Nevertheless, whatever had happened had apparently occurred soon after Crona had left.

'Then you disappeared. Which way did you go?'

'Through a passage leading to Björkstigen.'

'You returned the same way you came?'

He looked at me reproachfully and rubbed his nose, where an angry web of blood-vessels had appeared during the last hour as a result of the alcohol. Then wagged a finger in a roguish and admonishing way.

'Now, you know I can't answer that last question. It's beyond my power to judge.'

'Well, you said that you locked the door in the usual way and went out into the backyard, from whence you threw the key through the window, which the wind then banged shut. Okay, let's suppose all that to be true. We found the key in the morning. It was on the doormat inside the room. But how did you get out through the back door? Blom had locked that door one hour earlier and the chambermaid, who arrived in the morning, found it still locked. She had her own key and the other key was hanging inside the door on a nail. How did you do it?'

Crona's expression showed that he definitely considered me to be an idiot. That may well be true, but I don't like it to be public knowledge. I want it kept in the family.

'The door was wide open and I didn't shut it either.'

There were no two ways about it: either Crona was kidding or someone else was. Maybe, for the sake of uniformity, I should start to play jokes. Did you know, for example, that Stationsgatan isn't really a one-way street? It's just a farce on the part of the police. We put up the signs for fun and we collect the fines so as to inflate the crime statistics.

How can you conduct a serious investigation in a place like this where nobody takes you seriously? With this kind of an attitude, maybe all the police constables should start wearing red noses, starting next week.

'And then,' I said wearily, 'you made off, stealing a bike?'

'I confess. And I'm prepared to accept the consequences.'

I got to my feet and Gustavsson followed my example. The only thing we had found out during the long interrogation was that people are not to be trusted. Which we already knew.

Crona obediently got to his feet as well, and we found that he was more unsteady on his legs and more inebriated than we had realised.

Maybe the lingering faintness after the days and nights in the cottage without food had affected him. Be that as it may, we couldn't let him go home in that condition.

Gustavsson made a suggestion.

'Should we put Crona in the clink straight away, or wait a while?'

The question was primarily aimed at Crona. He looked quite thankful and then he nodded.

'Yes, please, if it's not too much trouble. May I have my usual room?'

We're never difficult at the constabulary, and cell No. 3 is more or less reserved for him. The two other cells are booked for Olle Asp, Vilhelmsson, Tinsmith, Stolt at the Old People's Home and other less frequent guests.

Gustavsson whispered a few words in my ear.

'Of course,' I said. 'And another thing, Crona. You did switch off the radio in Nilsson's room before you left, didn't you?'

As soon as the question had crossed my lips I realised that, based on recent experience, we could expect anything. For example, a statement that the radio had not been on.

'It was not switched on. The only thing I switched off was the light.'

'You say that it was not on, but we have several witnesses who are prepared to swear that it was heard through the door both before and after midnight. You have nothing to lose by telling the truth.'

Crona leaned heavily against the doorpost in order not to fall to the floor. He blinked in a friendly way with his best functioning eyelid.

'It wasn't on, Detective Sergeant. That's why I said it. Otherwise I would have said something else. Now may I leave? Good evening.'

After a courteous bow he meandered out into the corridor followed by Gustavsson. I hear that he made a great fuss about this being his last visit to the station. His new life would begin the next day.

I called Kerstin and told her that we had finished our work. The case was solved and I would be home on the dot. On my way out I heard indignant voices from No. 3, where Gustavsson was in the process of calming down Crona, who had dropped onto a bunk.

'What's going on?'

'Well, chief, Crona disapproves of us. He says that he can't trust anyone in the whole world and he threatens to begin drinking again.'

'Why is that?'

Crona got to his feet, his face white with wrath and disappointment. He stood in front of me, trembling and slobbering, eyes red and swollen with weeping.

'I thought that I knew where I had you, but what happens if I, sick and wretched, perhaps drunk and extremely unhappy, had needed lodging for a few hours? What if it had happened the other night and you had let someone else trespass on my room? Then, without a spot in the shelter, I would have been abandoned to get frost-bitten in the wilderness, at the mercy of my painful amnesia, left to ruin and destruction.'

He was, of course, practically paralytic. The next day he would clasp Gustavsson's hand on his way out and donate a twenty-five öre coin to the kitty.

'Why do you think that of us, Crona?'

'Look there,' he said dramatically and pointed at a note scribbled on the stucco wall.

"Magnus 1969."

I walked home through the nasty damp autumn weather. Next week Bengtsson would be back and I would resume my usual lousy job.

At home everything was peaceful, for a change.

Kerstin insisted on me having a bath while she cleaned the shrimps.

Of course I should have expected I would have a reason to become angry at least once more this evening. It happened when I was in the bath and found that my hair smelled of Kalles kaviar after a while. Kalles kaviar does not lather very well. Furthermore, it has no effect on dandruff.

9

The children woke us up at seven o'clock this morning. It seems that Mister Hedgehog had got himself into trouble yesterday and things had become critical. I pretended to be asleep and after a while the door closed.

Then Kerstin told me that she had reread the protocol from the last meeting of the Sunday Club during the week. Now she was beginning to wonder if the old men really were all that wrong. After all, what was so wrong about the doctor's theory?

I was a bit irritable that early in the morning and not in the mood to discuss their theory. I'd briefed her every evening since Sunday. Did I really have to wake up to it? Before I went back to sleep, I think I managed to say that everything that they could have misconstrued, they had misconstrued. We would draw up a report when we got the results of the post mortem and she could read it if she wanted.

At ten o'clock, Vivianne at the switchboard put a brown official envelope from the Institution of Forensic Medicine on my desk. The report was written in the usual incomprehensible gibberish. "The body was of a 52 years old man, height 179 cm, weight 63 kg. Normal post mortem phenomena. Besides a hematoma the size of a coin in the scalp over the right ear, there are no signs of external injury."

From then on it was mostly written in Latin, with the occasional word that was actually intelligible, such as prepositions and some minor conjunctions. Since I know that fracture means broken bone, I deduced that there was no fracture of the skull-cap, which probably has something to do with the scalp or the base of the skull.

The writer gave me to understand that the immediate cause of death had been *haemorrhagia cerebri invet. et recens*, but that Nilsson suffered additionally from both *hypertrofia cordis* and *cardionephroarteriosclerosis generalisata*. For this information I would like to thank him cordially. Fortunately, there was a summary:

"As is evident from the foregoing, death occurred as a consequence of cerebral haemorrhage, situated in such a way and of such proportions that vital parts of the brain were immediately affected, with instantaneous lethal outcome. The insignificant trauma we have established in the scalp probably ensued when the body fell, and it is

173

impossible that deliberate external damage could have led to a secondary cerebral haemorrhage. From a medico-legal point of view there is thus nothing to lead to a conclusion of death caused by a criminal activity.'

Below that was a handwritten note:

"Because of the failure to notify us immediately, a preliminary post -mortem could not be performed within reasonable time and because of that, the moment of death has not been possible to establish. After four days it is meaningless to analyse contents of the stomach. From the information about fully developed *rigor mortis* and the extension of *livor mortis* when the body was found, one could guess that between ten to twelve hours may have passed from the death until your grand intervention. But, considering the natural cause of death, these speculations are probably of no interest when it comes to the criminal investigation, which you will no doubt now wish to discontinue."

At the bottom of the page there was another addition, written with lead pencil: "When is Bengtsson back? That's what I really want to know."

The report was signed on Thursday, yesterday that is, by Dr. Mogens Nyegaard, docent.

With that the case was brought to an end, apart from some paper-work. We needed to produce an investigation report with a few official stamps here and there, so I instructed Gustavsson to write a short formal statement, which I would sign later on.

He was not at all happy with the assignment because he has no stylistic talent. Which means, as I pointed out, that he's in need of all the training he can get.

When I was alone again I made some calls. The first was to Göran Eriksson. I told him that the investigation had been wrapped up. I next called Nylander, who muttered something inaudible when I told him about the diagnoses. Then I called the office of the Public Prosecutor and reported the result of the last days' activities.

Gustavsson would take care of the remaining formalities.

There had been nothing in the newspapers, at least according to Ivehed. I strongly suspect that he had concentrated on the sport pages and they had not mentioned the case. I'd given him the chore of reading all the press reports as punishment for losing the picklock. It had been missing for months but he had not dared to tell me about it. No wonder he hadn't been able to open Nilsson's door. Maybe I'll report him for breach of duty.

In the end I asked for the pictures Gustavsson's photographer took at *The Little Boarding-House* on Sunday. I got them after many ifs and buts. The visual artist is a student living in the same house as Gustavsson, who has talked a lot in the neighborhood about objectives and perspectives and God knows what.

There were five pictures in total.

Two showed a vague and underexposed bundle on a floor.

They were supposed to be of the stiff itself, from different angles.

Another showed Ivehed in front of the rose bed. He was balancing his baton on his forefinger.

Then there was a group picture of all the guests, gathered on the front door steps of the hotel. They were arranged like a soccer team around Blom, who was waving at the camera. He was flanked by the schoolmistresses. Ivar Johanson was embracing Miss Hurtig-Olofsson from behind and Renqvist was standing in a stiff position at arm's length from Miss Söderström. Melin and Ivehed, the latter still with his baton, had been able to squeeze themselves through the doorway.

The last photograph was of a totally unknown girl on a sailing boat. As far as I could see, she wasn't wearing a bra.

The station has been calm the whole day. Crona left in an orderly way at eight o'clock this morning.

It began to drizzle after lunch, which was a hamburger from Rådhusbaren. Having nothing specific to do, I went to check on Gustavsson's progress and helped him to find "x" on the typewriter.

Then I sat down with our tape recorder for interrogations. Nobody has been able to get it to work. After juggling with it for a while I heard a click. At that I began to sing the song about the chimney-sweep, if you know that one. I rewound the tape, and, would you believe it, I heard the sound of my own voice!

I was just recording "You are my sunshine" when Vivianne came in. I barely managed to stop the recording. She asked what I was doing and I muttered something about summing up the Nilsson case. Then she said she was interested in learning how to transcribe from recorded dictation, and she promised to produce the material during Saturday, tomorrow in other words. There was nothing else to do but say thank you and try to look happy. Furthermore I'd promised Kerstin a report, which she needed as a counterweight to the old men's drivel.

Now I've been sitting here babbling for four hours. During the breaks I had had to oil my jaws with some beer, which I have ordered Melin to bring for me.

I'll be back for a while tomorrow afternoon to see if everything is completed. Then Kerstin can take over the whole mess. I hope that she'll give it to my old man the day after tomorrow. It should bring him down to earth. We're invited there on Sunday.

Because everything had been piling up, I was late for dinner. I called home and there was pork to fry and brown beans that could be warmed up. The kids had been somewhat uneasy. The boy had got wind of that thing about the Chinese: that one yellow one dies every time a certain button is pressed. He'd been secretly pressing the electric button in the living room most of the afternoon. At some point it had dawned on him that some Chinaman might do the same thing in return, so by the time I got home both kids were screaming with fear. I told them that they haven't got electricity in the Far East, they only use candles. Then they calmed down.

When Bengtsson returns I'll ask for a few weeks' leave of absence, so we can go to Mallorca. It would be great rolling over on the playa, leaving the trench coat at home and walking around in bathing-trunks. When Kerstin puts on her bikini the Spaniards will get misty-eyed, I shouldn't wonder. By the way, have you heard the story about Lundgren travelling to Spain last year? He returned home complaining loudly about the inedible food on the charter flight. It turned out that he hadn't realised he was supposed to remove the plastic wrapper. I think I've mentioned before that he's an idiot.

We just have to call the travel agency and make a reservation, take the kids and that wretched Mister Hedgehog to their paternal grandmother and board the flight.

(I wrote the last part for Kerstin's sake. It'll be a surprise when she reads it. She'll never get permission from the school to take the time off, but that's not my fault... I may go fishing for a week instead.)

PART THREE

Gjutarvägen, Sunday, November 2

1

I had thought of comparing this case with a modern piece of art in a picture gallery. The spectator could interpret it differently depending on the angle from which he viewed it. That was how we proceeded last Sunday, but the reality escaped us. The result we reached was a reflection of ourselves, distilled from our own imagination and our secret desires to be detectives.

The detective sergeant chose another method. He decided from the very beginning that the painting was non-figurative, but he was as much mistaken as we were.

We missed the point because nobody thought to turn the picture upside-down. If we'd done so, every detail would have been illuminated differently and seen in another context.

By using a new technology, I have exposed the murderer. It was ridiculously simple because the manipulation itself was so uncomplicated. He who accepts the original way of hanging the picture will never consider turning his head a half-turn.

Come to think of it, the picture comparison doesn't really work and isn't even original, so forget it. I'll try to find a better one. A good parable is like a magnifying glass. It frames the subject, clarifies it and mercilessly exposes the details.

On Monday I was still halfway convinced that Carl's solution was the correct one, but doubts began to nag at me and, purely by accident, I was soon able to establish the innocence of the son-in-law. I had called Nurse Ruth at the child-health station. She knows all the mothers with small children in the town and she discovered straight away that Rose-Marie Åhlund, under the name of Eriksson, had been coming to the station with her Yvonne since 1963. Her address was given as Tallåsvägen 19. I walked there in the evening in order to have a conversation with Mr. Eriksson, but happened to run into Dr. Rydin just as he was leaving, following a sick-call. He told me his patient had already been in bad shape on the Saturday. That settled it.

My weakness for detective stories is well known. I've half a mind to issue a Challenge to the Reader. In fact, Johan gives the answer early in his report, when mentioning the word "cheese," and an observant reader should be able to work it all out, provided he's been supplied with some advance information. Yet, even though I had that knowledge, the truth still escaped me a week ago.

If I ever decide to publish a book I could reveal the plot in the book's title, so that a small portion of our population, a few hundred people or so, would be able to anticipate the solution. One of my favorite writers, John Dickson Carr, performed this *tour de force* many years ago in such a crafty way that every reader, irrespective of knowledge and education, had the same chance of solving the puzzle.

Just think of the great discoveries: they're often the result of sheer luck. A sudden insight surprises, light falls in from a new direction, chance takes a hand. From my own professional discipline I only have to think of Röntgen and his X-rays and Fleming and his penicillin. And if I myself hadn't practiced medicine for almost half a century, following scientific progress and storing its jewels in my memory, maybe no one would have discovered the facts which, properly interpreted, shed new light on the problem.

It was as early as Wednesday when I had my inspiration. Maybe it was a unique combination of circumstance which opened my eyes at the right moment: a glass of port wine after the food, the scent of my lighted Corona and the temperature in the room combined to bring it about. I like to think of it as providence.

There, all of a sudden, was the solution of the riddle, the correct diagnosis. It dawned on me gradually without any fuss, more like an assurance than an inspiration. I experienced no triumph nor pride and absolutely no happiness—maybe even a touch of sadness, given the inevitable uncomfortable consequences. Young Mrs. Bergman's visit to my office earlier that day showed that she, too, had suspected something, vaguely and indistinctly, and her information came as a necessary missing piece of a bewildering jig-saw puzzle. Afterwards, my phone calls, field visits and enquiries were only by way of confirmation, and the last painful excursion was solely due to my own curiosity.

Many of my patients consider my methods to be old-fashioned. Well, as long as the treatment is the best I can give, they must accept that an old man is by nature conservative. If you don't like it, go elsewhere.

The proof that the therapy has been the right one is that the patient recovers. He may get well in spite of the treatment, but then my efforts won't have been wrong, merely unnecessary. Yesterday, I got the proof that the murder riddle was solved. It happened in the form of the murderer's oral confession. That's good enough, as far as I'm concerned.

We were supposed to have met at my home tonight, but unfortunately Johan couldn't make it. Over the last few weeks, the town has suffered from a persistent and unpleasant gastric influenza. It had been demanding many house calls of me, and prescriptions by telephone. When I paid him a visit, he was in bed with a woolen scarf around his neck, despite the fact that the flu was affecting his stomach. He really didn't have much to complain about: the fever was low, not even 38 degrees Celsius, and his strength seemed good. I suggested a most effective bismuth tincture to curb the frequent trips to the toilet, but my friend preferred boiled milk.

After half an hour I left him, with the understanding he would call Carl himself and tell him the bad news about our cancelled meeting.

So that way I ended up with a free evening.

After a while Carl called me. He'd obtained a copy of the police activity report for the previous week from his daughter-in-law. He gave me a short summary. They hadn't found much and what they had found was totally unimportant. Reality is something else.

There's no doubt that this is an example of a murder as a fine art. In my opinion, very little of what happened at the boarding-house in the hours before and after midnight a week ago had anything to do with the actual murder. The drama was performed with the curtain up, but on a revolving stage, where we witnessed an accidental improvisation which caught our interest and diverted our attention while the real action took place behind the scenes, where the murderer himself was hiding.

When I tried to penetrate the facade, I concentrated on the weak points. The weakest point was Nilsson himself, which was obvious long before the truth suddenly revealed itself on Wednesday evening, after I'd asked a couple of specialists for their advice and read up on some specialist literature.

Let's take a look at everything once more. If a certain fatigue has set in following the reports of the other writers, then follow my advice: forget their conclusions and forget what they wrote. We need to start from the very beginning and look at the case from a different angle.

Let me start by asking you this: isn't it perfectly obvious what Axel Nilsson was really after?

2

Let us recall the picture we have of Axel Nilsson, who, after an absence of many years, returned to his hometown. To put it bluntly, he had aged and changed almost beyond recognition.

It's true he stayed mostly in the boarding-house, but do we have any real proof that he deliberately kept in hiding?

Was he wanted? No.

Was he in great demand? Well, perhaps as far as the social welfare service was concerned, but he was obviously prepared to run that risk.

Was he eagerly awaited? Definitely not!

A week ago, we formulated the theory that he had everything to gain and nothing to lose by coming here.

Is there a connection between the fact that he had something to gain here, and the fact that he was no longer the same person as before?

He may have been a different person, but he was not a new individual in a literal sense. It was not Edvin returning home. That supposition was pure nonsense. Neither was he in disguise. What kind of changes do I mean? One may acquire new values and new interests, and one can mature and develop. Was it a regretful man who came back, anxious to atone for his sins? Was his conscience weighing heavily on him?

A moment's thought will force you to conclude that nothing had changed and that Nilsson was just as unreliable, egoistic and ruthless as before.

So, what do I mean when I say he had changed—and not just due to the deterioration that time imposes on us all? It's quite simple: he was sick. Now, I'm not the first one to make that observation: Blom remarked that he seemed to be broken, and we have already talked about him taking medicine frequently. The point that I'm making is that we never considered what the fact of his sickness meant to the whole case.

I've spent the whole of my long life working with sick people and I know what they have in common. Some take their suffering with serene calm and confidence. Others are anxious and feel alarmed. What they have in common is their feeling of helplessness in the face of their sickness, and their desire to be free of it and be cured.

So as far as I'm concerned, the simple truth is that Axel Nilsson was sick. That inevitably leads us to the supposition that he may have come here to get help. He simply wanted to survive as long as possible, and to that end he was prepared to stake everything.

He probably had nothing to lose in America and may well have preferred to stay there, but he simply couldn't afford the expensive private health care. He was a Swedish citizen and wanted to make use of the benefits at home. I am not moralising. Anyone would have done the same, myself included.

So a sick man came home in order to get treatment. Obviously, the first thing he did was visit a local doctor in order to get medicine. But what was he suffering from?

That is the question, the most important question in the entire case. It's so important that, if my conclusion is wrong, the murder would never have been committed because the perpetrator would never have been able to pull it off.

How was Axel Nilsson described? We were told that by Carl, who got it from his son, who got it from the boarding-house proprietor Blom. There's a party game in which each participant whispers a sentence which must be passed on to the next...and the next...and so on. At each step the meaning of the sentence is slightly altered, until it becomes unrecognizable. With that kind of risk in mind, I will nevertheless attempt to describe Axel Nilsson at fourth hand.

He was fifty-two years old, of average height, somewhat underweight, with a moustache and glasses. His clothes were worn and baggy. He limped and was in the habit of winking with one eye. His speech was often slurred. He appeared to be sick and was often quite intoxicated. It's not much to go on, but enough for a diagnosis which many of my colleagues would suggest.

Unfortunately, I didn't see it last Sunday. It was not until I received Johan's report that the truth about this and many other things became clear. There's also a detail in Detective Sergeant Bergman's own report which confirms the diagnosis. I learned about it in a conversation I had with Carl today.

Let's take a look at Nilsson's distinctive features. The moustache is a male decoration, which seldom reflects any sickness of its bearer. Spectacles are a sign of impaired vision. By the way, I often mislay my own somewhere. But what about the limp? It's been suggested that Nilsson had a wounded leg. I doubt it. My belief is that his wound was localized elsewhere and made him limp because it influenced the function of his leg. Which of them? The left one—and, *nota bene*, his left arm was also impaired by the same injury, resulting in a loss of some of its former strength. That's why he wore his watch on his right wrist.

According to Gunnar Bergman's report, the left arm had been twisted under the body, yet he could see the dead man's watch before the body had been moved. That means it must have been on the right wrist, contrary to the vast majority of the population. To me this fact suggests that the left arm was at least partly out of order. It was easier for Nilsson to perform the movement that turns and heightens the arm when you want to find out what time it is, by using the right arm.

His winking was surely nervous, but the slurring may not have been due to intoxication but to facial palsy weakening the muscles on one side of the face. That could very well have escaped the hotel guests' notice. They only saw Nilsson briefly and Blom himself never looked at Nilsson long enough to discern it. As you remember, Blom's eyes were always wandering.

I maintain that Axel Nilsson suffered from high blood-pressure and had had a cerebral haemorrhage—a stroke—in America. The left side of the body was still somewhat paralysed and, since he feared another occurrence, he wanted to be in his homeland, where he could get care at the local hospital.

I should have understood this last Sunday. Unfortunately, I failed to do so. Nilsson's medicine, Dichlotride-K, is to be sure a diuretic, but it's also used to a large extent for the purpose of lowering blood pressure. My regrettable neglect is no doubt due to the fact that, for many years, I've used other and more lenient preparations for hypertension and combined them with advice about low-salt diet— something my colleagues have differing opinions about.

Nilsson had taken blood pressure medicine for fourteen days before his death. The post mortem diagnosis was *haemorrhagia cerebri invet. et recens*, which means that he died of a cerebral haemorrhage, and that indications of an earlier stroke were visible in the brain tissue. Furthermore, he suffered from *hypertrofia cordis*, an enlarged heart, which is a common consequence of high blood pressure. His reduced vision could also have been a result of changes of blood pressure in the retina, which can be observed in many patients.

Can there be any further doubt that Nilsson was worried about his sickness, and that he carefully followed the prescriptions of his doctor in Göteborg?

Despite that, he succumbed to another stroke, just as he feared.

Sick, poor and alone, he reappeared after all those years, and his hope was that he would be helped. And even if he was not admitted to a hospital or a nursing home, the community would provide for him. As a citizen of small means, he could get a social allowance; as sick and unfit for work, he would sooner or later get a sickness pension. In this way, he benefitted from his handicap, but then so did the murderer. It seems paradoxical that Nilsson died from a stroke, despite taking all foreseeable measures to prevent it, including medicine.

Was the medicine ineffective? The answer is no. Dichliotride works, no doubt about that.

I willingly confess that real medication does not always hinder a sickness in its course. We can never guarantee that the penicillin we prescribe will kill the pneumonia, nor that the bicarbonate will prevent the emergence of a gastric ulcer.

Nilsson could never entirely avoid the risk of a stroke by treating his high blood-pressure as prescribed, but in his case the heightened tension and ultimate rupture of the vessel in his brain was triggered by another circumstance, the unavoidable consequence of which was death. And of this effect the murderer was guilty. That he has assured me.

I am sure that my intelligent reader thinks that I've spent too much time on the question of Nilsson's blood pressure. That's true, but I had a secondary purpose, besides giving you a hint of what really happened. With the best of intentions I also wanted to offer you a chance to discover a recently drawn wrong conclusion, which I will soon correct. I will also surprise you by saying it actually wasn't a mistake, other than for a certain person. And now that person is dead.

It's dark outside. Occasionally, sounds penetrate: the scarcely discernible breath of the wind through the leaky windows; the laughter of children passing by on the street; the less and less frequent sounds of the evening traffic; and the faraway hustle and bustle.

Now, did you discover my wrong conclusion? I gave you a short while to think about it.

Of course, it was that Nilsson could not have been taking his medicine properly during those two weeks if only a few tablets were missing from the newly opened medicine bottle!

Yet, at the same time, nothing was more important to him than taking his medication. Isn't this contradiction most puzzling?

3

Over the years, half the citizens of the town have passed through my clinic. Some have left my surgery unaided, many have been cured and others have gone out to die.

Even in my youth I never thought about any alternative profession. In my consultation room and during my home visits to various patients I have experienced most of the happiness, encouragement, disappointment and powerlessness life can ever grant a human being. It's a pity that Dr. Rydin, whom I hold in high esteem, didn't want to move in here and probably no other colleague will after me.

Videll's paint shop will probably turn it into a storeroom. The paint-dealer often looks up at my place when he stands outside his shop downstairs.

After my last patient left on Wednesday afternoon I finished up some routine work: sorting patient cards, sending out receipts and sterilising a few instruments. When I went out to water the flowers in the waiting-room, I found to my surprise that Mrs. Bergman was sitting there. She hadn't made an appointment.

'Excuse me, Dr. Nylander, but I've been thinking about the death case the other day, and I need to talk to a doctor to get my thoughts straight.'

I asked her to come in, whereupon I learned that she had a gap between lessons, that she'd read Johan's report and that she had things to add following her discussions with her husband. Since she had a lot to tell and I was an attentive listener, it took some time. We shared a cup of coffee I made in an Erlenmeiler flask in the laboratory cubicle.

When she came to the end, there was a deep and expectant silence.

'Why have you told me all this, Mrs. Bergman?'

'Because there's a disturbing detail in one part of the evidence.'

'Which would that be?'

'I was hoping that you would have noticed it yourself.'

She looked at me hopefully with her beautiful, expressive eyes. She's a charming woman, warm, personal and very wise. I'm unfortunately not an expert on women, besides my occupational experience and some theoretical anatomic knowledge, but I detected sympathy and an interest on her part.

'Why didn't you talk with your husband about this?'

'I wanted to hear your opinion first. He thinks the whole thing is a pure accident. Does the detail in question change anything?'

'It most certainly does.'

'And which of the interrogations of the witnesses contains that important piece of information?'

'That of the chamber-maid, of course.'

'Yes.'

She looked relieved. She hadn't come in vain.

'Then Axel Nilsson's medicines are important?'

'Of course. How did you arrive at that conclusion?'

'Well, Nilsson had only taken a few tablets of Diclo ...'

'Dichlotride-K.'

'... a few tablets out of a bottle of a hundred he'd obtained almost two weeks before he died. In spite of that, the maid testified that he was careful with the medicine, or as she put it: "with his medicines."'

'What did she mean by that?'

'That Nilsson took another medicine as well.'

'But probably he only used that other medicine, since almost all of the Dichliotride-K pills were still left. He kept both bottles on his bedside table, so the maid naturally thought that he was in need of both prescriptions.'

'Why two sorts of medicine? For what purpose did he take the other one?'

'For his blood pressure, I presume. When the bottle was empty he threw it away.'

Mrs. Bergman looked at me disappointedly. She twirled a lock of hair with one hand and absentmindedly permitted her tongue to wander along her teeth, maybe on the hunt for non-existent yellow tartar, or scraps from the teachers' lunch.

'So my discovery wasn't really worth much,' she sighed.

'On the contrary,' I said. 'I think I'll almost certainly be able to work out how the murder was committed now. Before, I only had a vague, hypothetical idea.'

'Do you mean the blood pressure medicine was poisoned?'

'Not at all. It was totally safe.'

'Then I don't understand....'

188

'I hardly understand it myself, but in a few days I'll be able to say something more, at least I hope so.'

'I'm glad to hear it.'

In a heartfelt way I assured her of my great gratitude for her contribution and escorted her out.

When I was alone, I threw myself at the telephone.

On the question of what the name of the second medicine could have been, the chamber-maid Mrs. Svensson replied that she was not in the habit of snooping on the guests' possessions. I rephrased the question, asking whether a person with her well-known powers of observation had observed anything about the medicine, especially since she most certainly dusted off the bedside table, where Nilsson kept his medicines. That bore fruit insofar as I learnt that the bottle, which had "a foreign label," had contained small pink pills with notches. I expressed my deepest admiration for her acute attention, whereupon she consulted me about memory problems with older people and treatment of teenagers' pimples. I recommended a fitting unction for the acne, which she might try for the other condition as well. On the question of where in such a case it would be applied, I suggested a thin layer on the temples three times a day. Then I hung up.

I looked through some annually published pharmaceutical catalogues and made an almost three quarters of an hour long call to the druggist Kvist, a personal acquaintance. Neither of us could make out what blood pressure medicine was manufactured in tablets which were pink and notched, and I was eventually forced to conclude that the preparation was not for sale in Sweden.

The father of medical science is Hippocrates, but necessity is said to be the mother of invention, and here I thought of arranging a temporary marriage of the two.

I arrived home later than usual, to find that my home help, Mrs. Storm, was still there. She is very reliable and conscientious, but usually not very talkative. All the same, she doesn't hesitate to give me a lot of quite irritating advice: on how to dress properly and how to avoid catching cold, for example. This day, she took the opportunity to deliver some admonitions about changing my underwear more often. I listened absent-mindedly while I ate my dinner in the kitchen. Her meatballs doubled in size in my mouth and I tried to swallow them as fast as possible. She must have had me under strict observation for, just as I was to stretch out to reach a cheese on the table she raised her voice to make it louder than the vacuum cleaner.

'Don't eat so much that you'll burst,' she cried.

'What?'

'Don't eat so much that you'll burst. Didn't you hear me?'

Her words coincided with something that had occupied my thoughts, and so her remark seemed of an almost visionary nature. I burst into a roar of laughter, which came as a sudden and unpleasant surprise. By the look on her face, I was confirming her long-held suspicion that I was suffering from a stealthy insanity, which had now all of a sudden broken out. She inched cautiously towards the door. When she got hold of her handbag and put on her coat, she asked anxiously if she should come the following Wednesday as usual.

'Come every day,' I shouted as she banged the door.

Too late, I realised the probable reason for her staying late. It was the agreed day for her monthly remuneration.

My laughter was caused by thoughts of cheese.

Not the safe cheese on my table, but the dangerous one in the boarding-house room.

Nilsson's cheese must have been at the back of my mind ever since it had been mentioned. I had unfortunately overlooked it until now because it seemed to be wholly inappropriate in the context of murder.

A common piece of cheese.

Now, don't think that it was poisoned. Like the red wine, or my forcemeat balls, it was not. Nevertheless it was an indispensable link in the chain I was in the process of forging around the neck of the culprit.

You will recall that we commented earlier on the cheese and the red wine in the room of the murdered man. And also on the paradox that two bums on a bleak Saturday in a third class boarding-house would feast in such a sophisticated way.

I spent the evening going through the case in all its details. With my eyes fixed far away, beyond my book case, my desk and the limits of the room, I completed the argument in my mind.

By the time my last cigarillo had burned itself out, the bottle of port was largely empty and the twilight had long reigned outside the windows. I knew how it had all happened and what measures should be taken. I even called the perpetrator, though I was almost certain he wouldn't answer. I honestly can't explain why I tried to call him. Did I want to prepare him for the worst?

At midnight I set the alarm-clock for eight o'clock for the purpose of getting in line in time at the State Liquor Store, where I had a reasonable chance to be at the front, as long as Crona wasn't there.

4

The following morning, I went to the largest liquor store in town.

The manager received me graciously in his small office. On the other side of the counter were storage spaces filled with all the different bottles they carried. It was a fascinating sight. Hundreds of colours glinted at me and the sun's rays, refracted by the glass bottles, threw reflections on the opposite wall. Big cardboard boxes of beer cans stood stacked on the floor, and on the rows of bottles on the upper shelves I read strange names, difficult to pronounce, from all the corners of the earth, on tempting labels from vineyards and *chateaux*. Here and there I recognized items that had sometimes graced my table: Estremadura, Bonita Sherry and Karlshamn's blue flag-punch.

Mr. Andersson sat behind a desk crammed with paper and brochures. He was a benevolent little man, round and bald-headed, with high colouring in his face, a man who no doubt studied his products in depth in order to be able to give an expert account of them. A dedicated businessman must know his merchandise inside and out.

I explained that, in my practice, I often encountered alcoholics of different kinds, and that I was, mostly for my own interest, doing a comparative study of the injurious effects of alcohol as compared to light wine and malt liquor. Mr. Andersson looked attentive, especially since I assured him that I did not aim to endanger his turnover, but had come in order to get his professional opinion about the Chianti wines. They seemed, I lied, to have certain specific qualities, positive to liver and other visceral tissues, and I wondered if he could tell me something about their composition and popularity.

'I am sorry, doctor, but I don't have much to tell you. The name comes from the province in northern Italy where the grapes are harvested. It is laid down to mature and has a full-bodied taste, with a dark red colour, almost like ox blood. The percentage of alcohol is just about the same as for other light wines, with the exception of Burgundies. Chianti makes me somewhat sleepy, but the experts consider it to be easy-going, fresh and simple.'

'Is there a demand for it?'

'Not very much, a few bottles a day, which is just a fraction of our total sale of wine.'

'Which is the most popular?'

'I would say the red wine, Chianti Ruffino.'

Since my purpose was trying to get to know who it was that had bought the bottle found in Axel Nilsson's room, my hopes were now awakened.

Were there security provisions for people working at State Liquor Stores, I wondered, and decided to proceed with the utmost care.

'Why do you think people don't drink more Chianti?'

'There are equally good Spanish and Algerian wines, and they are almost ten crowns cheaper per bottle. Tourists in Italy take a fancy to the picturesque bottles covered with straw, which are often used as vases or candlesticks. They try and recreate the atmosphere of the tourist hotel back home, but in my opinion it seldom works.'

'Do you recall any of your customers buying a bottle over the last few weeks? There can't have been many, and I'd like to get a few personal impressions.'

Mr. Andersson pursed his lips, which assumed the form and the appearance of a wild strawberry. If the colour of the lips had been bluish, which is the case when it comes to advanced forms of untreated heart disease, they could have been compared to a shrivelled grape. He looked thoughtfully up at the ceiling and tapped his plump fingers on the table-top.

'I'll ask the sales clerks.'

He disappeared and soon returned, triumphantly announcing that two well known citizens in our town, Carl Bergman and Johan Lundgren, had each bought a bottle from Miss Granlund in cash desk 1 three days ago, but she couldn't recall anyone else.

'Nobody last week?'

'Unfortunately not. Maybe you'd like a bottle from us, to be used in your scientific research, so to speak.'

'That would be very kind of you.'

I managed to suppress my disappointment, said thank you and left his office. With an effort I repeated this tour de force when Miss Granlund gave me a bag with a bottle and receipt for ten crowns.

Firmly resolved not to get charged for any unwanted cheeses, I crossed Rådhustorget to the market hall with the bag hidden under my coat.

As I walked past the different stands in the supermarket, my thoughts wandered to Zola's overblown descriptions of Les Halles in Paris. Ours were just like those, in miniature.

I stopped in front of a cheese counter. It offered a tempting sight. Big chunks of cheese looking like mill-wheels formed a semicircle, with smaller cheeses on top. The Edam, the Camembert, the Cheddar and our Swedish household cheese were all easily recognizable, as were the blue cheeses, Gorgonzola and Stilton. Others were covered with tinfoil, which meant I had to lean forward to read the name through the display-glass.

I was lost in thought in front of these delicacies. My friends often insinuate, unfairly, that I am a glutton. Rather, I am a gourmet, particularly as far as cheese is concerned.

I tend to favour the rounder, yellower and more solid pieces of cheese. They radiate good health and heavy dullness. It's possible my own unfortunate body perceives kinship and sympathy in their presence. They look prosperous and lucky in some way. We Swedes also talk about a lucky person as being a "lucky cheese" in the same way the English talk about a "lucky dog" or a "lucky devil." We also talk about "payback for old cheese," meaning getting one's own back on a person.

As I had studied about cheese the night before to pick up a few terms, that familiar quotation about old cheese kept coming back to me. It was not only that the murderer was getting his own back, he was also using an "old cheese" in the word's literary sense. And that was what I was after. I looked for an old cheese and wanted more information about it. The only thing we had learnt about the murderer's tool—and food often appears in detective stories, in some of Agatha Christie's mysteries for example—was that just a small and obliquely cut remnant of it had been found in Nilsson's room when it was searched in the morning.

To my mind nothing is more attractive than a fresh uneaten piece of cheese, and few things as repellent as the old remains, looking like the lopsided sole of a shoe, which, after a while in the open air, acquires curly, hardened edges and is sweaty on the surface. Over time it can even become mouldy and be transformed into a living entity, nasty and disgustingly smelly.

Edgar Allan Poe could have created such a diabolical cheese as the villain of a story. I can only theorise about the modest piece of cheese among Axel Nilsson's leftover belongings. It looked innocent enough, and may well have had its own period of glory in the past, but after having satisfactorily performed its task, it had been thrown in the wastebasket.

There are hundreds of different cheeses. Finding which kind the murderer had used was not easy, but at least I knew that it was a hard one. And it been cut, not handled with a cheese slicer. I also knew that it had to be old, i.e. long-stored. For the murderer had to get back at his victim for the sake of old cheese.

The proprietor of Blomberg's provision shop readily answered my questions.

'Ripe cheese?'

'That's right. What kind is the most ripe?'

'That depends. Our cheeses are stored for different periods. For the time being we have a most—.'

'Sorry, but I just meant on an average.'

'Maybe the hard Swiss-type cheese, hard granular Swedish cheese or Cheddar. Those have usually been stored for the longest time and they don't reach the market until after twelve months.'

'Is that also true about the hard cheese, those with a granular texture?'

He looked surprised and embarrassed. I lowered my gaze. The knowledge I'd learned by reading sounded forced.

'Well, yes, that's true. The longer the time stored, the more strength and taste, irrespective of the preparation procedure. The customer decides whether the cheese should be strong or weak. Our Swedish cream and household cheeses are mostly mild, and if the customer wants such a cheese as a dessert, they are very fitting, such as Tilsit cheese or some kind of processed cheese.'

'But if I want a well-stored cheese it would perhaps rather be a Suecia cheese?'

'That depends on what cheeses we have for sale at the moment.'

'How do you know how old the cheese is?'

'All Swedish cheeses are stamped by the dairies. Percentage of fat and date of production is included.'

'What about the self-service stores, where the pieces of cheese are packaged beforehand? Would the customer be able to make sure of the qualities of the cheese by reading the label?'

'I think so. We in the privately-owned retail trade have the pleasure of personally giving the wanted information about our line of products.'

A touch of haughty self-satisfaction was reflected in his face—a face which, because of the presence of blackheads, had a next to granular texture.

I thanked him heartily for his advice and looked at my watch. I had certainly not become much wiser, but in any case I had to make one last and decisive visit before my confrontation with the murderer. It was my intention to pay my colleague, Dr. Herder, a visit that afternoon. He's the chief physician at St. Katarina's. If it wasn't too late by then, I could pay the most important visit of all later that evening.

But, as everyone knows, I was summoned to the police station this Thursday, and the demand for my services reached me just as I was about to leave my home. My meeting with Crona was in many ways valuable and had given me some information of supplementary interest. His loss of memory was incontestable, but whether it was true amnesia due to a blackout caused by alcohol abuse, or just a gap in his memory as the result of such extreme intoxication that he ultimately dozed off, is an academic question.

Because of my conversation with the goldsmith, I had to postpone my visit to the murderer until the following day.

One has to respect other people's time. They may go to bed early.

5

Before I introduce you to the perpetrator, at long last, a number of obscure points need to be cleared up.

Johan embellished his report with speculations of his own, many of which turned out to be irrelevant, and Gunnar Bergman gave an account of actual events which he interlaced with personal comments and evaluations. Carl read out parts of his son's account during a phone call earlier today, so I know what I'm talking about.

My co-writers had no answers, at least not the right ones. I, on the other hand, have the answer but prefer—in accordance with longstanding detective tradition—not to reveal the murderer straight away, even though the newer English school often violates this rule and turns cases back-to-front.

Therefore, please accept my invitation to the street called Sandstensgatan, and let us see for the last time the events as they took place more than a week ago.

Sometime before eight o'clock Crona arrives. He has agreed to visit his old boon companion Nilsson for a drinking-bout. Knowing full well the hotel's policy prohibiting alcohol, he's anxious to get inside secretly. How does he manage that?

When Carl went in through the back door last Sunday after getting Blom into the reception area by pressing the door-bell at the main entrance, he was merely proving that a person cannot be in more than one place at any given time.

(I observe in passing that mystery writers have often dabbled with this and proved the opposite through brilliant manipulation of alibis and watches put back.)

But Carl's little experiment also proved something else: that from the reception area you can't hear the signal that sounds in Blom's room whenever anyone walks on the gravel pathways, either along the sides of the house or even in the passage leading to Björkstigen. The significance of this should be obvious to anyone. Crona must have opened the entrance door and caught a glimpse of Blom, who was at his desk, occupied with his accounts. He immediately withdrew, unnoticed by the owner. He didn't know about the alarm system, but the watchdog's presence at the front forced the goldsmith to walk over the garden towards the rear of the house, from whence he went upstairs to see the thirsty Nilsson, which turned out to be no problem at all.

By the way, did you work out why Nilsson was in a double room? It was simply because Blom wanted to earn an extra bit of cash on the side and therefore claimed that all the single rooms were occupied, but Nilsson could have a double room if he wanted. He had no idea that it was off-season and that half the hotel was empty.

Thus the old mates could settle down and the party could begin. A full-sized bottle of pure *schnapps* had been obtained for just such a purpose. Of the events after that, we only know that there was a quarrel and that the friends, or now enemies, wished to be left alone since they did not respond to Ivar Johanson's inquisitive knocking.

If anyone wanted to make the case that something important happened during these first hours, they would be totally wrong. The story about the plaster is the most irrelevant thing that happened during Crona's visit to the hotel.

The young Detective Sergeant's theory that Nilsson asked for the plaster in order to divert the host's attention while Crona slipped up the stairs is laughable. I won't burden you with detailed timetables— if you find that kind of thing interesting, pick up any book by Freeman Wills Crofts—but, according to Carl's account, the hullaballoo had been going on for a good half an hour before the need for a plaster occurred.

To eventually dispose of the question of the plaster, I need to reveal what it was used for. I myself initially assumed it was to cover a wound, and from that false premise I developed a theory which, in hindsight, is impressive only for its monumental stupidity. Now, if it was not for medical purposes, what was it used for? What are the qualities of a plaster? Well, it can be used to fasten things together or be affixed to something. Under what circumstances was such affixing required? Well, it happened during a quarrel between two alcoholics.

Now, your first thought was probably that something had been torn and needed temporary repair. But if an article of clothing or a piece of paper had been torn, you would ask for a needle and thread or a piece of sticky paper.

So, what did they quarrel about? We can't be certain because we weren't there, but let's hazard a guess, since we know what they were pre-occupied with: alcohol. What if they quarreled about the liquor? The most important thing in their miserable little lives at that moment was an expensively acquired bottle of alcohol. And, apart from the booze, they had a bottle of wine as well. Isn't it possible that after the first friendly discussion there was an argument about how to divide the remaining liquor evenly? Suppose Nilsson was drinking from the plastic mug and Crona from the tooth-brush glass, which were of different sizes. What would be needed was a measuring-glass and they decided to obtain one.

They borrowed a glass from one of the empty rooms on the same floor. It wasn't fit for the specific purpose, but it could be. How? By making a mark on it, crosswise! Lead or ink doesn't stick to glass, and using a transparent tape would not provide a distinct enough marking, particularly if visions had become blurred through alcohol.

So Nilsson goes downstairs and collects a plaster which he affixes to the extra glass at a suitable height from the bottom. Then they pour out equal amounts of the coveted fluid and begin drinking again. They also continue quarrelling, but the important thing is that neither of them has been wounded.

When Crona falls asleep around ten o'clock, Nilsson removes the plaster and throws it through the window. They no longer need a measuring glass. He then wipes the third glass clean, so that when he returns it in the morning it will look as if it hasn't been used.

Now we have to consider the next question, a most important one: when did Crona leave?

He's told us himself when and how. I don't need to repeat what he said to Gunnar Bergman, but soon afterwards he gave me the same explanation. There's no reason to doubt his account of what happened after he woke up around two o'clock, nor his statement about loss of memory. Nilsson was murdered during the hours while Crona was asleep, and when Crona woke up he found him exactly as he's described.

We don't know what Nilsson was doing while his guest slept. We only know one thing: he didn't listen to the radio.

How could this be possible, when different witnesses affirm that the radio was on in the room? On the one hand, it was on just after ten o'clock according to Blom, and at that time Crona would have been asleep. On the other hand, it was on just before one o'clock, according to Ivar Johanson, and at that time Nilsson would have been dead. I believe that he was murdered around eleven o'clock. Despite that, the radio was off when Crona woke up. And please remember that the battery was still working, for next day the police turned on the radio and heard the Sunday High Mass.

This circumstance raises the obvious question: on what programmeme is the High Mass transmitted?

I will answer it for you. Programmeme One.

But P 1 is not on the air at one o'clock in the morning, only P3 is, and it keeps going through the night.

Did the radio turn itself off between one and two, and change the programmeme from P3 to P1? No!

Now what happens regularly at one o'clock in the morning in *The Little Boarding-House*?

Well, Blom goes to bed and at the same time he normally closes the window. In any case, that's what he did that night, as well as the next one, when Johan saw him doing it from the backyard. Why was the window open in the first place? It wasn't because Blom was listening for footsteps on the gravel—for that purpose he had installed his signal system— but because he was warm and feverish and wanted to cool himself down. Remember how relieved he was when Gunnar Bergman opened the window during the interrogation! Nilsson's window on the other side was open until after two o'clock, a point in time when the wind, which had begun blowing after midnight, slammed the window shut. That was after Crona had thrown the key in from the backyard.

The truth is that Blom heard his own radio through Nilsson's room. His radio was on his window-recess and the sound was propagated through the two open windows, which are situated one above the other. The radio could be heard coming out of Nilsson's room, but not if one of those two windows was closed. When Blom stood outside Nilsson's room on the first floor, he heard the news being read from his own radio, which he had not yet switched to P3. He didn't do that until he was back downstairs again. Later that night, Johanson correctly reported hearing radio music when he listened from the same position as Blom had done a few hours earlier.

In other words the radio was Blom's, not Nilsson's, and the footprints Johan found in the garden after the rain belonged to Mr. Odestam and not to Göran Eriksson. The mistakes were made according to the same principle.

Now I turn to another puzzling matter, the dreary and hard-to-interpret whining sound that was heard by both Ivar Johanson and Warrant Officer Renqvist during the night the murder took place. It went on between twelve o'clock and half past one or two. It has been thought of as the death struggle of the murder victim, as someone crying and as the squeaking of the window that was open in Nilsson's room. That last explanation is the least plausible, for in such a case, why wasn't Crona woken up just as Johanson was?

You have actually heard of the one who produced those sounds, but you may not remember when and where. Therefore I will dwell a little on the subject in order to make it perfectly clear.

We can safely assume the only person in the house who could not have been the cause of the sounds was Nilsson, since he was dead. It is necessary to establish at what point of time this sound ceased, because it was directly linked to Crona's departure. How was it possible that he found the backdoor unlocked at just after two o'clock in the morning? The same backdoor, which he did not lock, but which the chamber maid found locked in the morning? That means that someone other than Crona must have left the house round about two o'clock in the night and left the door unlocked for a while. Who?

How long was the door open? When was it opened? Who had a reason to get out? The answer to the first question is trivial: enough time for the person who went out to be able to perform his or her errand.

What it was that needed to be done will be evident from the answer to the third question. The essential thing is that the door was open and that Crona could disappear. It happened around two o'clock, and just before that the sound had ceased.

Last Tuesday I met Renqvist at his regiment and after my conversation with him—you may prefer to call it a consultation, without him knowing it—I've been able to deduce that Renqvist's statement that the sound ended half an hour earlier was wrong.

I had passed through the barracks gates many times during my days as a part-time regimental medical officer. When I went there this time I was admitted by kind permission of the junior officer of the day, Staff Sergeant Holm.

In the surgery, I met another officer, who sent for Renqvist. It was at the end of the day and shooting practice was over. He didn't object to me asking a few questions, so we took off our outer clothes and went into the examination room in order to talk in private. I told him that there were still many unsolved problems regarding Nilsson's death and I needed one further piece of information. Whereupon, I bluntly asked if he was deaf.

'Deaf?' he said. 'Why do you think that?'

'You were originally an artillery man. Did you ask to be transferred to infantry, before someone else found that the deafness was causing problems with your work?'

'I'm not deaf. Who told you that?'

'I did. I assert that you're deaf in your left ear, but if you claim that's not true, would you be willing to submit to a test?'

'If you like.'

I asked him to stay at the other end of the room and cover his left ear. From a distance of five metres I whispered three numbers.

'8, 3, 7.'

'8, 3, 7,' Renqvist repeated.

He turned around and we repeated the procedure with his right ear covered.

'2, 9, 1.'

As he turned to me he had a somewhat ironic smile in his otherwise impassive face.

'2, 9, 1. Is the examination over now?'

I apologized. While I put on my overcoat, I wondered frantically how I could have made such a mistake.

Sometimes when you're grappling with a difficult problem, you can get a lucky break This happened to me when I suddenly realised I was without my spectacles and had to search for them for a while. It was when I returned to the problem that I had a flash of inspiration.

I rushed into the waiting room, out on to the barrack square and after the warrant officer, who had just disappeared into a grey building. I read 8 above the door. When I got there, I heard a nasty kind of clatter from the inside and twenty soldiers jumped out. They were wearing helmets with masking nets, green field uniforms and sub-machine-guns, and they formed two lines and began stamping on the gravel. I retreated behind the corner and bumped into a lieutenant. He was a polite man, who perhaps took me for a stray man doing his refresher course, so he showed me the way to the office, where I used a telephone. By the side of it was a list of numbers. I lifted the receiver and called the 8th company.

'The expedition, 8th company,' answered a young man. I could almost hear the youthful pimples in his voice.

'May I talk to Warrant Officer Renqvist?'

'Who's calling?' the conscript asked.

I thought of giving the name of a well-known military commander, but the only name I could recall in a hurry belonged to the main character in *Fänrik Ståls sägner*, a national epic written by the Finnish poet Runeberg in 1848. Instead, I played the role of someone at the top of the military hierarchy, invented by me on the spur of the moment.

'Colonel Ankarström!' I roared.

'Who?' he replied and then the warrant officer took over.

'Renqvist.'

'Colonel Ankarström here. Take down the following order until further notice.'

'One moment, Colonel.'

The silence lasted five seconds.

'Please go on, Colonel.'

At that, I whistled in a squeaky way a few bars from the second symphony of Beethoven, the trio of the minuet movement.

Silence.

'Hello, Colonel,' Renqvist said after a while.

'You didn't hear?'

'No, Colonel.'

'Are you deaf?'

'No, Colonel.'

'It's nothing to be ashamed of. Beethoven was also deaf,' I said and hung up.

Then I went home.

Renqvist had simply not heard my whistling and so he had escaped a totally unenjoyable musical experience. He had, of course, a hearing impairment of the higher frequencies, an occupational hazard of artillery men. When I had whispered to him he could hear it because the sound had a low frequency, but my shrill whistle had been inaudible.

I'd noticed that he was right-handed when he buttoned the coat of his uniform. After moving the handset from the right ear to the left one, as we right handed people do when we note down something during a phone call, I could establish that it was the left ear that did not react to high frequency sounds.

Therefore, Renqvist couldn't have heard the mysterious sound in the boarding-house after he changed his sleeping position around half past one. When he turned in his bed, he had obstructed the normal hearing of his right ear.

Of course, I wasn't going to report his disability to anyone, and he would surely be thankful for that. However, I will never know how comforted he was by my consoling words about his fellow-in-misfortune Beethoven.

Thus Johanson's statement that the sound ceased just before two was correct. It had a high frequency and we know from earlier reports that it sometimes disappeared—for example when Johanson went to the loo just before one o'clock—and then recurred.

Now I ask once again: who had an errand outside the house? What kind of squeaking sound could start at various times and urge someone to go for a walk? I'm assuming there's a connection between the ceasing of the sound and the fact that somebody went out and left the door unlocked.

There were seven people in *The Little Boarding-House*.

Axel Nilsson, who was dead.

Blom, who was asleep and had no reason to go out.

Crona, who doesn't count.

Johanson, who went up roughly when the sound had ceased and who got his alibi from the warrant officer in room 10.

Renqvist, who was in bed and was found there by the travelling salesman, who needed company.

Hurtig-Olofsson, who was reading aloud for Mrs. Söderström.

Söderström, who was listening to her woman friend reading aloud or....

You understand that I'm talking about the schoolmistresses. Mrs. Söderström, who was obviously a good deal more strong-willed, had succeeded in persuading her companion to let her take the dog for a walk. Especially since the dog had been whining for some time and had to be exercised and since Miss Hurtig-Olofsson was the archetypal anxious woman, afraid of the dark and reluctant to go out in spite of being the dog's owner. A telephone call to the caretaker at Miss Hurtig-Olofsson's home address, Ringvägen 88 in Stockholm, revealed that she possessed a Pekinese. The prohibition of both liquor and pets in the rooms of the boarding-house had made it necessary to smuggle in her little darling in the bag she always carried.

I stated earlier that you had indeed heard about what it was that created the sound. Do you remember that Crona developed his theory about *delirium tremens* from "a dog with slobbering jaws," which he did in fact see during his flight along Björkstigen? Mrs. Söderström, who herself was somewhere in the shadows, was walking the dog there, as it sniffed around trees and lamp-posts. Even though she'd seen Crona, she couldn't reveal that during the police interrogation. She had to prevent the unauthorised harbouring of the animal from being exposed. It was unusually cool of Miss Hurtig-Olofsson to keep her head while she was reading out loud alone in the room. Her voice should have broken now and then, for "Lilliecronas hem" is a very emotional story. She was aware of the fact that other people were still around at this time of the night and she'd probably heard Johanson knocking at the door of the next room. He may, by the way, have woken up a few minutes before when Mrs.Söderström passed his door with the whining dog on her way out.

By reading aloud, Miss Hurtig-Olofsson tried to give her friend an alibi during the short time of her absence. Needless to say, she had a really bad conscience over the dog's forbidden stay at the hotel, and perhaps she also feared that other guests, present as well future ones with allergies to furry animals, would develop painful, dangerous and ultimately even lethal reactions and....

Before I turn to discussing other things that happened beneath the deceptive surface and behind the scenes, a clarification would not be out of place. It is about lies—in particular, about one perplexing white lie.

If you want to get to the solution straight away, you would be well-advised to follow my example: take a deep breath and walk a few steps to and fro in the room. Such measures fill your lungs with fresh air and relax your joints and muscles in a most pleasant and stimulating manner.

And now the lies! Blom, who is a chronic liar at the best of times, made an unthinking statement at one point which unintentionally threw us off the track.

Do you remember that on Sunday morning he stated that Nilsson's door was locked? That was true, but he didn't see the key in the key-hole. Why? Because the only time he caught a glimpse of it inside the lock was during his rounds on Saturday evening at ten o'clock. By the morning, the key was on the doormat, having been thrown there earlier that night by Crona. Blom, who simply took it for granted that the key was still where he last saw it, decided not to look for it once again since at the time Johanson was watching him. If he had acted like a Peeping Tom, it would have seemed peculiar or suspicious to a guest. Under Detective Sergeant Bergman's questioning he had affirmed something he honestly believed to be true, but the information was twelve hours old. Ivehed believed him and didn't check the statement, for he was occupied fumbling with the key-hole using one of his private keys in the hole, pretending to use his picklock, which in fact he had lost or forgotten somewhere. Gunnar Bergman believed Ivehed, and we believed Gunnar Bergman and seized on that false notion, convinced that we had found the perfect locked-room situation we'd always dreamed about.

That was wishful thinking in the same way as when a piece of glass becomes a radiant diamond, or a random glance a secret sign of returned feelings of intense passion.

It's now time to introduce you to the murderer. I couldn't have presented him earlier, because he's been away all the time, but he was in fact talked about at length in Johan Lundgren's report and, in passing, we even suspected him of being the murderer!

6

Not introducing the perpetrator until the end of a detective story is something that few writers have dared to attempt. But in real life, the individual with the heaviest conscience always lies the lowest. The culprit who returns to the scene of the crime is a rarity, and in this particular case I had to call on him.

A small, nondescript man opened the door and peered short-sightedly at me after I pressed the doorbell button. He was wearing a shirt without a tie, striped trousers and slippers. The face was friendly enough, with small, blinking eyes under a furrowed brow. His jowls were rather heavy and he had a fleshy, veined nose. When he asked me to enter, I noticed that the denture in his upper jaw fit loosely, and he kept putting it in place with his tongue, which resulted in a continual sucking noise. It was many years since I had seen him. He was about my age, but less well preserved and more weighed down by worries.

After I had hung up my overcoat, he showed me into the small living-room without even asking me why I had come.

He didn't break the silence until I'd been shown the only armchair in the room and he had sat down as far as possible away from me on the sofa in front of the TV.

'Is something wrong, Dr. Nylander?'

'Yes, Mr. Åhlund, I'm afraid it is. I've discovered how you managed to do it.'

His features didn't become twisted beyond recognition, and he didn't rush at me with clenched fists or a cocked revolver. Neither did he run down to the furnace room for the purpose of hanging himself with a readymade running noose. He merely smiled in a melancholy way and gave a barely audible sigh.

Then he excused himself, offered me an ashtray and disappeared into the kitchen. I heard running water and the clatter of cupboard doors. There was a clink of chinaware, and then he returned with coffee cups, a Tetra Pak with thin cream and a sugar basin.

'I have no buns or cakes to go with the coffee. Would the doctor be put off by a few rusks?'

'A thousand thanks, it would be perfect.'

209

After that, he looked around with a puzzled expression.

'On the TV-set,' I said.

He picked up his spectacles with a smile. He looked embarrassed. Once more he disappeared, returning this time with a coffee kettle and some sweet fancy rusks on a plate. He poured carefully for us both. His hand trembled a little and he spilled a few drops on the teak table, but immediately mopped them up with his handkerchief. All in all, he seemed to be calmer than I was. He possessed a certain tranquility, and I felt a lot of sympathy for him.

For an observer, the scene must have looked like an everyday event. Two older men discussing the news of the day over a cup of coffee. Nobody would have guessed that one of them was a murderer who was treating his unmasker to a sweet fancy rusk or two.

The ornamental wall clock chimed loudly, exactly as at home. During my host's visits to the kitchen, I'd observed many mystery novels translated into Swedish on his book shelf.

'I tried to call you on Wednesday,' I said.

'I wasn't home until late. I'd taken my evening meal at my daughter's place after we returned from Stockholm. I went there on Friday the 24th.'

'I know. Did you hate him very much?'

'Well, actually I hadn't realised how much until he surfaced here a couple of weeks ago. I'd forgotten most of it. My sorrow had somehow been encapsulated, and I'd been forced to accept my new life. We'd been married for thirty years.'

'Quite a long time.'

'Yes, and a very happy time.'

He smiled to himself. A photograph on a chest of drawers showed husband and wife sitting on a sofa. It could have been taken on an important day, perhaps a wedding day anniversary. He rose, went over to pick it up, and placed it on the table, as if he wanted her as near to him as possible.

It was now ten years since he'd assisted her to the hospital where she had died. The face on the photo was filled with life and pride, hardly the same face she'd shown during her depression, with vacant eyes and blank features.

'What did he want?'

'He wanted my compassion. He was sick, he said, and placed his medicine bottles on the table, just about where the cream is now. Alone, sick and without anywhere to go. Maybe he'd hoped to stay here until his superannuation was arranged. If the circumstances had been otherwise I could have had space for him but, Doctor, I knew that after all these years he'd come for the sole purpose of trying to destroy everything again for Rose-Marie....'

'Wasn't it natural for him to want to see his daughter?'

'It would have been, if we'd heard from him during the past years. Ten years ago he was sitting here, smiling. Then he took our daughter away from us and returned her when she became inconvenient.'

'Did he kill your wife?'

'That was how I felt at the time, and I felt it again when he surfaced now. He couldn't be allowed to encroach on our family once again. That's why I murdered him.'

'I know that.'

'Was it revenge, or was it to protect those nearest and dearest to me?'

'Both, perhaps?'

'Yes, but I didn't want to think of it as revenge. Maja is just as dead as before. She may have been hit by a depression relapse in any case. Nilsson's intervention into our lives just helped to trigger the deterioration she never recovered from.'

He wasn't remorseful or heartbroken, just a bit puzzled, as if he was questioning his own motives. This was not a sick person who could plead temporary insanity in court. He had done what he considered to be the right thing without weighing his own chances. When his planning was over and the necessary arrangements were in place, he'd left town.

'Doctor?'

'Yes.'

'Did he really die as I had calculated?'

He hadn't even tried to find out. That's how little he'd cared. He'd thrown a hand grenade and walked away without asking if it had detonated, or if he'd set it properly.

'Yes he did, during the Saturday night when you were in Stockholm.'

'What's the punishment for something like that?'

'Difficult to say. Tell me how you did it.'

'You already know that.'

'I want to hear it in your own words.'

'It was simple, Dr. Nylander. I'm almost surprised that it worked. He appeared here on a Tuesday the week before last, I don't know

211

exactly why he paid me that visit. It was like an evil dream, but it wasn't as if I could shake my head or rub my eyes and wake up to find that he wasn't there. I couldn't deny his existence and sweep the memories of what he had done under the carpet. And now that he was here, there was no return! While he went to the bathroom, I saw his medicine bottle. It was then or never! I leant forward so eagerly I hit the table and almost caused the cups to spill.'

'What did the pills look like? What was the name on the bottle?'

'They were small and pink and they had a notch on one side. I've forgotten the name. It was an old bottle. The label was almost impossible to read. Anyway, the text was in English. It said "Welcome." *Välkommen!*'

He said it without irony. I nodded. The pharmaceutical manufacturer Burroughs-Wellcome had offered a blood pressure medicine for many years. I think it was called Darenthin and had been withdrawn because of side effects.

'He told me that the medicine was for blood pressure. It had been prescribed for him in America a couple of years ago, when he'd had his first cerebral haemorrhage attack. On the trip over, he'd felt sick and had had a headache. He may just have been seasick, but he'd thought that the blood pressure might be the cause of his symptoms and he began to take the pills again. When he arrived in Göteborg he felt better, but went straight away to see a doctor to renew his prescription and was then told to take it carefully since his pressure was at a dangerous level. Your colleague gave him another kind of medicine.'

'Dichlotride-K?'

'Maybe that was the name. In any case he couldn't use them because ... well, he had to run to the bathroom too often and....'

'So he continued taking his old pills?'

'That's right, the pink ones with a notch. He'd got it into his head that they were more effective, that's why he didn't dare to stop using them. They looked like Maja's old unused antidepressants in the bathroom cabinet. For some strange reason I hadn't thrown them away.'

'Niamidal?'

'Exactly. There were about thirty pills left in Nilsson's bottle and with a consumption of three pills every day they would last for ten days.'

'You substituted the pills?'

'Of course. I flushed the foreign pills in the bathroom and put Maja's Niamidal in the bottle instead. I made the substitution here, under the table, and Nilsson didn't suspect anything. He was too busy complaining. He had no money, so before he left I lent him a few hundred-crown bills for his hotel. He also took my old transistor radio to have some form of diversion in the room. He forgot to return it the following week.'

'So you met again?'

'Yes, that same Friday evening when I went to Stockholm. I'd asked him to come over and told him I'd a surprise for him.'

'A bottle of Italian wine?'

'Yes. But the real surprise was my announcement that his daughter would return home from her trip, and that the two of us would visit him on Sunday. He didn't know that Yvonne was in town with her cousins all the time. Needless to say, I hadn't mentioned that Rose-Marie was married to Göran. Had I told him that, Nilsson would have looked him up and caused problems. But I did my very best to prevent him from seeing any of my family.'

'And when he left you gave him the wine bottle?'

'Yes.'

'And the cheese?'

'A piece of strong Cheddar cheese, yes.'

'Well ripened?'

He looked at me in agreement. We knew where we stood with each other. There were never any attempts at excuses or lies. It would have been beneath his dignity.

'The ripest one I could find. "Here you are," I said to him. "Enjoy something extra tasty on Saturday evening." He left suspecting nothing. At what time did he die?'

'Round about midnight, it seems.'

'What will you do to me?'

'I don't know. Is there any more coffee?'

We talked for a while about this and that. He turned out to have an amazing knowledge of crime literature and, even though he preferred to tell me what he had heard about the need of utmost dietary precautions during treatment with Niamidal from Dr. Herder, who was in charge of Maja at St. Katarina's. I was more interested in discussing mystery stories with him. I asked him to join Carl, Johan and me that night and, believe it or not, he accepted my invitation.

When I had to inform him later over the phone that the meeting was cancelled, he sounded every bit as disappointed as Johan Lundgren.

It might have been high-handed on my part to invite a new member into our little circle, but I felt I would have the tacit consent of my friends. Sven himself—we soon started calling each other by our first names—had nothing against joining our little group, and he assured me that the risk of being questioned and stared at meant nothing to him.

On my way home, I went through the murder in my mind for the last time. Niamidal and other similar medicaments like Nardil and Catran, the so called Monoamine oxidase inhibitors, were used in the early 1960's as the most promising medicine against depression at the time. Unfortunately, they turned out to have dangerous side effects. A few patients were actually reported to have died of strokes. The explanation for this serious complication was that such preparations reinforced the increased blood pressure that some foods brought about, among other things. After that, they were mostly banned. However, in some places and under certain circumstances, Niamidal was still used.

I acquired my knowledge of this some years ago when I read it in a circular from the Royal Medical Board. It stated that red wines, especially the Chianti variant, and specific foods—among them well-ripened cheese and pickled herring —contained tyramine which, when given to patients treated in this way, could cause an increase of blood pressure and, at the very worst, a lethal arterial burst inside of the brain.

Nilsson had hypertonia and was hit by a stroke some years ago in America. He had been prescribed blood pressure lowering medicine in an attempt to reduce the risk of new, spontaneous bleeding. When he continued taking his pills, not knowing that they had been replaced, his blood pressure was not reduced at all, but remained at a high and life-threatening level. With Maja's Niamidal he saturated his body for ten days in a way that caused some of the forbidden foods to be perilous to eat. The murderer had, in fact, created a meal that was a virtual murder weapon. Sven Åhlund took into account that Nilsson would have downed all his Niamidal pills on Saturday and thrown away the empty bottle. A newly opened and seemingly innocent bottle of Dichlotride-K pills would be left in the room, together with an empty wine bottle and a piece of cheese.

Why did he save the Swedish medicine, if he wasn't comfortable with it? Maybe he wanted to show it to another doctor later on and ask for some appropriate and more enduring pill—anything but Dichlotride-K.

Maja Åhlund had had a difficult depression ten years earlier and all kinds of treatments were tried. She often stayed at home and, during one period, she was given Niamidal. When I talked to Dr. Herder I remembered what I had read about Niamidal and he told me that for her own safety he had asked her to cut off the cure. Sven was present at that consultation and received the same information. As her husband, he had been in charge of all her medicaments because of the risk of attempted suicide.

Sometime after that, she became worse and was committed to the hospital, where she took her own life. She managed to hang herself in a toilet in the ward, using the sash of her dressing-gown.

As I've already said, Sven was fully aware of the potential complications when it came to wine and cheese in connection with Niamidal treatment.

After Maja's death he had casually put the bottle aside in the bathroom cabinet, not for one second thinking that it would one day be handy for a very different purpose.

While I'm sitting here trying to formulate a proper conclusion, I find that all the alternatives seem to be sentimental and melodramatic.

I don't feel entirely satisfied now that the truth has been revealed, and I find myself to be irresolute. How to proceed?

My friends the mystery writers have often allowed the culprit to go free. The detective is overtaken by sympathy and withholds what he knows from the police, thus tempering justice with mercy.

It's debatable whether what I've discovered would be enough proof for a court. Maybe Gunnar Bergman is laughing at me by letting the matter rest there. I hope so.

A murder has nevertheless been committed and the murderer has been revealed.

The law should run its course, justice should be seen to triumph and one should atone for one's crimes; one's sleep shouldn't be disturbed by a gnawing conscience.

If I report the murderer he will suffer, yet his suffering deserves to be over by now. His own justice or retribution can't give him back his wife.

If I don't report him, I've betrayed my social duty by withholding valuable information, which I'm obliged to give as a law-abiding and loyal citizen.

Am I prepared to be an accessory to murder? A few days ago, I didn't even know him. Am I hesitant about an obvious course of action simply because he and I happen to share a common interest?

I'm not certain what I shall do, but I suspect I'll go to the police station tomorrow morning.

I would gladly have seen Sven Åhlund as one of our little club. He would have been an asset. Perhaps what he had needed was a sense of fellowship and solidarity. Now that our meeting tonight was cancelled, he probably won't ever be able to participate. Who knows how much time the law imposes in a case like this? Maybe the courts will show some tolerance? If he goes to jail it may take a long time before he's out. By then, our club may well have dissolved and we'll all be dead. We have, as we know, very little time left together.

Thinking about this case again I find another unexplained point. Who was the Axel Nilsson who lived at the boarding-house one and a half months before the murder? You remember that Johan called Blom last Sunday night and discovered that Nilsson had stayed there six weeks ago. That information surprised us very much at the time. Now I'm no longer surprised.

Johan Lundgren is a close friend of mine. I like him a lot, but I suspect that some people in this town may not appreciate him to the same extent, the proprietor of *The Little Boarding-House* being one of them. My conclusion is that our phone call made Blom angrier and more upset than he already was. It goes without saying that he recognised Johan's voice, with its rather characteristic whining tone, and realised immediately that the three of us were engaged in some kind of private murder investigation. So, in order to get us off his back, he decided to confuse us with a piece of false information. That's why he told us that the name of the guest who occupied room number 5 in mid-September was... Axel Nilsson!

This is sheer speculation, for what it's worth.

It's getting late. Most people in town are asleep and gathering strength for tomorrow.

I have a strong suspicion that I shan't sleep. I've had problems lately. It's as if the hours in the night are too valuable to be slept away. You don't know how many you may have left.

I can't take anything for it. Johan drinks lukewarm milk. I'd rather stay awake. I could, of course, prescribe myself some pills, but then I may not wake up in time.

My surgery opens in a few hours.

POSTSCRIPT

Stadsparken, Saturday, November 1.

My Dear Dr. Nylander,

I'm sorry for writing to you like this. You will, I think, get the letter with the morning mail. I thought of something. The memory returns—exactly as you said it would.

It's about the visit to Nilsson. We drank liquor, as I said. God help us, but I am not sure if he downed any red wine. I cannot swear that he did, but he said something about "sodding red dishwater." I don't remember if we ate much cheese either. Maybe we had some, that is possible, but I took some away with me, for there was a big chunk in my pocket that I was eating in the cottage.

This may not be of any importance but, since you were so kind to me the other day, I would like you to know that you were right about my returning memory.

Today I have relapsed into alcohol somewhat, but that is just for the time being and on Monday I will, thank Heaven, be sober again.

Maybe I should drop in this week sometime to be put on the sick-list? I'm too nervous to be able to work, unfortunately, and I still have difficulty with the amnesia. It will be better when I get rid of the alcohol, which is demoralizing for body and soul.

Elvy sends her greetings!

Yours sincerely,

Algot Emanuel Cronlund, former goldsmith.

ACKNOWLEDGEMENT

I wish to express my profound thanks to Bertil Falk for his exceedingly generous offer to translate this Swedish locked room classic.

Bertil is the editor and translator of *Locked Rooms and Open Spaces: An Anthology of 150 Years of Swedish Crime and Mystery Fiction of the Impossible Sort,* published in 2007 by The Battered Silicon Dispatch Box (www.batteredbox.com).

Additionally, he has translated similar short stories by, among others, John Dickson Carr, Jacques Futrelle and Melville Davisson Post into Swedish, as well as the essay "The Grandest Game in the World" by Carr.

John Pugmire
New York
November 2015

Made in the USA
San Bernardino, CA
21 May 2019